THE COAT

APRIL GRUNSPAN

Black Rose Writing | Texas

First printing

This is a work of fiction. Names, characters, businesses, places, events, and
incidents are either the products of the author's imagination or used in a
fictitious manner. Any resemblance to actual persons, living or dead, or
actual events is purely coincidental.

ISBN: 978-1-68433-438-4
PUBLISHED BY BLACK ROSE WRITING
www.blackrosewriting.com

Printed in the United States of America
Suggested Retail Price (SRP) $17.95

The Coat is printed in Baskerville

*As a planet-friendly publisher, Black Rose Writing does its best to eliminate
unnecessary waste to reduce paper usage and energy costs, while never compromising
the reading experience. As a result, the final word count vs. page count may not meet
common expectations.

DEDICATED TO

Hazel Rose and Evelyn Beatrice, the fourth generation

ACKNOWLEDGEMENTS

Many people informed, encouraged, offered words of wisdom, or gave constructive critiques. It would be impossible to thank every one of them. I can only mention those who went above and beyond.

The San Antonio Writer's Guild Saturday critique group members helped by providing a warm, friendly atmosphere where writers could discuss and improve their craft. In particular, I'd like to thank SAWG member Frank Hicks, for his constant encouragement, insight, and optimism.

Thank you to Stephanie Wittenbach, now-retired Texas A&M San Antonio librarian, for affording me access to the university's Mazal Holocaust Collection. Their extensive selection of research material greatly contributed to the historical accuracy of Seth's stories.

Finally, a world of thanks to my family, support system, and muses: husband Avie, son Dan, his wife Emily, and my daughter Alana.

THE COAT

THE COAT

CHAPTER ONE

BERESHITH
IN THE BEGINNING

My name is Seth Feinberg, and I write stories—ghost stories about a generation history displaced. I started writing what my grandmother would have called *meises* when I was twenty-four years old because of a coat—a Nazi officer's coat passed on to me when I turned eighteen. I write these stories because of a compulsion created by a history hidden from me by the very people who lived it.

I know my own story, just as everyone knows theirs. My parents' stories are ripe apples I can savor because my father or mother happily shared their narratives. My father's parents were different. They lived the majority of their lives as Holocaust survivors who maintained a stoic silence about their past, as though telling their stories would be like stepping into quicksand—a substance so saturated with pain they would no longer be able to resist drowning in the past's despair. With rare exceptions, their experiences remained shadows in the twilight, barely perceptible in the fading light of memory. When they died, their history died with them, buried in the soil where each grandparent was laid to rest, one next to the other. Ashes to ashes. Dust to dust.

During our shared years on this earth, I addressed them by their Hebrew honorifics—Saba for my grandfather and Savta for my grandmother. Saba was a mix of sarcastic humor and eternal pessimism. He reminded me of a locked book on the highest shelf. I wanted to read that book, learn its story, absorb its knowledge. I was only permitted to see its cover. Dignified silver hair fringing a balding head. A mouth forever set with gravity. Cloudy gray eyes that remained constant, even when he smiled, their shapes unaltered, their corners uncrinkled.

Savta was my father's gentler parent. Where Saba's body was sharp and angular, hers was invitingly soft and round. Perfectly bobbed, horsehair thick salt and pepper hair framed a face relaxed in sweetness. She smiled, hugged, and petted in English while she sang to us in Hebrew and Yiddish, a perpetual appeal for our affection. My sister, Ilana, and I often kept her company while Saba discussed politics with Dad, and Mom escaped by going to lunch or dinner with her Cleveland friends.

But my eighteenth birthday wasn't when I met my inheritance. The coat made its first appearance in my life the evening before my Bar Mitzvah, that stressful coming-of-age day when thirteen-year-olds take on the rights and responsibilities of a Jewish adult disguised as the opportunity for a great party.

Everyone came to Rochester for the occasion. Uncles and aunts, cousins, second cousins, old friends, school friends, people I'd only met once, people I'd be meeting for the first time ever. My parents hosted the weekend, but it was Saba who became the respected patriarch of the event, with Savta as his second-in-command. He luxuriated in the role. Everything had to be impeccable. Everything had to be perfect.

The festivities began with Friday night's *Shabbat* dinner. Over one hundred out-of-towners crowded into the Rosenbloom Social Hall, while Saba said the *kiddush* blessing over the wine followed by a catered family-style meal. Bowls of overdressed salad. Platters of fatty sliced brisket and boiled potatoes. Rich brown honey cake for a sweet life.

Speeches were made. Toasts were given. Saba told me I was the host. While everyone else enjoyed the food, he directed me from table to table, his hand resting on my shoulder giving it an occasional squeeze of approval, telling everyone what a wonderful, smart boy I was.

While the tables were being cleared, he led me over to a group of people he introduced as his greener friends. "This is my grandson, Sethy," he told them. "Seth, you already know my friend, Motek. These others are Perla, Sala, Chaim, and Frania. We all became friends in Europe and have remained close ever since."

Greener. I knew the word well. Saba and Savta used it when they referred to their friends from Poland, the old country, fellow survivors who'd migrated to the United States in the years following the Holocaust.

The woman he'd introduced to me as Sala reached out to shake my hand. "*Mazel tov.* I'm looking forward to hearing you *daven* your *parshat* tomorrow morning." she said.

I looked down, saw the tattooed number on her arm, and drew back, immediately ashamed of my involuntary movement.

Saba reacted quickly and took her hand in both of his. "Thank you, Sala. We're delighted you could come."

My cheeks grew hot. Maybe they didn't notice. I smiled and said, "Nice to meet you all."

As we turned to leave their table, the last of our rounds, I realized I was exhausted. Time had flown. It was eleven o'clock. Mercifully, people left. Thankfully, the evening ended.

After we got home, Dad and Saba took me upstairs into the room Dad used as his study.

"Saba wants to show you something," Dad said.

My gift! He'd given my sister Ilana five hundred dollars for her Bat Mitzvah. My parents made her put three hundred in the bank. Still, two hundred dollars to spend any way I wanted.

Dad opened the closet door and took out a leather coat.

"Great coat," I said, trying to make light of it, not wanting to show my disappointment. "But don't you think it's a little too big for me?"

"It's not yours yet," Saba said, fingering the coat's top button. "Right now it belongs to your father, but I want he should give it to you when you graduate high school."

I took a closer look. Dad held the hanger with his right hand, supporting the garment's weight with his left. The brown leather trench coat had a matching belt and a woven beige wool lining. I had to admit, it looked pretty cool.

"Where did it come from?" I asked.

Saba's hand moved to caress the collar, his fingers moving over its neatly stitched lapel. "It's part of our family history. Someday, when you're older, you'll appreciate what it stands for."

"What do you mean?" I asked.

Mom peeked into the room. "Guys, it's way too late to be doing this now. We have an early morning and a long day tomorrow. Let's all get some sleep."

"Your mother is right," Saba said, removing his hand from the coat and putting it on my head as though he was about to bless me. Instead, he took my face in his other hand and kissed me on the forehead. "I'll see you in the morning, *yingele*."

Sleep is difficult when there's a full day of excitement ahead. Later that night, I took a penlight from my desk drawer and went back into the study. Maybe the coat wasn't the gift, but the gift wrap. Saba and Dad's idea of a joke.

I opened the closet door, the tantalizing smell of the leather reaching my nose. I turned on my penlight and rifled through the pockets, figuring I'd find my check and we'd all laugh about it in the morning. The pockets were empty. I went back to bed, wondering about the coat, finally falling into a fitful sleep.

My Bar Mitzvah day started at six a.m. We all showered. Dad and Saba shaved, while Savta, Mom, and Ilana did their hair and makeup. I put on my brand-new suit and dress shoes while Dad tied my tie around his neck, then put it over my head and tightened the knot. By the time we all got downstairs, there was only enough time for everyone to grab a quick bowl of cereal and for the adults to gulp down their coffee before Mom said, "Let's go. We have to be at *shul* by nine."

Prayers. Readings. My *parshat: Bereshith*, the first chapter of Genesis. *In the beginning.* My *haftorah: Isaiah 42:5-21*. My *dvar torah:* a carefully crafted commentary on the week's reading. The rabbi's sermon, replete with congratulatory remarks and the congregation's usual gifts for the Bar Mitzvah boy: a pair of *Shabbat* candlesticks, a *tzedakah* box, and a certificate for a year's membership in the temple's youth group.

After the buffet luncheon and an afternoon nap, after the sun set and at least three stars appeared, it was time for my party. Once again, Saba relished his role as the reigning patriarch of the family. Dad gave the welcome speech, but it was Saba who traveled from table to table, making sure everyone understood what a wonderful job I'd done that morning and how I was going to grow up to be a real *tzaddik,* a *mensch,* a righteous person of integrity and honor. Dinner was served. The DJ was loud. People drank and danced and kept coming up to me, my parents, and Saba and Savta, congratulating us on a job well done. A wonderful party. We should all be so happy and so proud. So much *naches!*

"Only *simchas!*" they said, as the celebration wound down and they left, just before one in the morning.

The weekend finally quieted down after Sunday brunch ended and our final farewells were said. That evening, I went over to my father. "Dad, what's the deal with that coat you and Saba showed me?"

"It's a Nazi officer's coat, a *Ledermantel*. He gave it to me when I turned eighteen. He told me last night he wanted me to give it to you when you turned eighteen as well."

I didn't understand. There should have been no way this coat could be in my family, but there it was, upstairs in my Dad's closet.

"How'd he get it?"

"No idea. I asked him a few times, but you know how your grandparents don't talk much about the war."

"Did they ever tell you anything about their lives during that time?"

"Not too much. I know Savta and her sister built bombs for the German army in a labor camp somewhere in Poland. Later on, a Nazi officer took your Savta as his housemaid."

I didn't want to ask the obvious. Dad answered anyway. "He didn't abuse her, in spite of what you'd assume." Dad paused. "At least, that's what your Savta told me."

"And Saba?"

"A Polish family hid him in their cellar. He dug a tunnel for himself down there—he called it a *bunker*. He stayed in that dark hole for a long time."

"How long?"

"I don't know."

"I guess it's hard for them to talk about those things." My turn to pause.

Through the years, I came to understand pauses to be the expression of emotion most used by the emotionless. The pause. A time to change gears, abandon uncomfortable subject matter.

"If he wants you to give the coat to me when I turn eighteen, why did you show it to me now?"

"Your Bar Mitzvah is really important to him. He believes you're old enough to start thinking about what taking on your religious obligations really means." Another pause, this one ending the conversation.

Everything with Saba and Savta always came back to one plus one equals Judaism. My father and my Aunt Sarah were okay with it. They grew up that way—entrenched in the insular culture of the post-Holocaust diaspora. I didn't.

Sure, I loved my grandparents. But I never felt a deep connection with them. Anything interesting or funny was always in Hebrew or Yiddish. During our visits, the adults would laugh, while Ilana and I smiled as though we understood, play-acting to make our grandparents happy. Counterfeit happiness was the price we all paid as second and third-generation survivors—with one singular exception.

During baseball season, I would sit with Saba and Savta in front of their old Magnavox console television watching his and—by extension—my beloved Cleveland Indians. Saba, with his twisted sense of humor, had renamed many of the players from our team. Paul Assenmacher, a short-lived Indians pitcher, became "Assencocker." I used to assume he based his joke on the Yiddish expression for old fart, *alter cocker*. Now older and marginally wiser, I realize the pun might also have been Saba's bawdy combination of the Yiddish *essen*, eat, and the English word "cock."

We'd sit on the old brown sofa in their family room and watch the games together, cheering every run earned and lamenting each one surrendered. During the ads, Saba would stand up and perform for us, mimicking Jim Thome at bat or Jose Mesa on the mound. He'd stand on the room's orange shag carpeting holding an imaginary bat, butt out, shoulders angled toward the window facing the almost nonexistent backyard. He'd point his make-believe bat at a make-believe outfield, then resume his ready stance.

"Wait for your pitch, Saba," I'd say, fully participating in the charade. "Wait for it."

He wiggled his butt, his invisible bat moving in tandem.

"Ball one!" he called, his voice thinned out by several heart attacks, his slowly failing health showing in his overly lean frame and slowing gait.

"Mendel, sit down," Savta scolded. "Seth can't see the TV with you standing in front of it."

What Savta didn't understand was how much I enjoyed my baseball Saba. Those were the times I could forget the undercurrents of memory haunting my grandparents' household. Three hours of peanuts and popcorn and thankfully kosher Cracker Jacks while we watched the Cleveland "*Cockers*" play the great American pastime. Three hours during which I could catch a glimmer of the man who existed before persecution, war, and unspeakable loss colored his life. Once or twice a year, Saba and I forged a tenuous link.

The coat remained in the study closet while I finished high school. It continued its residence in my parents' home while I attended college. Like the coat, Dad's words about my religious obligation lay dormant until Saba passed away during my freshman year.

The four a.m. call startled me awake. "Hello?"

Dad's voice came over the phone. "Sethy, I'm so sorry. Saba died suddenly last night. We made reservations for you and Ilana to fly to Cleveland for the funeral. Your flight is at noon. That should give you enough time to pack a bag and get to the airport."

"What?" I must have heard wrong. Dad sounded so businesslike. Why wasn't he more emotional? Why wasn't *I* more emotional? So much to take care of. What should I pack? I'd have to email my professors. And what about the paper that was due the next day? Dad. What about Dad? "Are you okay, Dad?"

"I'm fine. I'll be fine. I'm more worried about Savta. I don't know how she's going to be. Your Mom and I are flying out in a couple of hours. Your cousin Matt will pick you up from the airport and bring you to Saba and Savta's house."

Coffee. What should I pack? No, first I needed coffee. "Okay Dad. I'll see you later today."

Saba's death was my first experience with loss. The graveside funeral, with Savta sobbing and Dad trying to console her, tore at me. My heart broke completely when the time came for us to drop shovelfuls of rich, dark earth onto Saba's wooden casket—such a hard and final sound. I held back my own sounds as tears slid down my cheeks and off my chin. Mom gave Ilana and me tissues to wipe our noses as the rabbi recited *El Maleh Rachamim* before we got into the limousine to return to the house.

We came home to a roomful of people in a house dressed for mourning. Savta and my aunt Sarah wore blouses with torn collars. Dad wore a tie with a torn edge. The three of them sat on low wooden stools. Someone had covered all the mirrors and lit a seven-day *shiva* candle. All this in a home that still smelled of Saba's cologne.

In the days following the funeral, I walked around in a fog. People made *shiva* calls to pay their respects or drop off meals. At the end of each day, Savta sobbed in her bedroom, while Ilana ran upstairs to hide from the sorrow.

During the rare quiet moments, I thought about Saba, then about the coat. Why had he kept such a thing? Why was it important to pass it on to Dad? To me? Was it enough to have a German officer's coat hanging in a Jewish family's closet or did I need a backstory to give it meaning?

My visit ended two days before the end of *shiva*. I went over to Savta, her usually perfect hair disheveled, her face even more wrinkled than I remembered. She didn't look at me when I kissed her goodbye—I don't think she heard me when I said, "I love you, Savta." I leaned over and gave her a final hug before Matt drove me to the airport and I returned to school.

THE JOURNEY

"Take or toss?" Mom held up the bag with my old karate belts.

I tried not to sound like a whiny six-year-old. "Can't you hold on to them? It's only one small bag."

"One small bag of belts, a small box of your undergraduate textbooks, your table tennis trophies. Dad and I are downsizing, Seth. You know. Smaller house. Fewer closets. Less storage space."

I pulled the belts out of the bag and laid them on the carpet—nine colors, white to black, each with three colored tape stripes showing my progress in the discipline over eight years. Did I want them? Did I need them? Was it enough to know I'd achieved the coveted black belt, or did I need something to prove it? "I'll take the white one and the black one. You can toss the rest."

Mom smiled as she put the seven belts into a large box against the wall across from the closet. "Great. We're making progress. Next, all these goofy ties you used to wear to *shul*."

"Grad school is pretty casual. Maybe I'll just take one or two, and you can donate the rest."

"Bar Mitzvah tie. Take or toss as one of your one or two?"

"I don't think a Cleveland Indians tie with Chief Wahoo on it would be appropriate these days, especially in Seattle."

Mom tossed Chief Wahoo into the same box as the seven karate belts. The loss of that small part of my childhood and its connection to Saba stung. I shook away the feeling.

At that moment, Dad walked into the room carrying…What to call it? Saba's coat? The Nazi officer's coat? Certainly not my coat. "Don't forget to pack this," he said.

I groaned. "It's so big and bulky. Can't you keep it until I at least finish grad school and have a permanent place of my own?"

"We've kept it long enough," Dad said. "Saba wanted you to have it when you turned eighteen. You're 23 now. It's time."

I pressed my lips together and paused. This coat had no more a place in Seattle than Chief Wahoo. "I'm probably not going to have room for it," I tried.

"You're going to have to make some," Dad said. "This is your coat, your gift from Saba. He was excited enough to show it to you before your Bar Mitzvah. It's time you took it with you."

Exasperated, I made a last-ditch effort. "What the hell am I going to do with it? I won't ever wear it."

Mom put a hand on my shoulder, her light touch calming the building storm. "You loved your Saba, and he loved you. This was his gift to your dad, his gift to you, and a gift for your son or daughter when, with God's help, you have children. Sometimes I agree with you and sometimes I don't. This time, I agree with your father. It's time you took the coat."

A couple of days later, the "toss" boxes had been dropped off at a donation station and we'd crammed the "take" boxes and bags into my ten-year-old Buick. I'd hoped to hide the box containing the coat in the trunk where I wouldn't have to see it during the drive. Mom, ever the pragmatist, disagreed. "You can fit way more bags in the trunk than boxes." Together, we stuffed the overloaded black trash bags—filled beyond a reasonable capacity with my shirts, pants, and bedding—into that space. Then, we tessellated the boxes on the back seat, the pile preventing any possible use of the rear-view mirror.

The car packed, my room and closet space emptied, goodbyes were said. With promises that I would visit sometime soon, maybe Thanksgiving, I hit the road at four in the morning.

With no CD or cassette player in the car, I blasted the radio—alternating between NPR (when I could get it), music (when I could get it), and right-wing, conservative radio talk shows (always accessible).

During the 85-mile-an-hour monotony of West Texas I-10, my mind drifted in random directions, finally straying to the smallest of the many boxes on the back seat of my car, the one into which my mother had carefully folded the coat.

It insinuated itself into my thoughts. Who was its original owner? Was he a decent human being forced into a bad situation? Or was he a vicious bastard, like the Nazi officer in *Schindler's List*? And what about provenance? What if the coat hadn't come to the family through Saba? What if it came through Savta? Could I find out? Saba was gone and Savta lived in a nursing home and suffered from pretty severe Alzheimer's. The window of opportunity had pretty much closed.

Approaching Van Horn, I pushed the search button on the radio and a crackle sounded, blessedly clarifying into Queen's "Bohemian Rhapsody." Perfect. I turned up the volume, drowning out my ruminations, and sang along.

Out of Texas into New Mexico. Overnight in Albuquerque. A late start so I could get some extra sleep. On to Arizona, then up into Utah.

In the second day's fading light, I passed oddly shaped, pastel-colored boulders balanced precariously on other boulders, and mountains eroded by rain into shapes resembling castles. My imagination morphed them into giant creatures of the night. I knew it was time to surrender to exhaustion when I thought I could see one of the silhouettes moving against the backdrop of the deep violet sky. Around eleven p.m., I reached Ogden, Utah. I pulled into a Motel 6 parking lot. It felt good to briefly stretch my legs as I walked to the entrance and went inside to get a room.

"May I help you?" asked the young woman behind the counter. Her dark skin in the sea of Utah whiteness made me wonder about her ethnicity. The absence of any identifiable accent didn't help. Native American? Middle Eastern? South Asian? I'd always heard Pakistanis and Indians owned a lot of motels across the country. But what would someone from Asia be doing in Nowhere, Mormonland?

"A single, please."

She slid a card and a pen across the countertop. "Yes, sir. Please fill this out. Queen okay?"

Broader nose, flatter forehead. I settled on Native American—most likely born and raised nearby. "A queen is fine."

"You can pull around to the rear of the building. Your room is close to the entrance back there." She handed me a small sleeve with my room card inside. "You're in room 135. Have a good stay."

Settled into my room, I turned on the television and flipped through the channels looking for some mindlessness before bed. The opening credits of *The Devil's Arithmetic* caught my attention. In the first few scenes the main character, a young woman, is reluctantly preparing for her family's Passover *seder*. Watching it brought back memories of being back at Saba and Savta's. I settled back into the room's armchair.

In the next part, when everyone greeted each other, the camera zoomed in on faded numbers tattooed on some of the family members' arms. Where was this going?

I enjoyed the scenes of the Passover seder, even though the main character rolled her eyes and refused to read from the *Haggadah*. I didn't buy this lack of respect in a family of Holocaust survivors. We never would have even considered behaving disrespectfully at Saba and Savta's. None of the grandchildren would ever have wanted to disappoint them that way.

It didn't take much longer for the movie to turn science-fictiony teenage-emo with the main character time traveling back to Lublin, Poland during the Holocaust years. Predictably, we discover the main character's relatives and new friends die in the horrors of Auschwitz. Enough. I hit the "off" button on the remote. It was late and the next day would be a long drive. I had every intention of pushing through to Seattle and needed to be alert for the curvy climb and descent through Washington's high mountains.

I slept fitfully. The movie I'd partially watched invaded my family's history and violated my dreams. I found myself in the asphyxiating darkness of a cave-like hole. I escaped into the gray light of the ghetto only to run and run, getting nowhere. I opened my mouth to scream, but no sound came. Panicking, I tried to control the direction of my dream— something I'd always managed to do before—to will an escape, find a doorway back to the present. Instead, I woke to my phone's six a.m. alarm, tangled in the top sheet, one of the bed's pillows on the floor.

I got out of bed, brushed my teeth, showered, dressed, and checked out of the Motel 6, handing my key to a gum-chewing blue-eyed young man who looked like he might still be in middle school. Before leaving the lobby, I filled a Styrofoam cup with complimentary lobby coffee and took a sip. It was way too bitter, but it was strong and would have to do. I was anxious to hit the road and needed the caffeine. The long drive would give me more time to think. I had to learn about the coat. I needed to understand Saba and Savta's lives, even though they'd never told their stories. Once I got to Seattle, I'd have the University's ample resources available for research.

Back in the car, the night's dreams filtered back. I turned the key, put the car in reverse, and pondered the possibilities.

CHAPTER THREE

MY *SHIKSE*

Amelia and I are a study in contrasts. My eyes are muddy brown, while hers are a cerulean blue. Her hair is a fine, straight strawberry blond, while mine is a mass of dark, untamable curls. My last name, Feinberg, is unmistakably Jewish. Hers, Wisniewski, is unequivocally Polish. Our shared one-bedroom basement apartment in the Greenlake neighborhood of Seattle always smelled of lavender and tea tree oil instead of fried onions and boiled potatoes. She is the sweetest of forbidden fruits, my pomegranate in the Garden of Eden. She nourishes me and offers me the promise of mainstream normalcy.

I'd met Amelia years after Saba's funeral and months after Savta's. With the loss of my grandparents, Dad's words from my Bar Mitzvah weekend had germinated. I spent time thinking about the coat, my grandparents' years in Europe, the horrors of their youth, and the specter of their history. I needed to fill the narrative void.

I watched documentaries, listened to professors, fellow students, and TED lectures. My ongoing research took me to different resource collections offering books and articles about the history of the Holocaust, human nature, culture, and epigenetics. Amelia just happened to work as a library aide in the University of Washington campus's Suzallo and Allen Library.

I loved working in the library's reading room, with its hanging brass lamps and long oak study tables sheltered by the umbrella of a huge vaulted ceiling. I also delighted in watching the facility's petite library aide replace books on the hundreds of shelves located just below the tall stained glass windows. My weekly visits there continued, even after I'd exhausted the collection's relevant materials.

Eventually, I felt comfortable enough to speak to the attractive employee. "Excuse me, I'm looking for a specific article in the February 2011 issue of the *Journal of Cross-Cultural Psychology.*"

She put her finger up to her mouth and whispered. "This is a silent reading room. Let's step outside." Once outside, she said, "You asked if we had that specific journal?"

I nodded. I knew damn well the article would be in a different campus library. The question's purpose was to impress, not to research.

She thought for a second while I looked into her bluest of blue eyes. "I don't believe we have anything like that in our library. I could check the campus database for you. I'm pretty sure what you need can be found at the Health Sciences Library—but I'm not sure that's really what you wanted."

I smiled. "You're correct. I still think you can help me, though." I paused. Was this the right way to do this? Already half committed, I went all in. "How about giving me your number so I can invite you out for coffee sometime?"

She smiled back, and I left with her name and number penciled in her slanted handwriting on a library request slip she'd pulled out of her pants pocket. I was gratified to see she didn't use tiny hearts instead of dotting her i's.

We began dating. In time, I fell in love. A year later, we moved in together. Now, together two years, I believe she might be the one.

Amelia has never been shy about asking the hard questions, ones I'd grown up avoiding. My previous girlfriends always shied away from my patrimonial history. Amelia attacked it with a passion.

"Where did your father's parents live?" "Why didn't they leave when they realized what was going on?" "How do you think they would have felt about me?"

Some of her questions I can answer. "They lived in Stopnica and Lodz before the war," I told her.

"Where are those?" she asked. "I mean, I know they're in Poland. But where in Poland?"

"One's in eastern Poland, and the other's in the southern part."

"That's not very specific."

"Look, I don't like looking at a map of Poland. When I see Warsaw, I can only picture the failed uprising. Lodz can never mean anything more than the ghetto that would have killed my Saba had he not managed to escape. Then there's Auschwitz, Treblinka, Dachau."

As to why they didn't leave, I never answered that one. Too many permutations exist for the answers, and I refuse to fall into the easy trap of blaming the victim.

As to how my grandparents would have felt about Amelia's and my relationship, a relationship with someone whose pedigree might well include the active participation in—or the passive disregard for the destruction of my family, I knew the answer but didn't want to hurt her feelings. My grandparents would have been horrified. If I marry her, a non-Jew, my children won't be Jewish. A *shanda*!

My parents once said, "You could try dating a Jewish girl now and again."

I answered, "You're right. I could." It's useless to argue. Agreeing without agreeing is the Jewish way.

But my grandparents are gone now, and my family hopes this is a passing phase—that, when I marry, it will be to a nice Jewish girl who will keep a kosher home and light the candles every Friday night. That's not Amelia. She offers the lightness missing from the burden of being a Jew.

Our first December together, she put up a Christmas tree in her apartment, arguing it was a pagan symbol which has nothing to do with Jesus. That Friday evening, she handed me her box of decorations.

"Go to it. Knock yourself out," she said, then laughed at my ineptitude when I had difficulty hooking the different shapes onto the shaky, prickly branches of a small, pinelike tree.

I reciprocated at Chanukah, bringing my menorah and a box of candles to her place, and challenging her to fix the candles into the too-small, wax-filled holders and light them in the correct order.

"Why the hell does the order matter?" Amelia challenged.

"I don't know. It just does." Of course it matters. In Judaism, everything matters.

Growing up, Chanukah made up the winter chapter of the sacrosanct trinity of visits to Saba and Savta's every year. Fall visits coincided with either *Rosh Hashanah* or *Yom Kippur*. Spring was Passover.

Back then, we'd drive from Rochester westward to Cleveland, sometimes on dry roads, other times on roads covered with snow, always stopping at the Angola, New York, travel plaza. The plaza sat on a large median strip between the eastbound and westbound lanes of I-90. Two pedestrian overpasses, one for each side of the highway, connected to the main building which, in turn, offered us lunch, last-minute gifts, and dozens of pamphlets we'd always collect for places we'd never visit.

Our ritual was to stop in the middle of the pedestrian overpass, stand by the large windows overlooking the highway, and wave at the approaching semis. If we got lucky, the driver waited until he was directly under us, then he blasted his horn, the sound and its vibration provoking our triumphant giggles. Then we'd all stroll into the main building for our last meal of American fast food until the drive home, the return trip offering the palpable relief of having survived another brush with the specter of the past.

Things changed when Saba and Savta retired from their jobs at the Dalton clothing factory and decided they'd had enough of Cleveland's winters. They became snowbirds, purchasing a one-bedroom condo in the same Florida complex as their greener friends. The Cypress Chase complex in Lauderdale Lakes became their winter residence and the new setting for our Chanukah visits. They decorated the condo with white furniture and pink art, everything accented with Judaism. A photograph of Jerusalem. A pure white tablecloth decorated with embroidered Stars of David. The large, silver candelabra for the *Shabbat* and holiday candles. When we walked in, we were always met by the odor of fried onions and potatoes, a staple in every single kosher meal Savta cooked.

Cypress Chase became their retirement *shtetl* where they could sun by the pool, socialize in the clubhouse, or attend services with that particular season's intern rabbi. Once or twice a week, Saba played late-afternoon poker with his friends in the clubhouse, wagering nickels on straights and full houses. When we visited, he invited me along. I'd sit next to him while he joked with his friends in Yiddish. In between hands, he'd offer me a banana or a piece of candy and ask if I was having fun, believing me when I smiled and said, "Yup."

In the evenings, we sat around the table in the apartment's dining room, where Savta had set up the Chanukah menorah. Every night, Ilana and I took turns putting in the candles and lighting them. Saba supervised, talking us through the way things had to be done.

"What night of Chanukah is it?" he'd ask.

We'd answer in unison.

"Take out the number of candles we need."

Ilana and I always had different plans. She picked two colors and alternated them. I used as many colors as I could.

Once we had our choices laid out, Saba said, "Put them in from right to left and light them from left to right. We always light the newest candle first."

We never thought to ask why, and Saba never told us. It was what it was. This was how you did it. That was all we needed to know.

Now, a few feet from the Christmas tree, Amelia chose to use all the white candles, inserting them into the menorah. She pointed at me. "Hey, aren't you supposed to wear something on your head?"

I grabbed a paper napkin in lieu of the *kippah* I didn't have. My head comically covered, I began the prayer.

Amelia picked up the candles' blue box and read along, using the transliteration printed on its back.

With the mandatory ritual complete, Amelia said, "Wait here. I have a surprise for you." She ran to the refrigerator and pulled out a plate of potato *latkes* she must have made earlier in the day. "I called your mother, and she talked me through her recipe. I hope they came out okay."

We popped them into the microwave, then we ate them, topping some of them with sour cream and others with applesauce.

As we carried the dirty dishes to the sink, I leaned over and kissed her. "That was better than okay. Thank you."

Her smile shone as brightly as the candles we'd lit a little while before.

As we cleaned up, I flashed on the eighth night of Chanukah moving across 39 global time zones, a contagion of tiny lights traveling from longitude to longitude over a 24-hour period—one of so many Jewish holidays celebrating freedom from our oppressors and the promise of a new world. I thought about the coat, that brown leather *Ledermantel* my grandfather had held on to and passed to my father, then to me.

I hung up the dish towel. "Do you need help with anything else?"

She shook her head. We weren't living together yet, and we both had early morning commitments. I grabbed my jacket and my menorah and kissed her goodbye at the door.

"Text me when you get home," she said.

When I arrived at my own apartment, I obediently texted Amelia. Then, I went into the bedroom and opened my closet to look at the coat. I forced myself to touch the thick, hard leather. With Saba's death, the coat's true story had been lost forever. How many different ways might it have come into our family? I thought about the books I'd read, the documentaries I'd seen, and the copious notes I'd taken. Imagination transported me, not to the experiences of the Holocaust, but to the experiences of survival—the experiences of my grandparents who made it to the other side. How many stories could I weave? I could weave them through with slender threads of details my grandparents had let slip in moments of inattentiveness. As I stood there, one of the threads stirred. I sat down at my computer and began to write.

CHAPTER FOUR

IN WHICH THE COAT
IS A GIFT OF FAREWELL

1942

Remnants of the gray winter light filtered through the cracked window. It was just before sunset, time for seventeen-year-old Mendel, his younger sister Ida, and the five people who lived with them to light the candles celebrating Chanukah, a commemoration of liberation. Standing in the fading light, they would recite the prayers and fulfill the ritual, even though this year's holiday held no joy. Any celebration of freedom was meaningless under the heavy reality of the Lodz Ghetto in December, 1942.

Three months earlier, eight days before Rosh Hashanah, The German-appointed "King Chaim" Rumkowski had gathered the entire population in the nearby square and made the announcement condemning 20,000 people.

"A grievous blow has struck the ghetto," said the German-appointed *Alteste der Juden*. "They are asking us to give up the best we possess—the children and the elderly."

A murmur arose from the crowd.

Rumkowski, in his bowler hat and warm herringbone wool coat—with the required yellow star sewn on—continued. "I must perform this difficult and bloody operation. I must cut off limbs in order to save the body itself. I must take children because, if not, others may be taken as well, God forbid."

The crowd's reaction amplified as Rumkowski sharpened his scalpel's blade. The very young. The very old. The very sick. A sacrifice all must make so the rest could survive.

Protests from parents of the young and children of the old rose to a deafening intensity.

"We will not let the children go!"

"We will all go!"

Rumkowski shouted over the crowd's cries. "You may judge as you please. My duty is to preserve the Jews who remain. I do not speak to hot-heads. I speak to your reason and conscience. I have done—and will continue doing—everything possible to keep arms from appearing in the streets and blood from being shed. The order could not be undone. It could only be reduced. But put yourselves in my place. Think logically, and you'll reach the conclusion that I cannot proceed any other way. The part that can be saved is much larger than the part that must be given away!"

Uniformed ghetto police came alive, swinging truncheons, forcing the crowd away from the cobblestoned square into their overcrowded buildings. The *Gehsperre*, had begun. That night, and during the following eight days of curfew and seizures, wails resounded through the emptied streets, a resurgence of the ongoing cycle of mourning over those being ripped away to a destination unknown.

That first *Gehsperre* train transport had taken Ida and Mendel's parents—Ida's infant daughter, Bella, in their arms, her screams piercing their hearts—the sound so horrendous the siblings never spoke of it again.

That memory still echoed, as Mendel and Ida stood in the candles' dim light, the tiny flames barely illuminating the darkness of their living quarters on Zielna Street.

The small apartment on the third floor would have been adequate for a single person or a newlywed couple. Now, seven people lived among yellowing walls, cracked windows, and inadequate plumbing. Photographs of past times and lost relatives hung on the walls next to a shared calendar which allowed them to mark the passage of time—when to light *Shabbat* candles, upcoming holidays, and new moons signaling the end and beginning of each Hebrew month.

The group remained stoic through the prayers and the lighting of that first night's candle. Liturgy carried the gathering until they began singing *Maoz Tzur*.

The women's too-recent losses silenced their voices after the first few lines.

Mendel and the other men doggedly continued singing in Hebrew. "Restore my House of Prayer, and there we will bring a thanksgiving offering, when You will have prepared the slaughter for the blaspheming foe." At this point, their singing stopped as well.

The brother and sister leaned into each other. Ida sobbed for the loss of her parents and her infant child. Mendel contemplated an alternative to what he suspected lay ahead.

Just that afternoon, he'd come home to find Ida breaking up a stool. They'd been using it as an end table, since that had been burned as heating fuel during the chill of November. "That would hardly warm up the kitchen, let alone the entire flat," he said.

"Not for heat," she'd replied. "To melt the frozen drinking water."

In spite of the losses, shortages, and hardships, life continued for the ghetto's ever-shifting population. Twelve hours a day, Ida and Mendel labored together at one of the ghetto's factories, manufacturing uniforms for the German military. Every morning, they trudged past bodies lying where they'd fallen, having died of starvation or disease. At work, only their midday ration of watery soup and weak, yellowish coffee interrupted the nonstop hours of cutting and sewing. Over time, their bellies contracted, and their feet and fingers swelled, making it increasingly difficult to work.

Rumkowski regularly spoke to his citizens, telling them, "My long-standing slogan, 'Work,' has proven itself from the start. We have seen, many times over, that only work brings calm. Experience has made it clear that, in our times, the basic law is that work protects us from annihilation."

So they worked. And they starved. And they suffered day after day, month after month.

Nearly another year had passed when a fresh rumor began circulating. Yossel, another worker in the factory, said, "There's a rumor the Germans have plans to modify an old factory to produce ammunition and armaments. I wonder who they'll select when the time comes? I sure hope it's not me. I'm happy enough sitting quietly at my sewing machine. I have no desire to *shlep* around heavy pieces of steel."

That evening, Mendel wrote a letter requesting an appointment to meet with Rumkowski.

"Is this true, what I hear about a new factory?" he asked, after he'd been admitted to the chairman's large, well-heated office.

The *Alteste der Juden* studied Mendel. "It is a possibility."

Mendel raised his head toward the ceiling, drawing himself up as far as his emaciated body would allow. He needed to appear tall, healthy. He riveted his eyes on Rumkowski, willing the *Alteste* to do what he wanted, what he needed. "I must work there. My time is being wasted sewing. I am a trained mechanic and can be useful first to the renovations, then as a production worker."

Rumkowski nodded. "I am glad you understand the importance of work to our survival. Would that more of our residents did as well. Leave your name with my secretary. My office will notify you when we are ready to begin."

Back in their apartment, Mendel shared the news with Ida.

She grabbed his arm. "You lied to him."

"I had to. Saying I have experience working with machines gives me a much better chance of being transferred to the new factory."

"You can't. You must stay with me. If you change jobs, I'll be alone all day, every day."

"You have friends in the factory. And we'll still be together in the evenings. I must find a way to get us out of here. Sewing uniforms offers nothing to that purpose. Fixing machinery requires tools. Manufacturing munitions requires tools. Those tools will be useful."

Ida covered her face. Her shoulders shook as her hands muffled her anguish. "I've lost so much, so many. Our brothers, Shmuel and Avram, off to fight with the Partisans. My husband shot for simply asking about the bread trucks. Mother and Father. My dearest infant, Bella. And now you want to leave me, too."

Mendel took Ida into his arms. Her hip bone stabbed at his thigh through the fabric of her dress. How thin she was. "*Sha, sha, maydeleh.* This will be a good thing. You must trust me."

She lowered her arms to her sides, her hands balled into fists, and slowly nodded.

How pretty she'd been before the ghetto—long, dark lashes shading soft gray eyes. Now, her tearless face reminded him of the dead lying on the streets waiting to be gathered up by the overworked gravediggers. How much longer could she go on?

A few months later, Mendel's bravado paid off. A letter from the *Alter's* office ordered him to report to the factory renovation project.

Conditions in the new building offered the same gray cold, the same watery portions of soup. But, he no longer pushed meters of fabric through a sewing machine. Steel replaced textiles. Levers, hand drills, and metal shears took the place of needles and pins. Mendel modified parts, repaired components, and replaced bearings. He worked—watching, waiting. Eventually, someone would tire, become careless, leave a tool lying where he could pick it up and tuck it between the worn fabric of his pants and his wasted body. Once that chance came, he would have to move quickly.

Weeks passed. The high snow drifts of winter melted, leaving streets covered in mud. As the weather improved and the early spring mud abated, the more ambitious planted crops of cabbage. The hot summer brought about swarms of insects who devoured the tender leaves, leaving little behind for the gardeners. Flour delivered to the ghetto was moldy. The store of potatoes, no longer frozen, was now rotten.

In late August, notices appeared. *Due to ongoing shortages, the ration of one loaf of bread will now have to last for ten days.* This, combined with the growing numbers of Jews and Romani being transferred into the ghetto each day, made the implications clear.

It was time for Mendel to share his plans with Ida. "I was right about the factory. They give us real tools. I think we have a good chance at escape."

"What are you talking about? Are you *meshugge*?"

"Ida, something bad is coming. I don't know when, and I can only imagine what. But I keep hearing rumors and I believe them. We need to leave before more deportations are ordered."

"I don't want to go. It's too dangerous. Whatever you think you know, I don't believe it. People on the transports are simply being taken to another place in the countryside, away from these overcrowded conditions. If we go we might even find Mama, Papa, and Bella. Rumkowski wouldn't lie. We'll be safer here. We're both good workers, and he promises work will keep us all safe. He's been right so far." Ida's eyes seemed to be gazing past Mendel's face, beyond the walls of their apartment and the borders of the ghetto. "They've only taken away the ones who could no longer do their jobs because they needed a healthier place to live. If I go, I might even find our family." She returned from her reverie and returned her eyes to Mendel's. "Stay. When they get that new factory up and running, you'll have work until the war ends and we're all free again."

"Or until the Germans change their minds."

Ida crossed her arms across her chest and stood in stubborn protest. "No, I'm right. I don't care what you want to do. I'm staying."

Mendel began leaving the flat earlier in the morning. Three kilometers to work and three kilometers home, he studied where it might be easiest and most inconspicuous to cut through the two barbed wire fences surrounding the ghetto's perimeter. Keeping a safe distance from the fence itself, he made sure the patrols saw him and got to know him. He hoped familiarity would make him invisible when the right time presented itself.

In December, Mendel watched as two SS officers escorted Rumkowski to a waiting black limousine. He returned two days later. No reports. No speeches. No promises. New rumors flew. Mendel didn't need to hear them. Nothing good ever came from any of Rumkowski's mysterious absences.

Six days later, Chanukah returned to the Ghetto. This time, there were no candles, no prayers, no songs of celebration. There was nothing to celebrate and nothing to celebrate with. Every day, new bodies appeared on the streets, rigid from the cold, lying where they'd dropped. Every morning it became more and more difficult to wake, eat the smallest slice of the shrinking ration of bread, and go to work.

"Ida," Mendel said one evening in late February. "The time is coming. Please change your mind and come with me."

"When? How? Even if we managed to get out alive, where would we go?"

"To the forest. I've heard about bands of Jews who have managed to survive in the forests around Poland. Better to take our chances out there than to be passive victims in here."

Ida's voice choked. "No. Rumkowski promised."

"He made no promises in December."

"Because there was nothing new to promise. You speak of rumors. I hear there are negotiations for more factories, more work. The Germans would never think of destroying their army of free labor. That's us. We're that army."

Mendel shook his head. Every week, people received their 'wedding invitations' to board the cattle cars taking them away to places unknown. "With you or without you, I am going to try and escape during the new moon of *Rosh Chodesh*. The darkness will provide cover, and I've spent months studying the movements of the patrols. All I need now is the right tool, a way to cut through the fence."

Ida looked down while her thin fingers plucked at Mendel's shirt. "Stay here. With me. We'll be safe."

"I can't."

Her forehead furrowed and her right eye twitched as she tried to contain her emotion. Her voice was almost a whisper. "Then, wait here. I have a gift for you. I wanted to give it to you for your birthday. But, now that you're leaving…"

She went into their shared bedroom and came back with something wrapped in the remnant of an old sheet and tied with a length of dirty string.

Mendel undid the tied bow and pulled open the worn fabric. Inside was a brown leather coat with a wool lining. He drew in a breath. "Did you steal this?"

"No. We've been making these as special orders. I traded some of my better dresses and my old pair of blue shoes with Gitla. She works in the tannery and, over time, slipped me the pieces of leather. I made this in between the coats destined for the *Wehrmacht*."

Mendel held the coat up against his body. "How long have you been working on this?"

"Almost a year. I wanted to make you something special for your birthday. Try it on. Let me see how it looks on you."

Mendel manipulated the heavy coat, slipping his left arm into one sleeve, his right into the other.

"I made it a little big. *Baruch Hashem*, when this is all over you can get back to your normal weight."

"I…" The emotional wave coursing through Mendel's body prevented the words from coming. He pulled his sister to him, wrapping her in the warmth between the coat and his body. The leather's redolence lent a fleeting lushness to their otherwise barren world. "It's perfect."

The moment passed. He kissed Ida on her forehead. Together, they wrapped the coat back in its sheet and placed it under the cot that served as Mendel's bed. He lay down, agonizing over his decision.

April came, along with opportunity. Someone at the munitions factory left a pair of tin snips lying on a nearby work bench. Mendel held his breath as he walked over and grabbed them, tucking them into his waistband. For the rest of that afternoon, he watched. If the guards or ghetto police caught him, he'd be shot where he stood. Maybe Ida was right. Maybe he was *meshugge*, but he couldn't continue living under the ever-worsening conditions of the ghetto.

When the long work day ended, he returned to their flat and checked the calendar. The night of April 23rd would be *Rosh Chodesh*, the new moon. The streets would be dark. He told Ida it was time.

She sighed. In a flat voice she said, "I can't change your mind?"

He tried one last time. "Come with me."

"I'll be fine here."

The days passed. The time came. Mendel took his clothing and removed the yellow stars from the front and back of each shirt. The stars left vibrant halos on the otherwise bleached, worn fabric. He took some ashes from the stove and rubbed them into the fabric, softening the contrast. Then, he layered as many garments as he could, topping everything off with the coat Ida had labored over so lovingly.

She accompanied him down the stairs, where they stood together on the street. He reached into his pants pocket and pressed some papers into Ida's hand. "These are my ration coupons. Use my portions of bread and soup to put some *fleisch* onto those bones of yours."

A silent space stood between them, each trying to memorize the other's face. Then, the siblings embraced and kissed each other on the lips; a final, ephemeral moment of intimacy.

Mendel turned to go.

Ida grabbed him and whispered, "Be well, Mendel. Stay safe. *Zol zayn mit mazel.*"

When he didn't turn to face her, she released him. He walked away. From her. From the ghetto. From Lodz.

He would never see Ida again.

CHAPTER FIVE

THE VIDEO

"Let's play the taste game," Ilana said to me one rainy day, when I was five and she was seven. "Close your eyes and guess what I'm putting in your mouth."

I squeezed my eyes shut and opened my mouth wide. A spoonful of something powdery was poured onto my tongue. A salty bitterness filled my mouth. I ran to the kitchen and spit into the sink. The game ended before it really began, with me crying and Mom yelling at Ilana.

As we got older, my older sister's persecution of me downgraded to mild harassment. Eventually, we became friendly, though never as close as those happy families in TV sitcoms. Distance and busy schedules defined our relationship. For years, I was an undergrad in one city and she was a ballet teacher in another. We'd call each other every couple of weeks and see each other a few times a year. We'd share news about my classes or her current boyfriend. It was during one of those casual conversations that I learned about the video.

I was 26, she was 28, and we were both home for a weekend visit. I sat with my cup of coffee while she sat with her iced sweet tea.

"Hey, Ilana. Do you know anything about that leather coat I got from Saba?"

"The Nazi one? I know you should wear it."

I wanted to roll my eyes but willed them to remain fixed on my sister. "Let me rephrase. Do you know anything about Saba and Savta's lives during the Holocaust?"

"I know about Savta's. It's on the video I made when I interviewed her."

Wait. What? "What video? You interviewed her? When?"

Ilana looked at me with her 'you're crazy' look. "You don't know about that?"

"How could I? Nobody ever told me."

"I interviewed her for over an hour when I was, like, fifteen. Dad let me use the video camera for it."

I remembered that video camera, a big black and silver contraption Dad called Two-ton Tessie. "Why wasn't I there? It isn't as though their house was so big that I could have missed something like that."

She shrugged. "I think you and Dad went off to an Indians game that day."

"Why didn't anyone tell me about it?"

"I dunno."

"Where's the video now?"

"I have it. But it's a VHS tape. If you want to watch it, I'll have to find a way to convert it unless you have a working VCR."

I'm not sure if Ilana felt guilty, generous, or sorry. But several weeks later, a DVD arrived in the mail, her barely legible chicken scrawl in black marker on the front of the disk: *Interview with Savta.*

I popped the disk into my computer and the drive whirred. The video had no title, no introduction. Just Savta appearing on the screen exactly as I remembered her. Perfect hair. A face with no makeup, other than a little lipstick. An immaculate white shirt decorated with sequined flowers.

She sat at the kitchen table and read from a piece of lined notebook paper in her hands. "My name is Leah Feinberg. I was born in Stopnica, Poland, on July 20, 1925. I had a very happy childhood in a very comfortable home with an older sister, Shoshana, and my two parents, Sara Szulman and Yaakov Kalman."

The camera panned over to three framed photographs hanging on the wall—I knew they were Savta's mother Sara, and Saba's parents, Aron and Julia. I recognized the whisper of familiarity in my great-grandparents' portraits. Saba's angular face. Ilana's soft almond eyes. My own sharp chin and high forehead.

The camera panned back to Savta's face. Her expression remained passive, her voice matter-of-fact. "In 1939, when I was fourteen years old, the Germans came." She impassively spoke of them seizing all the merchandise from her parents' store. The Germans taking all the men from the village. The fear of the women and children when they heard intermittent bursts of gunshots. Her terror that her father might be one of those lying dead in the nearby woods. Her joy at his return.

Through it all, her expression never changed; the cadence of her voice never wavered. Savta told her story like one might tell a fairy tale, with a lilting, far-away voice belying the horror of the Pied Piper leading the children away from their families or the wolf devouring Red Riding Hood's grandmother in a single gulp.

Savta stopped reading. She looked up at the camera as her memory took over.

"The Germans told us to pack what we needed. They forced us from our comfortable home into the ghetto. We were happy to be together. Then, one day, they separated Shoshana and me from our parents." Tears filled her eyes. The lilt in her voice broke, becoming an infantile whine. "They took the young people to Skarzysko to work. They told us, 'We'll bring the parents tonight.' I stayed awake all night waiting. They never came." She dabbed at her eyes with a crumpled tissue.

Ilana's voice: "Is that the labor camp where you made bombs?"

Savta nodded. "After six weeks, my parents bribed someone. One morning, at the usual five a.m. count, the official called Shoshana's name and then mine. We thought they were going to kill us." Her voice returned to its fairy tale distance. No more tears fell. "He told us, 'One sister can go to see the parents.' Shoshana said I was younger, so I should be the one to go."

"How did you get there?"

"They took me in the back of a truck. When I saw my father, I didn't recognize him at all. He was so small, so hunched over, like he was trying to disappear."

"How long were you there?"

"A few hours. When they took me away, I banged my head against the truck. I didn't want to live without my parents. I wanted to die."

I recognized our family's habitual pause before Ilana asked, "How do you know your parents died?"

"A man in Siemiennowice saw them put on a train. We knew that meant they were going to be killed."

Savta's demeanor broke. Her face transformed from my sweet grandmother's to that of a building's carved grotesque, the grief flowing from her eyes and seeping around the corners of her quivering lips. At that moment I wished there were photos of my Savta as a young girl. Try as I might, I couldn't transform the familiar grandmother on the screen into the teenager she'd been before the Holocaust ravaged her young life. I wondered how she dressed. How she wore her hair. Did she wear a necklace with a gold, Jewish star?

A cut in the video. A change of scene, this one in the Cleveland living room with its 1950s green wool carpet and coordinated upholstered furniture. Savta was composed. Face washed. Hair brushed. Fresh color applied to her lips.

Ilana eased back into the interview. "How much older than you was Shoshana?"

"Three years."

"How long were you in the labor camp?"

"Four years."

Ilana returned to the harder questions. "What was it like in the camp?"

"Torture. We lived without shoes, without clothes, without nothing. We were given one piece of bread all day."

"Didn't Shoshana save your life?" Ilana shifted her focus. Had it been as uncomfortable for her to conduct the interview as it was for me to watch it?

"I had typhus. Many people got sick. They put me in the hospital. Not really a hospital. It was where they treated the animals. They kept us on straw, the same as the animals."

I felt as though I were in a vacuum, the air being sucked out of my lungs. I knew how this story would end, but didn't know what else would happen before then.

"What did Shoshana do?"

"First, she hid me so they shouldn't take me to the hospital. Once they took me away, she bribed them to let her stay with me."

"What did you use?"

"Mommy and Daddy had given her a pin—a gold fish with a diamond eye. She hid it in her braid. We both had very thick hair. She gave someone that pin."

"How long were you in the hospital?"

"Seven days. It was terrible, terrible. My friend was there, also with typhus. They took her away with the dead while she was still alive. She never came back."

"Didn't you work as a maid for an officer later on?"

"Yes. I worked for him about a year."

"Was he good to you?"

"He didn't do anything bad to me."

Another cut. During the rest of the video, Savta shared her single most treasured possession—her box of old photographs. Ilana took a close-up of each photo as Savta described it. I'd seen the photos before. Savta enjoyed sharing them with us. Just like baseball with Saba, her photographs were her way of connecting with us.

I needed a break to think about everything I'd watched. I needed to find a way to reconcile the duality of Savta—grandmother and survivor. I shut off the video and looked down at my phone. Two missed calls from Amelia a half hour apart. I called her back and made arrangements to meet at her apartment.

A bus ride. A short walk. A knock on the door. A kiss hello.

"Do you want some coffee?" Amelia asked.

I nodded.

While the coffee brewed, we sat down at the tiny two-seater table at the edge of her kitchen counter.

"I just watched an interview my sister had with my grandmother."

"Wow. How did that go?"

"I survived. I mean, I watched the whole thing without losing it."

"Really?"

"Yeah. Savta was pretty dispassionate most of the time. There was a real disconnect between the story she was telling and her emotionless telling of it." A question percolated in my brain. I didn't mean to blurt it out. "Did your grandparents ever talk about their lives in Poland during the war?"

Amelia leaned back in her chair and away from me. "No, they didn't."

"Did you ever ask them about it?"

"I did once, a long time ago. They told me they didn't like to talk about those years."

I shouldn't have pushed the subject. I could see she was uncomfortable. I loved this woman. But I was on a mission. "Did they ever seem antisemitic? Did you ever get a sense of anything like that from them? I mean, it would probably have been something they weren't even aware of, just part of the popular sentiment at the time."

"Holy shit, Seth. It isn't fair to make assumptions just because they were Polish. The Germans were the ones who killed the Jews. The Germans killed plenty of Poles, too, you know."

I couldn't believe it. Amelia was educated, had a degree. How could she not know about how quickly the Poles jumped to help the Germans free Poland from its Jews? Among the few things Savta shared was how the

Poles and Ukrainians treated her worse than the Nazis. They wanted to be *Judenrein,* clean of Jews—even more than the Germans.

I looked at the familiar stranger sitting across from me. Her grandparents' lives during the war weren't her life. She couldn't be held responsible for anything they did or didn't do any more than I was responsible for my grandparents' survival. I needed to back away from the conflict.

"Sorry. I'm just a little sensitive right now." I reached across the table, my finger tracing around the random freckles on Amelia's hand, trying to gap the disconnect I'd created.

Amelia pulled her hand away from mine. "I understand we're from different backgrounds with the whole Holocaust thing. But my grandparents are good people. They would never have done anything to hurt anyone. I'm sure about that. I couldn't love them as much as I do if I ever thought they were capable of such evil. The fact they don't want to talk about the war probably means they're as disturbed by it as much as you are."

A silence lingered between us. Time to change subjects. "Here I am going on about the video and I never asked why you called earlier."

Amelia wasn't having it. "Look, I know you're trying to find your way through this whole coat thing. But looking for people to blame won't get you there."

"I'm not looking for people to blame. I'm just searching for a story."

Amelia stood up, shut off the coffeemaker, and grabbed her purse. "Let's call a truce. How about going to Saigon Deli to get some *banh mi* sandwiches and *ca phe das*?"

We took a bus down to the U District and got our food to go. Then we Ubered back to my apartment, where we watched the entire video together.

This time, I watched it with an academic eye, trying to collect information I might have missed during my first viewing. Savta's telling made no accusations, assigned no blame. She spoke calmly, laying down the facts, crying only when she spoke of her parents, dry-eyed and dispassionate when she told of everything else.

While I made mental notes, Amelia cried her way through the story. When we got to the part where Savta began showing her photographs, I shut off the video.

"Why'd you do that?" Amelia protested as she got up for a tissue to wipe the wetness from her face.

"You don't really want to see an hour of family photographs, do you?"

"Damned straight I do. I never got to meet your grandparents. I want to see everything."

I turned the video back on, and Amelia settled back into the couch while Savta showed her extensive collection of photographs. This time, she didn't merely name people, the way she did when we used to look at them together. On the video, she included dates and places.

Amelia laughed when we got to the photos of my dad as a child. "Look at that one of your father on his bicycle," she said. "You look a lot like him."

By the time we finished, it was dark. "I guess you have a lot to think about," Amelia said at the bus stop, just before she headed home.

"I do. Sorry about earlier."

"It's okay. I'll get over it. After watching your Savta's story, I can understand how you felt. I just hope you can understand how I feel."

"I do. I'm so mixed up. Seriously—that damned coat."

I looked away. Amelia grabbed my arm. "We'll figure it out together. You go back inside and find something to do other than overthinking things. Listen to music, watch TV, or read a trashy book."

"What I really need to do is grade some exams."

"Then do that. You can try to make sense of what you learned another time."

Amelia's bus pulled up. She gave me a quick kiss and climbed on.

Back in my apartment, I didn't grade exams. I didn't listen to music, watch TV, or read a trashy book. Instead, I sat down and watched the video for the third time that day.

CHAPTER SIX

IN WHICH THE COAT
IS A PROTECTIVE TALISMAN

1944

The shock of the warmth against Leah's face made her tremble as they entered the cottage. She wanted to rub that gift into her bone-thin arms, but dared not move. Even the slightest twitch had consequences. So she stood there, just inside the doorway, rubbing her tongue against the roof of her mouth to distract herself from the unexpected comfort.

"Good morning, Kommandant Pollmer," said her escort, a tall, thin guard with stark blue eyes and narrow lips. "Kommandanten Fuks said you wanted a young woman to be your housemaid."

"Yes, yes. Leave her here and come back at seven tonight. I have a full day of work for her."

"Thank you, Kommandant Pollmer." After a click of his heels and a straight-arm salute, her escort walked away, leaving Leah standing alone in the entryway.

She glanced up from the ground to sneak a look at her new overlord. He looked softer than most of the other Germans in the camp—his nose not as beak-like, his eyes a cool steel gray rather than the usual icy blue.

She startled when he spoke "I am *Werkschutz* Kommandant Pollmer. You'll be working for me." He pointed toward the kitchen. "There are dishes in the sink to be washed. When you're done, scrub the floors down. Whoever lived here before left this house a filthy mess." Without another word, he walked into a different room, closing the door behind him. Music began playing. An orchestral piece by Brahms. Leah recognized it from the collection of recordings her father used to have.

Leah walked to the kitchen to find cleaning supplies. The cottage was so different from the house she had grown up in before the Germans had come. This one seemed claustrophobic, with its dimly lit foyer, small kitchen, and dark, rough wood floors. Her family's two-story house had been opulent—the downstairs illuminated by tall arched windows or, at night, by crystal chandeliers. A grand staircase led to the upstairs bedrooms—one for her parents, one for her sister, Shoshana, one for her, and another for guests. And their kitchen—Anka, their cook, made sure it was filled with activity preparing their meals and baking their pastries. Gone now. All gone.

She used to hate those who stripped her of her previous life, but the brutality at the Skarzysko-Kamienna labor camp had worn her down, numbing her feelings and killing her spirit. This new work assignment would be a new form of degradation—working as a maid for a German officer.

She walked into the kitchen. Days of dishes sat in the sink, a rag and a bar of brown soap on the shelf behind them. No flies buzzed above the collection. The Polish winter was too cold for any of them to have survived. A bucket and a scrub brush sat in the corner, a spider, wisely avoiding winter's frost, using the conjoined walls as an anchor for its home. She set to work.

After the dishes were dried and put away, she filled the bucket with water. Getting down on her knees, the soap and the scrub brush helped her work on the floor. True to the Kommandant's word, it was filthy. Leah scrubbed the wood three times before the natural color revealed itself. By the time the floors were finished, so was the bar of soap.

Her mind raced. Everything was valuable during a war, even to a high-ranking officer. There had to be more soap. She needed to find it before she was accused of stealing. She opened the kitchen's cupboard. Nothing but dishes. Where else to look?

Leah dragged over a chair and climbed up to check the cupboard. Only dust and mouse droppings. She wet a rag and made short work of their disposal. "How easy it is to clean away something you know is worthless," she thought, as she rinsed out the rag.

The desperation for more soap eclipsed her fear. She cautiously walked over to the door separating her from the German officer. The exuberant strains of Mozart's *Great G Minor Symphony*'s first movement drifted through the closed door. She stood listening to it, listening to her breath, trying to work up the courage and find the right words. Body tense, eyes closed, she knocked.

"Enter," the Kommandant's voice commanded.

She opened the door and waited.

Pollmer lifted the phonograph's needle. "Already done with the dishes and the floors?" He paused, studying the gaunt, washed-out figure standing in front of him. "What shall I call you?" he asked.

She stood there stiffly at attention, uncertain, afraid to speak.

"Well? Your name?"

"Leah," came her voice, barely a whisper.

"Speak up, Leah."

"I'm sorry, Kommandant. I don't mean to disturb you. But it took all the soap I could find to wash the kitchen floor. I wonder if there is another bar somewhere so I could continue cleaning the rest of the house?"

His laugh jarred her. She stood in place, waiting for something else unexpected.

"I told you this place was a filthy mess. To be honest, I'm not sure where there might be more soap. I can certainly requisition it. Meanwhile, there happens to be a feather duster in the smaller bedroom's *Kleiderschrank*. There are at least ten rooms' worth of dust in this four-room house. See to that."

Pollmer walked over to the phonograph and Mozart sounded again as Leah closed the door.

The bedroom—terrible things can happen in the bedroom. Then again, terrible things happen in a kitchen, in a study, or even under a cold, blue winter sky. Nothing terrible had happened this morning. Perhaps she would make it through one more in an endless series of days.

True to Pollmer's word, a feather duster hung on the inside of the free-standing closet's doors with a broom angled next to it. Leah couldn't help but study the few garments hanging on the other side—two olive green officer's uniforms, a brown wool suit, and a heavy, brown leather coat. The coat demanded her attention. What a treasure for these freezing days. She reached out to touch it, then drew back. What if Pollmer caught her?

She snatched the duster and closed the door. She moved the duster across the window sill, the lamp shade, the small bedside table on which the lamp sat. The room grew hazy. Leah knew the dust would only settle again, becoming an infinite, endless task. She needed more than feathers. Nevertheless, she moved from room to room and dusted until the day ended and another German soldier arrived to return her to her barracks and her people.

The next several days passed much like the first. A German guard brought her to Pollmer's cottage, where she cleared and scrubbed and dusted. Soiled laundry. Dirty dishes. Scuffed floors. Smeared windows. Then, on the fifth day, Pollmer strolled into the kitchen where Leah stood scouring the burnt remains of the previous night's dinner from the stove top.

She flinched when his voice boomed, "So, Leah, how is your cooking?"

The truth was, Leah had never cooked a day in her life. Anka had always prepared their meals, except for the Friday night *challah*. Her mother had always insisted on baking this herself. How Leah had loved the smells of the bread just before it came out of the oven. "Yes, Kommandant. I can cook."

"Good, good, because I have been most unsuccessful with my attempts. There is a chicken in the ice box and some potatoes on the counter. If you need anything else, there are more potatoes and some onions in the store room out back. See what you can do with them."

He returned to his study and Bach's *Brandenburg's Concertos*.

The potatoes were dusty and the chicken slimy. Leah wrinkled her nose as she butchered the chicken and considered the different iterations of what Anka had made every Friday for *Shabbat* dinner. What would be easiest? Chicken stew seemed simple enough. She only needed an onion.

She went out back to grab one. The potatoes in the adjacent basket tempted her. She considered stealing a couple and hiding them under her shirt to share that evening with her sister, Shoshana. They could take the place of her now-withered breasts, a pair of edible replacements guaranteeing a sure, swift death if discovered by the guards. Sighing, she selected a single onion and returned to the kitchen.

While slicing the onion, its pungency brought tears to her eyes. Raw emotion threatened to unmask her stoic façade. *Aba* and *Ima* dead. Shoshana left to slave without her in the munitions factory. Sobs welled up. Never to see her dear parents again. Never to have any life but this until she died of typhus, or starvation, or a cruel guard or *kapo's* whim. Leah's focus returned to the potato. She held back her sorrow and allowed only the slightest cough to escape.

When all the ingredients sat in the pot, she added a small amount of water, remembering Anka once saying, "You see, Leah, stew is like magic. You put in a little bit of water and you wind up with twice as much broth!"

As the aroma of real food filled the house, Leah's stomach groaned, and her mouth watered for a taste. She went over to the stove. After all, one must taste food while it's cooking. She dipped the spoon below the frothy scum forming on the surface, blew across the liquid she extracted, and took a taste. Her stomach seized with desire. Did she dare take more?

Rather than more broth, she drank the scum she skimmed off the surface. When only the broth and solids remained, she walked down the hallway and scrubbed the windows by the entrance, in the parlor, in the bedroom. Anywhere but the kitchen, where temptation simmered in a speckled enamel pot.

The day ended. A guard came just as Pollmer sat down to his dinner. Leah returned to her barrack, guilty for having tasted real broth while her sister only ate a stale piece of bread dipped in swill.

The following morning, Pollmer startled Leah when he came out of his room and sat down at the kitchen's heavy oak table. "Where was your home before you availed yourself of our hospitality?"

"Stopnica, Kommandant."

"Herr Pollmer will do." A pause. "Stopnica. I wonder how much is left of your town?" Pollmer continued as though in a dream, staring off beyond the kitchen walls. "You know, the Hasag factory has been here a long time, I believe since the late 1800's. But the barracks were built following the destruction of a town, probably one like yours. This house was spared, unlike its former occupants. You people really should have left before mine rounded you up like cattle."

Left? Where could they have gone? Even with money, there was nowhere to go. She kept her eyes lowered, directing her flood of anger at the floor.

Pollmer continued, his fingers drumming on the wooden table top. "I have no taste for the brutality surrounding us here. I did not become an officer in the German military for this. That is why I choose to work in my residence rather than my office in the factory."

The empty, soundless space demanded a response. "Yes, Herr Pollmer."

The sound of her voice startled him back to the kitchen. He slapped both his hands down on the worn wood of the table. "What do you know about sausage and eggs?"

Leah knew very little about them. Anka used to prepare eggs, but Leah's family had never eaten sausage. "I'm sure I can fix them, Herr Pollmer."

"Fine. You will join me. A walking skeleton needs nutrition to help her do her job."

Leah had no response to the shocking statement. Instead, she merely took out the food and carried it over to the stove.

Pollmer sat and studied her while she cracked the eggs into a bowl and mixed them with a wooden spoon. "How old are you?"

"Sixteen, Herr Pollmer."

"How long have you been here?"

Sausage sizzled in the cast iron frying pan. Time was difficult to calculate—one terrifying day followed another, each one with the impossibility of prophesy. One more or one less meal? A beating? A new humiliation? These past six days had been wonderful by camp standards. A warm house. No brutality. But she continually mourned the loss of her parents and worried about Shoshana working under constant threat. And now, Pollmer's offer of real food.

"So?" Pollmer's voice interrupted her thoughts.

"I believe about two years, Herr Pollmer."

"A long time, I think. No typhus?"

A turn of the sausage. A splatter of grease on the stovetop. "I did have typhus, Herr Pollmer."

"Enough of this constant 'Herr Pollmer,' girl. Speak with me as you would anybody else. You survived your typhus, eh?"

"Barely, Herr…barely. I was put into the infirmary; really an animal hospital where they put sick prisoners."

"Yes, I'm familiar with the place. I marvel you survived it."

"My sister refused to leave me and prevented them from taking me out with the dead bodies." Leah stopped speaking rather than tell Pollmer how burning the still-alive with the already-dead was a common occurrence.

"You speak of a sister. Is she still alive?"

She poured the eggs into a small pan and stirred them as they coagulated over the heat. "Yes. She still works at the munitions factory in Werk A. We used to work there together."

Pollmer nodded.

The tantalizing smells clawed at Leah's stomach. She yearned for the freedom to eat the meat, but sausage was *treif*. Pork was not permitted. Leah's mind struggled to find a loophole, a way she could bring herself to consume what was forbidden. Many people in the barracks ate the cockroaches and beetles. Surely she could force down some pork.

Leah plated the eggs and sausages and carried them over to the table.

"I invited you to eat with me. Bring another plate and sit down."

Leah did as she was told. Pollmer pushed half of the eggs and a large sausage link onto her plate.

Her thoughts did battle with her stomach. To choose between observing the laws of *kashruth* or obeying a German officer and temporarily mollifying years of starvation.

She watched as Pollmer ate methodically. He cut a piece of the sausage and pushed some of the egg onto it, putting the combination into his mouth. He pointed his knife at Leah's plate. "Eat. Eat."

She picked up the fork and took a bite of the eggs. A drawing rush of saliva pulled along her jawline. She swallowed, ignoring the sensation, and wolfed down several more mouthfuls, finishing the eggs on her plate.

"You must try the sausage. It is quite good, and so difficult to get these days."

Leah tentatively cut a small piece and put it in her mouth. An intense wave of nausea made her jump up and run outside, her body rejecting the taboo protein. She fell to her knees and vomited violently, purging both the permitted and the forbidden. When her body was done with its revolt, she returned to the kitchen and rinsed out her mouth.

Pollmer tsked, the smallest of smiles teasing the corners of his mouth. "Perhaps a slower start would have been better."

"May I please get back to work?"

With a flicked wave of his hand, the Nazi officer dismissed his maid.

The days passed. The house became cleaner, the work load lighter, though it seemed Pollmer hosted more and more meetings during the evening hours. Leah often arrived to find empty glasses and bottles smelling of beer littering the kitchen table. What plans did such men make and how might they affect her and Shoshana? Better not to think of such things. Better to place the bottles out back, wash the glasses, and scrub down the table.

The first signs of spring came one sunny morning, when a warm breeze ruffled Leah's stubby hair as she and her escort walked to the cottage. The sensation against her scalp stirred up sorrow over the loss of her beautiful, thick hair, shaved off during her bout with typhus.

At the cottage, Pollmer was already in his study, Beethoven's *Fifth Symphony* playing from behind the door. She stepped into the kitchen and began the day's work by doing the few dishes and washing the springtime mud tracked all over the entrance and kitchen floor. The sun rose higher in the sky, beckoning through the tiny window, the luxury of feeling it on her face too strong a lure.

"Surely Herr Pollmer won't mind if I go out for just a few minutes." Having spoken it aloud surprised Leah. It also emboldened her.

She opened the kitchen door, leaned against the door jamb, and raised her face, eyes closed, to welcome the warmth of the late morning sun. A breeze carried the springtime songs of birds searching for their mates. How wonderful to do nothing but take pleasure in something so simple.

"Enjoying your little break in the sun?" Pollmer's voice was so close his breath tickled her ear.

As Leah turned, he was on her. He grabbed her arm and dragged her into the kitchen. She cried out. "Herr Pollmer. I'm sorry. The sun. The warmth. I swear, I was only outside for a minute."

"A minute of my time. My time! Not yours!"

Pollmer threw Leah to the ground and grabbed the handle of the broom. "Who. Do. You. Think. You. Are?" he shouted, striking her with each word. Her legs. Her back. Her head.

Leah covered the back of her head and neck, a defensive posture learned from beatings she'd received during her time in the ghetto and then the factory. "Please, Herr Pollmer," came her muffled plea. The thick straw bristles drew blood where they pierced her skin.

"Jew!" shouted the German as he continued striking her. "I should have known your true nature would come through. I should never have allowed myself to trust even a little. First the pig Russians practically at our doorstep, and now you. Now this. How dare you take advantage of all the kindnesses I've shown you?"

As abruptly as it began, the beating ended. "Ach! Look what you forced me to do," He threw the broom to the ground as if it had burned his hands. "You caused me to lose my temper. I am not a man who likes to lose control. Get out of my sight."

Leah struggled to her feet, trying not to shake, forcing herself not to cry. She hadn't thought Pollmer capable of violence. But now…

Her body stung from the blows as she walked as calmly and as steadily as possible out of the kitchen and into the small bedroom. She heard a door slam. Music. Wagner's Overture to *Tannhäuser*.

A pair of Pollmer's boots sat in the corner. She opened the closet where the shoe polish and brush were kept. Good. A simple task to focus on and calm her nerves. Her eyes fell on the brown leather coat. She reached over and touched it, expecting the leather to be supple and soft. Instead, it was stiff and unforgiving. Tears spilled over onto her cheeks. Nothing was what it seemed. There was no understanding the world. Shoshana should have allowed the typhus to take her, rescue her from softness turned hard, where kindness could transform into brutality in a split second.

Over the next several weeks, she and Pollmer reverted to a more formal relationship, though the strain showed when he continued to demand she keep him company at mealtime.

One day, she arrived to find an empty cottage. More dishes than usual sat in the sink, and the crushed butts of cigarettes filled a small flowered bowl.

As the morning hours passed, she worried. She'd been alone in the cottage before, but Pollmer had never been gone for more than a couple of hours. Unsure when he would be back, Leah took out a few links of sausage and sliced them into thick rounds. That way they could either be put back in the ice box or cooked up quickly and served with bread when Pollmer returned.

Hours ticked by. He still did not arrive.

Leah busied herself with sweeping and dusting. Finally, as the sun sat low, she heard Pollmer enter the cottage.

"Herr Pollmer?" she called, surprised at her relief.

He entered the kitchen and nodded, dropping down into his usual seat at the table.

The words left her mouth before she could stop them. "You were gone all day."

"A long meeting. The Russian front is advancing, and we can't seem to hold them back. This is a bad thing for us and a worse thing for you. We have orders to begin evacuating the camp."

Evacuation. So many people. How could they transport everyone? And where? "I took out some sausage. I can cook it up, if you'd like."

"No. Someone will arrive soon to return you to your barrack. I have much work to do. I will see you tomorrow."

Rumors spread through the camp. People claimed the Russians were advancing even faster than the Germans had anticipated. Shoshana and Leah worried they would be separated in the inevitable upheaval.

Word came of the occupants of Werk B being forced to march away from camp, the weaker ones dropping from exhaustion; those who survived relocated to another factory further from the Russian line.

Pollmer grew haggard. Bags from lack of sleep developed under his eyes, and he often came to meals unshaven, his hair disheveled.

One early morning roll call a guard called out, "Leah and Shoshana Kalman!"

They gripped each other's hands and stepped forward.

"Come with me," ordered the German.

He led them the familiar distance to Pollmer's cottage amidst the distant whistling and booming of mortar layered with cracks of gunfire. The sisters looked at each other, eyes wide, unsure what to expect.

Pollmer answered the door wearing the brown suit she'd always seen in the closet. He brusquely dismissed the guard and led the sisters to the kitchen.

Leah walked over to the sink and gestured for Shoshana to start cleaning the stove.

"Not today." Pollmer said. "Sit."

All three at the table, Pollmer lowered his voice. "The Russians are only a few miles away. Plans are to evacuate the entire camp. I expect most on that march will die, either by God's will or our hand. Leah, you've been a loyal worker for me, and I see no reason for you or your sister to suffer that fate. Wait here."

Pollmer left the kitchen momentarily, returning with the heavy leather coat and one of his uniform jackets.

"I will be leaving the camp and you two will come with me. We will enter a world with no knowing. These coats would only identify me as an enemy officer." Pollmer gave a wry smile. "Much better for me to travel incognito. Now, you two—these coats will serve you well. Wear them or barter them. One way or another, you'll soon be free, whatever good or ill that brings. Just know, the Russians are not your friends, nor are the Poles. I'll escort you until we're a few kilometers from the camp. Then we will part ways. I will remember you, Leah. I hope you will remember me with some kindness."

With a sharp click of his heels and a quick bow, he opened the door and the three of them walked out to face the unknown.

CHAPTER SEVEN

LIBERATION IS NOT FREEDOM

Passover. My 29th, to be exact. Why was this night different from all other nights? Tonight I'd be conducting a *seder* by myself for the first time. How hard could it be? I'd certainly been to enough of them to remember the flavor of Savta's food and the tenor of Saba's leadership.

None of my invitees were Jewish. Michael was a Catholic chemistry major, Susan an Episcopalian biologist. Amelia had invited Laurie, a fellow atheist she worked with at the Pacific Science Center. Most of the fifteen people attending had never been to a *seder*. A few didn't even know what Passover was or what it commemorated. I'd carefully gone over the *Haggadah*, marking in the margins what to read, what to skip, and jotting in commentary I wanted to expound upon or group discussions I thought we should have.

I surveyed the dinner table with the improvised extension of two borrowed folding tables and the desk Amelia and I moved from the study area. Instead of Savta's fine white linens and gold-trimmed porcelain *kiddush* cup, our plastic-backed tablecloth, paper napkins, and two-piece plastic wine cups had come from the party goods store. *Fifty percent stronger than the leading comparable store brand paper plates* replaced gold-trimmed china. Amelia had insisted on the tacky ones, the plates with the blue trim and a big Jewish star in the middle, adding to the illusion the food would be kosher (it was not) and the participants would know what they were doing (for the most part, they would not).

She'd done a great job, working from Pinterest photos of other families' holiday tables and website recipes. She'd made a traditional European *charoset* with apples, walnuts, matzah meal, and sweet red kosher wine. The concoction looked like brown crap, but tasted wonderful—tart, sweet, and nutty, all at the same time. Our brisket was brown too. In fact, most of the food we'd be eating that night was varying shades of brown. Only the fresh greens on the *seder* plate would add some color to the meal. I ran to the *Haggadah* to jot down another note. *The food is brown, like the sand of the desert, like the mud of the labor and concentration camps. Why, then, do we dip bright green karpas into salt water representing our tears? Talk about the eternal sorrow of the Jewish people blended with our eternal hope for peace.* I also reminded myself to speak about the fact that Jewish slavery was not limited to the years after Joseph brought us down into Egypt. After all, Savta and her sister Shoshana had been slaves in a German munitions factory, until some Nazi officer brought Savta into his home as his housemaid.

I thought back to one special Passover when Shoshana had come to the United States from Israel, a rare visit between two orphaned sisters. It was the first and last time I would meet Savta's sister, quite a contrast with the Savta I'd known all my life. Savta was short, not much more than five foot two. Shoshana, with her slim build, seemed to be so much taller. But, where my grandmother walked with her head up and back straight, Shoshana walked with a beaten slouch, as though she needed to match her sister's height, rather than tower over her. In spite of her hair, dyed a red that would never exist on a natural head, in spite of the heavy makeup covering the wrinkled skin and baggy eyes, she seemed much older than the two years that separated them.

Before the *seder*, I sat with the two women as the house filled with the odors of stuffed cabbage, chicken soup, and brisket. The flavor of their reunion sweetened the room with animated conversations drifting from language to language—Yiddish, Hebrew, Polish, English.

"How are Yizhar and Ika?" asked Savta.

"*Beseder.* They're good. Ika's kids, *kein ayin hara*, are fine. Yizhar's wedding is next year. *To dobra dziewczyna.* I hope you and Mendel can make it out."

Savta sighed.

Shoshana changed the subject. "What can I help? You want I should set the table?"

Savta smiled over at me. "That's Sethy's job. Wait 'til you see how beautiful he makes the napkins."

The word "beautiful" came out in four distinct, heavily accented syllables: bee-you-tee-ful. The smile—the compliment—were my cues. I got up and went over to the china cabinet where the Passover dishes sat on display along with Savta's treasured lead crystal goblets.

Shoshana came over and sat on the dining room chair at the head of the table. "Seth," she said, as I took the white linen napkins and folded them into origami fans. "I am very happy to finally meet you. You are even more handsome than the photo sent to me by your Savta. She says you are a wonderful *yingele*." Savta's familiar Yiddish word coming from the mouth of a near-stranger.

I looked up at my great-aunt and grabbed at an opportunity. "You were together in the labor camp with my Savta, weren't you?"

Shoshana's face tensed. A change came over her, as though she'd become a different person. The smile disappeared, and she pulled at the fingers of her left hand with her right—Lady Macbeth trying to remove the stain of death. "*Nachon*. We were together in that place."

Should I continue? She deserved more than a series of questions, an interview, even though I wanted to ask so much. Precious little had ever been said about any of their time during the war. In fact, little had been said about life before and after the Germans invaded and destroyed my grandparents' world. Better not. Who was I to force anyone to speak of those times?

"I just wanted to thank you for being there for her. She probably would have died if she'd been all alone."

"I maybe die as well, if I did not own the responsibility to keep her alive." Shoshana stood up. "Speaking of my sister. I must go and help with food. I promised to make Israeli *charoset*."

That was the only year we ate *charoset* made with dates and mashed bananas. The Sephardic-style mixture kept company with the rest of the ritual food on Savta's treasured *seder* plate. Her treasured china, silverware, and crystal, the sets used only for Passover *seders*, gilded each place at the table.

We took our seats, and Saba began. We read every word on every one of the twenty-eight pages in the *Haggadah* before eating—the subsequent twenty saved until after "The Festive Meal." Ilana and I looked at our cousins and each other, telepathically praying for a break from the annual marathon. This passage in English. That one in Hebrew. Lifting the *matzah*. Pointing to the shank bone. Never skipping a song, a prayer, a word. Never getting to the actual food until well after nine.

At *my seder*, at *my* table, unlike Saba, I would skip. Rather than plodding through the ritual, I'd lighten the burden with an interactive evening. My *seder* would be an intellectual pursuit, using the foundation of the writings to inspire an understanding of the Passover story for what it is—an important allegory. Passivity versus action. The horrors of slavery. The truth about freedom. The importance of asking, and telling, and passing on.

At my table, we'd use my *seder* plate, the one I'd made in Hebrew school kindergarten with a five-year-old's interpretation of the ritual foodstuffs in brightly colored markers on a melamine blank: The shank bone, the egg, the bitter herbs, the *charoset*, and the *karpas*. My teacher had sent the plates off to be "finished," making the final product food and dishwasher safe.

"At least the dishes are all *pesadick*," I told Amelia, after she came home and took her purchases out of the party store bags.

"Pesa-what?"

"Kosher for Passover."

Amelia still looked confused.

"Because of the prohibition against eating anything with leavening, or anything else resembling flour, we have to use special dishes which haven't come in contact with those types of ingredients."

"Wow," she said. "Passover is one tough holiday. How many days can't you eat normally?"

"Well, if you're an observant Jew, you can never eat 'normally.' There are all these rules about what we can and can't eat, not to mention all the different fast days. Then there are food traditions. Dairy on *Shavuot*. *Hamantaschen* on *Purim*. Lots of liquor for the adults on *Simchas Torah*." I grinned.

"And you grew up that way?"

"Not really. My parents were traditionalists. We celebrated most of the holidays but weren't strict. Like, they never bought kosher meat, and we only fasted on *Yom Kippur*. I think they wanted my sister and me to grow up with some connected understanding of our culture. The only time things got strict was when we visited my father's parents for the holidays—*Rosh Hashanah, Yom Kippur*, and Passover."

"And Chanukah," Amelia added.

"And Chanukah."

The doorbell rang. Our guests began arriving. We handed each one a cheap satin *yarmulke* we'd borrowed from the University's Hillel House. We had several different *Haggadahs,* their different covers resulting in a colorful mix. Emily had laid one at each place setting. I'd grabbed several free Maxwell House Coffee ones from the local grocery store. Amelia had snagged a few of the free ones put out by Maneschewitz. I'd be using the *Passover Haggadah: New English Translation and Instructions for the Seder* by Rabbi Nathan Goldberg, published in 1984.

When everyone was seated, the time had come to see if the years of holidays spent with my orthodox grandparents had paid off. I watched as my guests flipped through the pages of their *Haggadahs,* pausing as if to parse the meaning of this unfamiliar language. I opened my own *Haggadah* and took a sip of water.

I began. "Welcome to this semi-conventional Passover *seder*. Many of you have probably never participated in a *seder* before. So, if there are any questions during the evening, please feel free to ask them. As for me, this will be my first time leading. If any of you would like to chime in or volunteer to help with any of the prayers or songs, please do. After all, this is a holiday celebrating freedom, so let's not be afraid to break with the canon."

I heard my own voice echo all the years of listening to Saba read the introductory prayers. I blessed the first cup of wine, and we all drank.

Amelia got up and brought over a basin half-filled with water and a large red plastic cup so we could wash our hands while seated at the table. The ritual continued. Celery dipped in salt water. The breaking of the middle matzah. The lifting up of the *seder* plate. The pouring of the second cup of wine.

"Now for the Four Questions. *Ma Nishtana*—why is this night different from all other nights? The youngest child at the table usually sings these questions. Why? Because that's what makes the most sense. Usually, the adults at the Passover *seder* are pretty familiar with the story, while the children are still learning and need an explanation for what it's about." I surveyed the guests seated around the table. Our youngest was a Baptist sociology student from a small town in South Carolina. What did he know from Hebrew, or *seders*, or anything Jewish? I decided the job fell to me. "Tonight, I'll sing the questions in Hebrew. You can follow along using the transliteration, then we'll all read them together in English."

As I sang, I closed my eyes and pictured myself at fourteen years old, Saba mouthing the questions along with me, and Savta taking a break from plating food in the kitchen, her arm around Shoshana's waist, their heads touching, their lips pursed in pride over me; their hope for the future—the grandchild who'd inherited the coat, its legacy, my responsibility.

All those years ago, when Shoshana visited, her Passover gift was the tiniest whisper of my Savta's secret past, the unspoken years in Europe, the impossibility of true freedom.

CHAPTER EIGHT

IN WHICH THE COAT
IS BARTERED

1945

Mendel emerged into the stark light of day. He squinted with the sudden glare; it had been so long since he'd dug that *bunker*, that hiding place in the Polish family's basement. So long since he'd seen sunlight. Earlier that morning it had rained, and the air, the cool, cleansed April air, inflated his lungs and expanded his soul. All around him were the celadon greens, intense yellows, and liquid blues of spring, even while his pallid skin matched the gray-white snows of the barely-passed winter.

How long had he been in that tunnel, that narrow hiding space he'd dug into the basement's dirt floor and shared with the rats and their fleas? Long enough that his fingertips would never forget every detail of the *bunker's* rough dirt walls. And to survive all that time on the smallest piece of bread or potato peel dipped in the stalest of leftover grease.

Closing his eyes, he angled his face upward. A momentary spasm caused his empty stomach to seize. Not hunger. Those pangs had disappeared months ago. Anxiety. It would take time to adjust to the open space of freedom and accept an approximation of normalcy.

Normalcy. What an odd word. He wondered what might be left for him from his life before the Germans imprisoned his family with barbed wire ribbons. His life before they'd taken away his parents and his infant niece. His life before he'd stolen a pair of tin shears and cut his way out of the Lodz ghetto.

Before the confinement, his older brothers, Shmuel and Avram, told him they were off to join the partisans, and advised sixteen-year-old Mendel to take the remaining family members and travel east.

"The Russians might not be much better than the Germans, but they're certainly an improvement over the Poles," said his oldest brother, Shmuel. "You will stand more of a chance there than if you remain here in Poland. Keep off the road. Travel through the forest. Stay alert."

The brothers embraced before a separation of unknown duration, preparing for the not knowing.

What was left of the family didn't think much of Shmuel's plan. "How can we go into the forest? At least the ghetto offers us shelter and food."

So mother, father, sister, and youngest brother remained in Lodz until they were only two, then one, after Mendel snipped four strands of barbed wire and slipped through the darkened streets, beyond the city's buildings, and into the countryside.

He hadn't traveled far before he came across an elderly man trying to fill a burlap sack with fallen sticks and branches. Mendel watched as the man bent over, picked up a piece of wood the size of the peasant's forearm, and slid it into his bag.

Mendel inched closer. Cautiously. Cautiously. "Could you use some help?"

The Pole's bright blue eyes studied the gaunt teenager who stood a couple of meters away. "Thank you. There's almost no fuel in the village. The coal they sell is more than anyone can afford. We need something to cook with. And, more importantly, winter will be here soon enough. I can't carry much weight, even if I sling this bag on my back. But what am I to do? My cart is useless because my horse is dead. Almost no food for us; even less food for him."

Without adding to the conversation, Mendel joined the man in gathering wood. Once the bag was full, Mendel swung it over his own back while the Pole carried an additional bundle of wood in his arms as they walked together.

The man scrutinized Mendel as they trudged through the sea of leaves covering the path, making it indistinguishable from the rest of the forest floor.

"So, my good helper, I'm Teofil. You?"

"Mendel." A sharp intake of breath. He'd forgotten himself and given his real name.

"A Jew!" The man's eyes opened wide. He pressed his lips together and nodded. "It's been a difficult time for your people. I was sure you'd all been taken away."

Mendel was trapped. Should he drop the wood and run? He decided to take his chances. "Are any Jewish people left in your village?"

The man put his wood on the ground and crossed himself. "None. Many Jews used to live in my town. About a year ago, the Germans came, forced them into the synagogue at gunpoint, and burned the building with all of them inside. Everyone could hear the screams and the smell lingered in the air for days. It was sickening. I wished I could have done something to save them. But what to do without endangering myself, my children, and their families? I could only pray to not get caught up in the abomination." He kissed his knuckle before picking up the bundle and walking on, the only sound their muffled footfalls against the damp leaf litter.

As they approached the village, the man spoke. "When we reach the edge of the village, lay the bag down, and I'll take care of getting the bag to my cottage. You stay in the forest for now. Teofil pointed to an opening a short distance from where they stood. I'll come to you tomorrow morning around sunrise with some leftovers. We can meet over there. But you must understand, we can't spare much. The Germans monitor our rations."

Mendel nodded. He understood the consequences perfectly. He'd frequently seen the same monitoring in the ghetto. Transgressions didn't allow for second chances.

Evening came, followed by a black sky filled with pinholes of stars filtering through the towering trees. In the twilight of sleep, Mendel drifted between memory and dream. His family used to watch for the first three stars in the sky on Saturday nights so they would know if it was time to light the *Havdalah* candle and celebrate the beginning of the new week. He saw Ida holding the candle aloft while they sipped from the cup of wine, smelled the sweet spices, and watched the glow of the candle's reflection on their fingernails before snuffing out the flame in the *kiddush* cup's remaining wine.

Mendel slept in spurts, always listening for Germans who might have been alerted to his presence by a Polish villager. Germans never came. Morning did, as did Teofil. "Good morning. I told you I'd return with a sorry meal."

Mendel rose to his feet.

Teofil continued. "I hope you're all right with last evening's crust and the peel of a boiled potato, though I'm sure you would prefer sausage and eggs. Unlike my horse, my chickens are still alive. However, they're living—well, I hope living—with some Germans instead of at home with me."

So began their bridge of trust. The connection grew until, one evening, Teofil signaled for Mendel to follow him to his house at the edge of town. Once inside, he led Mendel down to the cellar.

"I can no longer sit and do nothing. It isn't right. It isn't righteous. God sent you to me for a reason, so I must respond. Right now, the Germans are leaving our little village alone. I guess they believe we are what they call *Judenrein*, clean of Jews. I can't offer much more than this hiding place. But, if I ever feel…" Teofil had paused, then sighed. "I need your promise you will leave if I request it. If not…"

Mendel remembered taking Teofil's hand in both of his and kissing it. "Thank you. I promise to protect you the same way you offer to protect me. Thank you. Thank you."

Mendel's thoughts returned to the present. It had been an unknown chasm of time. Now he stood next to Teofil with the sun on his face, fresh air filling his lungs. The two men hugged in bittersweet farewells. He took Teofil's hand in both of his, kissing it the same as he'd done so long ago— the burden of concealment lifted from them both—thanking Teofil for the *mitzvah* of saving even one life in a world gone mad.

Mendel left the village. Where Germans had walked weeks ago, now there were Russians. Their muddy language replaced the previous guttural one. They sang and laughed and smoked and spit. For now, they were liberators—but liberators often become conquerors. Keep moving. Find the way back to Lodz. If his brothers and sister had survived, he knew that was where they would go.

As the day dragged on walking with muscles atrophied from disuse changed from arduous to painful. The need to keep moving forced him to trudge along with the masses of emaciated survivors, all of them stepping aside at the sounds of approaching vehicles. The forest's decimation, the limited stands of trees among the remaining stumps and their useless spreads of roots, reminded him of the world's sacrifices to the gods of war.

So many people on the road. Where were they all going? There was no home anymore—only a directionless wandering, the faintest hope of finding a familiar face or someone who recognized a name.

Along the way, he spoke with others like himself. Every conversation searching for the same type of information.

"Do you know Shmuel, Avraham, or Ida Feinberg from Lodz?"

"Do you know Ewa, Rozia, or Pinchos Chmielnicka from Lublin?"

"I'm from Tarnopol. Have you met anyone from that city?"

The air buzzed with inquiries; only names and villages changed; the answer always a glance down at the ground and the shaking of a head.

His legs ready to give out, Mendel sat down on a tree stump at the side of the road, putting his small bundle of clothing—his parents' photographs tucked inside—on the ground next to him.

His body ached and his neck felt stiff. He leaned back and stretched his face upward. Overhead, a flock of pigeons wheeled about. He'd once raised birds exactly like these. Even though the door to their coop was left open, they always came back. An intense sadness overwhelmed him as he realized no such haven existed for his own return.

He looked down, trying to relieve the tension in his neck by touching his chin to his chest. He saw the combination of the road's dirt, the recently-melted snow, and the morning's rain, crusting his shoes with hard, wet mud. He reached down and used a stick to scrape off the clotted dirt.

"At least I have shoes," he thought aloud, "rather than the rags some people have wrapped around their naked feet."

He looked at the road. So much mud. The Russian convoys of trucks and tanks splashing through the unavoidable muck, spattering it onto everyone's shoes and clothes. He turned away from the mass migration. The contrast of the nearby seedlings, newly green from life-giving moisture, gave Mendel hope that even a gray skeleton of a man with muddy shoes might come back from the near dead.

The spontaneous thought yielded an involuntary response—he suddenly needed to relieve himself. Even though others used the road as their latrine, Mendel craved a respite from the swarms of people and vehicles. A nearby patch of surviving trees enticed him, offering a break from the road's hard reality. He put his bundle under his arm and walked into the stand of alders, his steps silent on the soft covering of the previous summer's leaves.

As he reached the edge of the woodland, a movement behind a tangle of shrubs caught his eye, the motion coinciding with the shouts and songs of another passing Russian convoy. The invigoration of the sun, the air, and the smell of spring—combined with the tenuous security of the convoy's presence nearby—emboldened him. He walked toward the source of the movement. A rabbit would make for good eating, if he could catch it. Creeping closer, he froze when he saw what had attracted his attention.

A German officer in a brown leather coat sat on the ground, awkwardly leaning against a sapling barely thick enough to support his weight. The German looked up, pulled out his gun, and leveled it at Mendel's chest.

Mendel froze. A bitter tang filled his mouth. Every nerve in his body strained to attention. He pushed away the rising panic. God had kept him alive all this time, would He really allow things to end like this? The sun cast speckled shadows through the trees. What to do? Gnats buzzed around his ears and hair. Think clearly. The pointed gun, still and steady. Stay calm. His own hands slowly rising in surrender while he examined the German.

Short blond hair. Narrow blue eyes. Unbuttoned leather coat with a gray uniform beneath. Two legs splayed out in a V—one of them bootless, revealing a swollen ankle. A perceived advantage. *Chutzpah* replaced fear. Mendel formulated a plan. What other choice did he have?

"You would really want to end your own life this way?" Mendel asked, his voice muted and even. He slowly lowered his arms as he jerked his head in the direction of the road. "Shoot me and the Russians on the road will hear the sound and come running. I'm sure they have no interest in taking an injured viper like yourself prisoner. You'd be quite the burden to them."

A lie. The Russians wouldn't hear anything above the sounds of the convoy's engines and their own loud voices.

The German kept his gun raised but still hadn't fired. Could he believe such a lie? Mendel continued talking. "If you stopped pointing your weapon at me, I could just continue down the road. Nobody would ever need to find out about your being here so alone and vulnerable."

The German squinted toward the sounds of the road. He placed the gun in his lap, keeping his hand on the grip. "Do you have any water or bread?" he asked. "A sip of water. A piece of bread. Even a small piece would do."

A long pause. Let the bastard wait. Seconds passed. "No water. But, yes, I have bread."

"Well?"

"Not for you. You can eat the Sorrel growing around you. However, I will offer you something I'm sure you value even more than bread or water."

The German leaned forward, wincing from the unexpected pressure on his injured ankle. "*Ach!* Enough with your riddle. Come to your point."

A breeze cooled the anxious droplets on Mendel's forehead and upper lip. The hobbled officer's irritation let him know he'd gained the upper hand. "How much do you value your life?"

"Remember, I'm the one with a gun."

"Remember, the Russian army is within earshot, only a few meters away."

The German leaned back against the tree and sneered. "So, you believe you're free. Where do you think you can go? There's nobody for you out there. You can, maybe, find work shoveling horse shit. But your kind will never find a place in this world. Go ahead. Walk away."

Mendel spat on the ground. His hands itched to slip around the German's throat and squeeze the life out of him, but his heart had learned the value of survival over revenge. "You're right. I'm free—free to offer you a deal. I won't tell those Russians you're back here. That coat you're wearing is the price for my silence."

The German's eyes darted over to the movement on the road and back to the stony stillness of the man standing over him, a man for whom it was obvious the coat was several sizes too large. With a sigh, he placed his gun on the ground next to him and carefully removed the leather garment, flinching when he moved his ankle to pull the coat out from under his legs.

Mendel stepped closer and took the coat from the officer's hand. "Now, my hobbled friend, I will go my way and you are welcome to go yours." He gave a curt nod to the man on the ground then headed back to the road.

CHAPTER NINE

SHAWARMA ALABAMA

I loved the district around the University of Washington, better known as "The Ave," the perfect place for a poor student like me to eat. In between study bouts at one of the local coffeehouses, I could choose from a wide variety of inexpensive international cuisine. Crunchy Vietnamese *banh mi* sandwiches, nutty *pad thai*, every imaginable variety of ramen noodle bowls, and amazing shawarma.

My favorite shawarma place on The Ave used to be Al-Malik's. At least once a week, the enticing smells of the meat and its seasonings lured me to the hole-in-the-wall restaurant's counter. A rotating cast of laid-back Anglo college students always took my order. I'd always get their lamb marinated in special spices, grilled to perfection, stuffed into a crispy, warm pita bread, and garnished with garlic sauce, onions, tomatoes, and pickles.

A different vibe came from the back. The kitchen spewed forth the harsh, guttural sounds of Arabic. Some rumors said the owners were Maronite Christians from Lebanon. Others claimed they were Palestinians. That unknown factor always left me with a nervous gnawing in my stomach as I carried away a meal prepared by hands I suspected might just as easily build a bomb.

That wasn't the first time I'd experienced what others might call bigoted anxiety. The knee-jerk reaction reminded me of what my mother and I experienced a decade earlier when we'd driven from Rochester to San Antonio.

Before the drive, we'd made a pact, agreeing to eat only at locally owned restaurants during the four-day road trip. We looked forward to enjoying regional specialties along our route. With no Yelp and no smart phones, billboards and the usual "Food-Gas-Lodging" signs on the side of the interstate were our guide. Successes included Cincinnati chili in Ohio, pit barbecue in Kentucky, and fried chicken with waffles in Tennessee.

We hit Birmingham at noon and, a little more than an hour later, found ourselves searching for a place to eat in the middle of rural Alabama.

Infrequent commercial travel plazas mocked us, offering only fast food in the form of burgers or pizza. Signs along the highway touted easy offs and ons, all to large chain restaurants with more of the same. Our mouths watered for soul food, not greasy pizza or overcooked hamburgers and over-salted fries.

Two o'clock. "Maybe if we take an exit and try a nearby town?" I suggested, the sounds in my stomach making my growing desperation apparent.

Mom nodded. "I'll bet that's where we'll find something authentically Alabamian. Is that the right word?"

I laughed. "Authentically or Alabamian?"

The town name on the next exit sign read *Epes*. Coming from a background well-sprinkled with Yiddish, we both knew *eppes* meant "something."

"*Eppes essen*," Mom joked.

"Something to eat," I translated back at her. "Sounds like there are distinct possibilities."

Two-twenty. The turn signal clicked as we exited onto a two-lane road with no shoulder. About a mile into our detour, we wondered how much farther Epes might be.

We passed a white double-wide trailer home with a rusting metal roof. A rope strung between two trees awaited laundry, while a metal-grate on two sawhorses functioned as a lonely table whose chairs had gone missing. We made light of the stereotypical '68 Chevy sitting on cinder blocks on the other side of the trailer.

Further down the road, we saw another trailer, this one's tragic character enhanced by several large holes in its hail-pocked shingle roof.

As we drove on, things deteriorated, going from sorry to worse. The homes more ramshackle, their sparse, grassless yards browner and dustier.

"Damn it," Mom said. "How far could the town be?"

I wondered if this *was* the town. It couldn't be. A town would have something—a gas station, a post office, a restaurant. "Do you remember seeing a mileage marker anywhere?"

She shook her head. "We must have missed it back on the highway."

Worse and worse. Houses farther and farther apart. Peeling paint on worn wood siding. No cars on the barren properties, not even any of the earlier-seen stripped down steel skeletons with their metal guts long ago sold off as spare parts. No people livened the dusty yards, or the cracked windows, or the road.

I wanted to get out of there, but Mom kept driving. "I need to find a safe place to turn around."

Finally, the asphalt ended at some railroad tracks, a gravel road on the other side. A little ways beyond stood a mule confined to a property surrounded by a low chain-link fence. The relaxed mule stood on three legs—the fourth held up off the ground—as it watched two dumb Yankees in a New York Subaru trying to decide what they'd gotten themselves into. Beyond the mule sat a dingy yellow house with what looked like a faded pink flowered sheet hanging in the front window. A few feet to the side, tied to the top of a tall PVC-pipe flagpole, fluttered a tattered Confederate flag.

We sat, engine idling, while the overwhelming smell of manure wafted through the car's air conditioning vent.

No cars in front of us. No cars behind. A fifty-six year old Jewish woman wearing an Israeli dance camp shirt driving along a deserted road with a just-out-of-high school kid sporting a Cleveland Indians baseball cap with a prominent Chief Wahoo on it. The two of us headed—where? To Epes? To something?

Two-forty. Mom and I looked at each other and laughed uncomfortably—better to laugh than admit to the caution spurred in us by history-driven fear. We crossed the tracks, made a U-turn, and headed back to I-59.

Looking back, it was entirely possible my mother and I could have knocked on any of the doors along that road in Alabama and asked where we might find a nearby restaurant. The people might have smiled and given us directions to the best meal of the trip. It's also entirely possible that her shirt with Hebrew writing and my hat emblazoned with the image of a Native American might have invited a very cold shoulder and a whole lot of undefined grief. At the time, with no idea about what might happen, I could only base my reactions on things I'd heard about the past.

My U-turn moment at Al-Malik's arrived one rainy Seattle day during a particularly contentious time in the Middle East, when missiles rained down on Ashkelon and Israel retaliated with attacks on Gaza. I'd heard it all while listening to the nightly news, but we lived in the United States, so what did it really matter?

But, that day, as I walked up to my favorite shawarma corner, I saw a medium-sized poster prominently displayed in the restaurant's window. It was a photograph of Benjamin Netanyahu, the Prime Minister of Israel, his eyes printed in a satanic red, horns sprouting from his head, and fangs dripping blood from his mouth. As if all that wasn't enough, a swastika had been superimposed on his forehead. The words, *Stop the killing of Palestinian babies,* screamed in bright red letters along the poster's bottom.

"Shit," I breathed.

"What?" asked Steven, a fellow grad student who had joined me for shawarma that day.

I needed to leave, be anywhere but in front of that poster. "Let's go somewhere else."

"Why?"

"Don't you see what's in the window?"

Steven shrugged. "So?"

"I can't go in there."

"Why not?"

Didn't he get it? "I'm Jewish."

"Jesus, Seth. You've been in there plenty of times before. You're not Israeli. That poster has nothing to do with Jews and everything to do with the illegal Israeli occupation and their fascist oppression of Palestinian lands."

He didn't get it. The poster was only cloaked in anti-Israel sentiment. Its clearly antisemitic message screamed at me.

"Steve," I said. "Don't you see the innuendo?"

"That Netanyahu is evil? Sure—the devil eyes, the vampire fangs."

"Those refer to the ancient accusations of blood libel in Europe and Russia; Jews murdering Christian children and using their blood as part of the Passover ritual." I couldn't even bring myself to comment on the horns and swastika.

"You're being paranoid."

Discomfort morphed into anger. Anger that he refused to listen, blindly accepting antisemitism as a political statement with recalcitrant political righteousness. "Hey, Steve, you ever hear what someone once said about paranoia?"

"What?"

"Sometimes paranoia is simply having all the facts."

He dismissed me with a wave of his hand. "I'm going in for some shawarma. You?"

"I'm going to take a permanent pass."

We parted ways, Steve happy with his anticipated lunch, me obsessing over the poster I would be walking by for weeks to come.

Just as the threat was perceived back in Alabama, so did I perceive a threat at Al-Malik's—not the type of threat endangering my physical well-being, but a threat of escalation—the possibility that people could begin to accept hatred if cloaked beneath something else. Something charitable. Something empowering a perceived underdog. When does the underdog gain the upper hand? When does that upper hand rewrite recent history?

How would I feel living with that sort of threat on a daily basis? My imagination traveled across time. Back to Europe. Back to Lodz.

CHAPTER TEN

IN WHICH THE COAT
IS CHARITY

1945

"Filthy Jew. We thought they burned you all in the ovens." The threatening group of men followed their insults with a barrage of rocks. People stood in doorways or on the street, watching in silent approval. Nobody made a move to help the tattered target.

Mendel protected his head with the small bundle of his possessions and ran.

"Get the hell out of here or you'll get worse than stones next time!"

The Poles' angry voices couldn't fade quickly enough.

When he reckoned himself a safe distance from the attack, Mendel stopped and looked back. The group hadn't followed. Mendel lowered the bale of clothing, retied the frayed string holding it all together, and continued down the road away from yet another in what seemed an infinite sequence of dangerous villages.

It felt as though he'd been traveling back to Lodz forever. He had to return, if only to see if he could find Ida or his brothers. There could be no other destination.

He traipsed along dusty roads. Past overgrown fields. Past the remnants of war-ravaged forests. One among thousands, maybe millions of displaced people. He stopped in villages and begged for food or shelter, not knowing whether to expect help or harm. He hauled water in exchange for a sleeping spot on the manure-covered straw of a barn floor, volunteered to feed pigs so he might pick out some potato peels from their slop.

One couldn't depend on good will even though, sometimes, Russians would give him a real meal and, sometimes, fellow travelers along the road would offer a piece cut from their own meager loaf of bread with a thin slice of cheese or a precious spoonful of jam.

Rumors abounded. Fellow survivors told of returning to their villages to find no family, no other Jews, no friendly faces—their property stolen by former friends and neighbors. Other rumors claimed the horrifying *lagers* were being used as places of refuge. But rumors were not information and information was scarce.

Not only had lives been disrupted, so had transportation. How to get around with no passport, no identification—no identity? So he wandered, dependent on people's innate kindness or defensive remorse or fear of retribution, even though a living ghost has no means by which to take revenge.

Other wraiths wandered the roads—some in worn, striped uniforms, others in rags. All with sunken faces capped by the stubble of shaved heads or tufts of straw-like hair. All reeked of filth and decay. He wondered if he stank as well. So much time before, in a *bunker* without water or a latrine. So much time after, wandering with nothing but ice-cold river water or muddy puddles. How long since he'd bathed?

It took four days to reach Lodz and no time at all to find what was left of the ghetto, first ravaged by the Germans, then devastated by the liberating Allies' mortar and bombs. The old building on Zielna Street still stood, but had fallen victim to marauders—black market scavengers pillaging whatever Jewish property they could find. Doors were missing. First floor windows had been smashed. A miracle nobody had stolen the apartment itself.

Three stories up, Mendel ran his fingers along the apartment's familiar surfaces. The small nail that had once held up the calendar still stuck in the wall, fixed in place, the calendar gone. Who would want an old calendar? Maybe used as a fire starter. A few photos remained on the wall. Among them the two of Mendel's parents, formal portraits, their subjects wearing stiffly-starched collars and serious expressions. He stared at them, trying to conjure up the sound of their voices or the smells of his father's hand-rolled cigarettes and his mother's soup. He only smelled the building's weakened wood after years of seeping rain and snow.

Mendel removed the precious pictures from the wall, took them out of their frames, gently folded them into quarters, and tucked them into his bundle.

He continued to look around. Something lying in the corner caught his eye. The stub of a pencil—possibly the very one Ida used to mark days off as she kept track of the ebb and flow of the seasons. He picked up the remnant and deliberately wrote on the wall: *I am alive, Mendel Feinberg, Lodz.* He tucked the stub into his pocket before throwing his meager roll of possessions onto the dust-covered floor. Laying his head on the bundle, he fell into a nightmarish sleep filled with rats, lice, and interminable hunger.

He woke to the lightest of breezes against his face. Light leaked through the cracked, dirt-streaked window. How many hours had he slept? No matter. Today. Tomorrow. The day after. And after. And after. He'd stopped keeping track eons ago.

Belongings tucked under his arm, he wandered back down to the street. Hunger pricked at his stomach. Perhaps someone would trade a morsel of food for one of his two shirts—food other than hard, stale bread, and a drink other than muddy water.

He headed away from the ghetto and came upon a market filled with hundreds of people speaking dozens of languages. The maelstrom competed for fragrant loaves of dark brown bread, small measures of sugar, black market sausage, and clothes; so many clothes. A woman of indeterminate age stood at one of the many tables, a filthy scarf covering all but her graying widow's peak, strands of wiry hair escaping the fabric's confinement. She scowled at him, her nearly toothless mouth revealing a crone's snaggletooth.

He held the shirt and pointed at the bread. "Will you take this shirt for that loaf?"

She shook her head and held up three fingers. "Cigarettes. Thirty cigarettes."

"I have no cigarettes."

She shrugged and moved on to her next potential customer.

Behind him, through the commotion and noise, so close the whisper caressed his ear: "*Amcha.*"

He stiffened. He must have misheard. *Amcha* was Hebrew for "your people." Mendel remained frozen. Waiting.

Now singing in the softest of tones. The same voice. The melody and words of *Hatikvah, The Hope,* caressed his ear. After a few bars, the voice spoke again. "*Amcha.*"

Mendel turned. A tall, broad young man—an unquestionable bravado in his posture—stood there. Fierceness smoldered in dark brown eyes. Mendel nodded, unsure how to reply.

"Come with me," the man said. "I can offer you bread, coffee, and fresh clothes."

"Your name. What is your name?" Mendel asked.

The man's expression softened; a small smile worked its way across his mouth. "Come with me. Let's go to a place where we can talk."

To follow a stranger? He'd done it before. It saved his life then, who's to say it wouldn't do so again? They zigzagged through the crowded market and walked back to the old ghetto and into a building he recognized as Rumkowski's former headquarters. The room they entered was crowded with people filling every available space on the many chairs and benches around every available table. People attacked bowls of soup, cups of dark, rich coffee, and pieces of brown bread smeared with ruby red jam. The man gestured for Mendel to sit down, went into the next room, and came back with a generous portion of the same.

Mendel fell on the food, unable to stop himself. Streaks of soup dribbled down his beard. He tore pieces from his serving of bread and dipped them into the sweet jam, then stuffed them into his mouth, swallowing them whole.

His deliverer reached out and grabbed Mendel's shoulder, shaking it lightly. "Slow down, *meyn brieder*. You will become dangerously ill. The food is not going to disappear, except into your own mouth by your own hand."

Mendel nodded and gulped the coffee. "I'm just so hungry."

"I see you've completely forgotten about needing to know who I am. Don't worry. I'm quite used to this type of neglect at this point in my relationships." The man winked. "I'll let you continue eating while I tell you. My name is Menachem Smulovitz."

"Why me?" The question muffled through a mouth stuffed with a piece of bread.

"Why you? Because you looked like one who has need of what we offer."

"Who are 'we?'" A lick of some jam smeared on a finger.

"We call ourselves Operation Swallow. Our Zionist brothers are spread out across Europe, working to help the *Sh'erit ha-Pletah*, what we call all of you—the surviving remnant of our people—find your way home."

"I am Mendel Feinberg." He spoke, his mouth full of the final bite of bread which he'd used to sop up the last droplets of soup. "This city, then this ghetto, was my home with my family. Is it possible you've come across any of them? Any other Feinbergs?"

Menachem shook his head. "I'm sorry, friend. But many people work within our organization. Perhaps someone else can offer you better news."

"I'm beginning to think such news doesn't exist."

The buzz of the room filled the silence between the two until Menachem spoke again. "Perhaps not better news, but maybe a better path."

"How could any path be possible? There are pogroms in the villages. The cities have been destroyed. We have no money, no papers, no means by which to travel, other than by foot."

Menachem paused.

Mendel almost stopped breathing in anticipation of what he sensed the man was going to say.

The pronouncement came. "Palestine."

It was Mendel's turn to pause. Where his body had screamed out for food, now his soul screamed out for the enormity of such an idea, one he'd worshipped in *shul* so many years ago. An idea they'd talked about and planned for in his Zionist youth group. *Hatikvah*—The Hope. Was it even possible? "How?"

"You are interested then?"

"How?" he repeated.

"Come upstairs to my office. There we will talk."

They climbed the stairs and entered a room furnished with a few chairs and a worn wooden table covered with masses of papers.

Menachem gestured for Mendel to sit. "Our *bricha* organization is quite extensive, and we've established contact with *shlichim* from Palestine. They help us with the needed materials and funding for these journeys. If you desire to travel with us, you will be playing a decisive role in the re-creation of *Eretz Israel*."

Mendel knew *bricha* was Hebrew for escape. He sat, curious to hear more.

"The journey will be long, tortuous, and carries no guarantees. We have a network of operatives who help with money, documentation, and movement. Where are you staying? Do you have a place?"

"Right now, I guess I'm staying at our old apartment on Zielna Street."

Menachem pushed a piece of paper across the table. "Write your name and that address on this. When you leave here, go to the building with the yellow star on it across from Balucki Square and tell them I sent you. They'll take your photo so our people can work on the documents you'll need for transit. After that, go back to your apartment and we'll be in touch."

"Clothes. When we were still in the market you mentioned clothing." Mendel's voice dropped. "Do I smell as badly as the others?"

Menachem laughed—a gentle laugh, an *I understand* laugh. "I did promise you clothes. You attend to that paper and I'll be right back."

Mendel picked up one of several pencils from the table and wrote the few lines of requested information. Menachem returned to the room just as Mendel was pocketing the pencil.

"I'm sorry we can't accommodate sizes perfectly. We make do with what we scrounge from the German military storerooms in the area. It's amazing what the *Wehrmacht* left behind. Very considerate of those bastards. Here—see what you think."

Menachem laid a pair of olive green wool pants, a white shirt, and a brown leather coat over the table and its papers. "Here," he said. "These are for you."

Mendel picked up the shirt and held it up to his nose and mouth. The clean smell was as sweet as fragrant flowers. Then he reached out and fingered the heavy leather of the coat, teasing it open to see the perfect wool lining inside.

Menachem gestured at Mendel's feet. "I would offer you a pair of shoes as well, but yours appear to be in decent condition, unlike the painful wooden clogs the *katzets* from the *lagers* wear. I surmise you weren't in any of the extermination or labor camps."

"I was hidden in a Polish citizen's house. I dug a *bunker* for myself under his basement floor."

Menachem nodded. "Then what you have on your feet will have to do. Shoes are in such short supply. Meanwhile, let me give you another address for one of our local transit points. You can wash yourself and your old clothes there."

Tears filled Mendel's eyes. He grabbed Menachem's hand. "Thank you. What you offer is more than simply food and clothing. You offer salvation and hope."

Menachem put his free hand over Mendel's. "This *Pesach*, may you not have to say 'Next year in Jerusalem.' With *Hashem's* help, you will already be there. Now, go. Clean up and get that photograph taken. We will contact you soon."

As he walked down the stairs, Mendel's mind filled with the anticipation of what he'd been offered. Food. Clothing. Papers. Palestine. If only he could find family, he might be offered a future as well.

CHAPTER ELEVEN

CAN'T YOU TAKE A JOKE?

"Okay, so there's this barber…"

The joke was being told by a fellow graduate student, a blue-eyed business major with an Abercrombie model's perfect build and a hipster wardrobe to match.

"One day, a Buddhist monk walks into his shop and asks to have his head shaved. When it's done, the monk rubs his head and says, 'Wow! This is the smoothest shave I've ever had. How much do I owe you?'

"The barber replies, 'You're a man of God. There's no charge.'

"The following day when the barber arrives to open his shop, he finds a dozen gemstones sitting on his doorstep.

"Later that day, a priest comes in to get a haircut. When it's done, the priest looks in the mirror and says, 'This is the best trim I've ever gotten. How much do I owe you?'

"The barber replies, 'You're a man of God. There's no charge.'

"The following day, when the barber arrives to open his shop, he finds a dozen silver coins sitting on his doorstep.

"Later that day, a rabbi comes in to get his beard trimmed. When it's done, he says, 'Wow! You did so good a job. What do you want I should pay you?'

"The barber replies, 'You're a man of God. There's no charge.'

"The following day, when the barber arrives to open his shop, he finds a dozen rabbis waiting on his doorstep."

Everyone standing around him with various alcoholic drinks in their hands laughed. With a bottle of beer in my hand, I laughed as well. A complicit laugh. An uncomfortable laugh. A laugh that instantaneously made me wonder. Why didn't I speak out, protest the dehumanizing nature of jokes such as this one, jokes that reinforced the stereotype of Jews as conniving and cheap?

I thought about a conversation I'd had with Amelia a few months prior, one pointing out that the Scrabble-like game on Facebook doesn't allow the use of proper nouns with a singular exception.

"They don't?" she asked.

"No. They don't allow the words Hindu or Christian or Muslim. But they allow the word Jew."

"Why is that?"

"I'm pretty sure because it's a verb. Now, does that verb mean intelligent or learned or righteous?"

"By your tone, I assume not," Amelia answered.

"It means sneaky and cheap. As in 'to jew someone down.'"

I willed my attention back to the present and took a sip of my beer as I walked away from the joke-telling party-goer—who was starting another joke about a Frenchman, a Greek, and a Polack—and joined a group debating the merits of IPA beer: micro vs. nanobreweries.

"Have you tried the Berlinerweisse Sour with that raspberry syrup? It's like dessert," asserted a heavyset blond.

"Too sweet. How about the Eldorado Pale at Northwest Peaks?"

It was no good. The conversation felt as sour as my mood. The barber joke had embittered the evening. I left the party, making excuses about an early morning loaded with work, more afraid of offending someone than letting anyone know I'd been offended.

As I waited for my bus in the cool darkness, my mind rambled. It settled on an interview with a mass murderer I'd once read in some medical office waiting room. The interviewer had asked, "How were you able to commit so many murders so easily?"

The killer answered, "Because people are more concerned with being polite than with being safe."

Is this how hatred spreads? Do we hear someone denigrate a group of people and, wanting to be liked or accepted, smile and nod? Does going along with a tide of sentiments eventually permeate our own beliefs, until we become Eric Hoffer's true believers—unconditionally following a dogma, be it right or wrong?

But there are also people who fight those instincts. The Polish couple who risked everything, including their lives, when they hid my Saba in their basement. The remnant of decency in the German officer who might well have saved the life of my Savta.

When I got home, I opened my laptop and clicked my way into the university database. It didn't take long to connect to a page on confirmation biases. It talked about people like that blue-eyed business major who thought his joke was funny because, deep down, he believed Jews are, indeed, cheap. It only took another few minutes to link to an article on the bandwagon effect which explained why everyone, including me, laughed—because everyone else did. Another article on authority bias. I continued down the rabbit hole. Herd instinct. Superiority bias. Self-serving bias.

As I scanned article after article, I came across a paper written by a Harvard professor on the behavioral effects of Nazi propaganda and its successful use of all these concepts. I remembered some of the illustrative posters I'd seen at the Holocaust Museum in Washington, D.C. when I was 13-years-old.

My trip there began one obscenely early spring morning when I joined about forty of my fellow eighth-grade Hebrew school kids in Temple Beth El's parking lot where, after unwanted parental words of guidance and embarrassing hugs and kisses, we boarded the charter bus.

During the long ride, we sang camp songs from the summer, gossiped about who had a crush on whom, and guessed about the food they'd serve once we reached our destination. Cold cuts or pizza? Kosher or not? Maybe we could find a way to sneak out and grab a burger.

My assigned "buddy" and roommate for the weekend was Jake Frankel. We were in the same class at Hebrew school, but he and I had never been friendly. It wasn't that we didn't like each other. We just had different interests and ran with different crowds. I went to Brighton schools, he to Pittsford. I played table tennis year-round. He played football in the fall and soccer in the spring. He was a full head taller and about forty pounds heavier than I was, and had absolutely no interest at all in this trip.

"Ya know, I'm missing a big soccer game for this," he complained.

"Didn't you tell your parents?" I asked.

"My fuckin' parents knew. They forced me to come, anyway. Said it was something important I needed to learn about." He air-quoted 'something important' and gave a big sigh.

Not being a jock, I figured it might be cool to have one as a friend, so I lied. "Yeah. My parents forced me to come too."

"Ugh!" he said.

"Yeah, ugh!" I confirmed.

I spent the final hours of the ride to Washington agreeing with Jake's complaints about the bus, the kosher bag lunches, and Mrs. Levin, our teacher/chaperone. Jake made fun of Mrs. Levin's accent before stuffing his sweater under his shirt to make fun of her large breasts as well.

After a box lunch at a highway rest stop, he changed the words in the after-meal prayer. "*Leolam va'ed*" became "*leolam* drop dead." "*Asher bara*" turned into "I swear I saw your bra." We all laughed, a few of the kids even coming up later to slap Jake on his back and tell him what a riot he was.

The rest of the bus ride was subdued—the food in our stomachs resulting in most of us catnapping to the sound of the bus's drone. Jake snored lightly. I thought that particular sound was a big improvement over what had been coming from his mouth earlier in the trip.

We pulled up to the hotel around four in the afternoon. Mrs. Levin must have known what was up because Jake and I were assigned to the room between hers and Ms. Gold's, successfully leveraging a strategic position of supervision.

After a dinner of kosher pizza in the smallest of the hotel's conference rooms, followed by a repeat of the after-meal prayers, we went back to our rooms. I settled in to do my homework. Jake pulled out his Gameboy and spent the rest of his evening with Super Mario.

Six a.m. arrived with the harsh sound of the room's telephone ringing. Jake startled awake. "Shit! They arranged fuckin' wake-up calls for us."

We washed, dressed, and met in the lobby for morning prayers and breakfast. Then we boarded the bus for a driving tour of Washington, to be followed by our visit to the United States Holocaust Memorial Museum.

During the tour, Jake remained locked into his Gameboy, while I looked out the window at the sights, excited to finally be seeing so many of the buildings I'd only read about or seen in photographs.

"Jake, look. There's the Capitol Building."

Jake grunted, as he pushed the console's button to make Mario jump.

I settled back to enjoy the tour. If he wasn't interested, that was his loss.

After a picnic lunch, we arrived at the museum. As we entered, our loud, rowdy group grew silent. We hadn't anticipated what confronted us. We were passing through the gates of Auschwitz. Over our heads was a metal cast that seemed to have been taken from the original entrance to the infamous death camp topped with the words *ARBEIT MACHT FREI*. The interior's red-brick construction with unfinished ceilings was unsettling. Strategically placed spotlights cast eerie shadows—dark corners broken by accented horrors. I was entering a dystopian nightmare.

As we passed under the gate and into the exhibit area, each of us received a card with the name, photo, and background of a European Jew who'd been sent to Auschwitz. I became *Viktor Ullman, born January 1, 1898, in Prague, Czechoslovakia. Composer, conductor, pianist, teacher, music critic. Deported to Theresienstadt concentration camp on September 8, 1942, where he helped to organize cultural life. Transferred to Auschwitz on October 16, 1944.* The photo showed the torso and face of a tired man, shoulders slumped, wearing a dark suit and nondescript tie. In the three-quarter view, his eyes looked directly at me. I quickly tucked the card into my pants pocket. I didn't want to look at his tragic expression any more than I had to.

Arbeit Macht Frei. Work will free you. Room after room surrounded us with artifacts and photographs. A railway transport car. The naked wood bunks of the death camp. Mountains of men's, women's, and children's shoes. Eyeglasses piled upon eyeglasses piled upon eyeglasses, reaching a height taller than the tallest student in our group. Faded black and white pajama uniforms. Yellow stars. Voices and faces. And faces and voices. And films of testimony with faces. And faces upon faces of victims. And more victims. And walls filled with framed photographs of even more victims.

The tour seemed to last forever. At the end of forever, I learned Viktor Ullman's fate. He'd—I'd—been transferred and murdered in the gas chamber at Mathausen.

After forever, we stepped out of Nazi Europe and back into the sinking afternoon sun of 1999 Washington, D.C. I squinted as the sudden brightness strained my eyes.

Desperate to talk with someone about my experience, I turned to Jake. "That was tough," I said.

"That was bullshit," he spat back. "Who gives a flyin' fuck? That stuff all happened way before we were born. I missed my soccer game for this shit. Fuck them!"

What was wrong with him? Of course "that stuff" mattered. It mattered almost more than anything else. This happened to my family. We needed people to remember so it wouldn't happen again. "C'mon, Jake. You don't have to act so frickin' cool all the time. You have to know that learning about this stuff is important."

"Fuck you," he said, before walking away and boarding the bus.

My solemn mood continued through dinner and into the evening. In no mood to socialize, I was happy when Jake ignored me by continuing to concentrate his attention on his stupid handheld game.

On Monday's bus ride back to Rochester, I sat next to Nicole Rose. Those of us who didn't sleep on the ride home read, caught up on homework, or talked about anything other than the previous afternoon's experience.

I looked at the scenery along the highway and thought about one of the questions on the wall near the end of our time at the museum. *What is your responsibility now that you've seen, now that you know?*

Now, sitting at my desk in my Seattle apartment, I turned my attention back to the evening's party and the barber joke, and my reflexive desire to fit in. I considered the bandwagon effect and herd instinct. Why some people are good, and how even the best of people might leverage others' lives into bargaining chips for their own survival.

Unable to think about sleep, I reluctantly turned to my American Literature class homework, an assignment due on Monday morning—an essay on Steinbeck's *East of Eden*—the author's retelling of the Cain and Abel story.

I wrote. I redacted. I rewrote. Concepts eluded me. Nothing satisfied me. I closed my eyes and tried to picture Steinbeck's prairies shouting grass and waters slipping twinkling over yellow sands in the sunlight. My mind transformed it all into putrid mud shouting bones and water running gray with ashes—the ashes of strangers from whom I'd received my DNA.

I opened a new file on my computer and left Eden behind. I wrote instead about the Land of Nod, the place to which God exiled Cain, even while the mark placed on Abel's pariah brother identified and protected him from harm. I wrote about limbo and the possibility of a reawakening of hope.

CHAPTER TWELVE

IN WHICH THE COAT IS ACCEPTED
IN SPITE OF ITS PROVENANCE

1945

People clotted every area of the Radegast train station. Their odors assaulted Mendel's nose and stomach. Rotten teeth. Sweat. Urine. Excrement. The stink of people who hadn't known cleanliness for an eternity. The essence of people who'd eluded their own deaths.

Mendel stood and peered into the gaping doorway of the train's box car. Inside, someone had placed evenly spaced rows of wooden benches separated by narrow aisles barely wide enough for one person to squeeze through.

He looked away from the darkness of the compartment and studied people's feet, a habit he'd developed of late, trying to parse their stories— shoes always the seminal clue.

Wood clogs meant he or she had come from one of the camps where unspeakable horrors took place. The stories infected his dreams. He'd wake, unable to move, terrified at the images of his parents or Ida agonizing in such a hell, their screams disguised as his own.

Well-fitting shoes in decent condition hinted at someone like himself, one who'd spent the years in hiding unable to move or speak or breathe. Shoes don't wear out when you're in a cellar, an attic, a sewer, or a hole dug deep underground.

Others wore mismatched shoes, or shoes with soles tied on with filthy scraps of cloth, the binding fabric rotting with damp. These people had trudged many miles in slave labor camps, fought with the Partisans, or been conscripted into one army or another.

Then there were those who walked barefoot or wrapped their feet in rags, even though there was often a pair of shoes tied together with string hanging around their necks. These were the cautious ones who had received footwear from charities along the way or pilfered them from vacant homes or long-closed shops.

While the mob waited for their *bricha* leaders' instructions, a woman came up next to Mendel and, when she saw the gaping mouth of the train car, she stopped, then stiffened. One hand flew up to her heart, as though she needed to shield that vital organ, and the other dropped her small, tattered suitcase. A sound—a moan from deep within—rose in pitch until it became a scream of anguish.

Mendel gently removed her hand from her chest and stroked her cheek. "*Sha, sha*. It will be okay. Nothing bad will happen here."

The woman spoke, her voice almost a scream. "Those trains. I know what they are. What they're for. I've been on them. I know where they're going to take us." She pulled her hand away and waved her arms in the air. "Don't get on the train! They can't take me again. I'll kill myself first!"

A short, dark, muscular young man, pushed through the crowd and put his arms around the woman. "*Mameleh*. Don't be afraid. I, Velvel Baran, am one of your guides. I promise you, on my life, you will be safe with me." No doubt, Velvel had seen behavior like this before and experienced the memories box cars could awaken.

Velvel yelled over the cacophony of the crowded station, still holding the woman close. "*Chaverim*, why are we just milling about? Come! Let us gather up fresh branches with green leaves and fragrant pine needles, and see if you can find some flowers. We're going to decorate our train so it looks like a train of life rather than a reminder of death. We'll transform it from a transport of the sad past to the caravan to our future in *Eretz Israel*."

His arm still around the woman, Velvel led her away as he began singing in Hebrew with a deep baritone voice:

> "Never say this is the final road for you, though leaden skies may cover over days of blue.
> As the hour that we longed for is so near, our step beats out the message, we are here!"

Mendel leaned over to the singing men. "What is this song?"

"It's the Jewish Partisans' Anthem. They say it was written in the Vilna ghetto to honor the fighters of Warsaw."

Those who knew the song joined in as people walked to nearby trees and bushes, breaking off branches, placing them in the rungs of the boxcar ladders and tucking them into the spaces between the wooden slats. The cars gaily decorated, Velvel announced it was time to leave.

The cars filled. Then, doors still open, the train jerked as it began to move. People broke out in song anew.

"*Chalutzim, greyten zikh far Eretz Israel.*"

Mendel smiled. "Pioneers, prepare for *Eretz Israel.*" Maybe there would be a life for him after all.

The man sitting next to Mendel opened his satchel and pulled out a loaf of dark bread. "Look here," he said. "What else can we scrounge up so we all can have a decent meal?"

People began pulling things out of their suitcases and bundles. Cloves of garlic. A slab of salami. Pieces of fresh fruit.

"Where did all this food come from?" Mendel asked.

A man sitting across from him laughed. His nearly toothless mouth stank from years of suffering. "The Poles, of course. Whenever my companions and I..." He nodded to the two men beside him, "passed an empty house, we'd go inside and help ourselves."

Mendel nodded. He'd done the same. They'd all done it. It was the only way to survive in this new world.

With a piece of bread in his hand, Mendel approached a small group of people he'd seen singing the songs and asked them to teach him the melodies and the lyrics.

The train traveled in fits and starts. Between the short distances it managed to travel, it would frequently sit motionless on the sidings to allow other trains to pass.

After what seemed like a million stops and starts, the train jerked to yet another stop and Velvel stood up. "My group, it is time to exit our luxurious transportation. Accommodations and a good meal await. To those who are traveling on, I wish you a good journey."

Mendel, along with twenty-nine others, jumped down from the boxcar. He turned back to the open door and yelled over to his new friends, "*Nu?* You're not coming?"

They shook their heads and broke into a new song as the train jerked back into motion.

Mendel looked around at the people in his group. Eleven pairs of wooden clogs. Fourteen pairs of real shoes, some with soles so worn they served almost no purpose at all. One teenager, his feet wrapped in rags. Like himself, three people wore decent footwear.

Velvel spoke. "Welcome to Katowice. Our people here are preparing papers which will enable you to cross into Austria. For now, we'll be spending a few days at a transit camp. Our gracious hosts will be members of the International Red Cross. They'll give you food, new shoes, and fresh clothing. Follow me and try to stay together."

The group hiked a little more than three kilometers to what had once been a school, the faded wooden sign over the door reading *Szkoła Podstawowa nr*. The school's number was missing, probably used in someone's fireplace or stove. The building and its grounds—crammed with people and more people—served as a way station. Men and women lay on the ground or stood around, seemingly waiting for something. What? Food? Papers? A sign from God?

A babel of languages filled the air. Mendel recognized some of them. Polish. Russian. Yiddish. Others he didn't. But he understood the questions, those same ones he'd been hearing every day since liberation.

"Do you know so and so?"

"Did you happen to meet my sister? Her name is Fanny Neumann."

"My brother?"

"My cousin?"

"My parents?"

Velvel shouted over the noise. "Go. Get food and get clothing. Meet me back here, in this spot, in the morning, so I can let you know what comes next."

Mendel didn't rush to the food or the clothing. Instead, he studied his surroundings. So many people. Several of them carried their possessions in one hand and a bowl and a spoon in the other. Other people sat on the ground emptying their bowls as though this might be their last meal. People in the other line were being handed clothing and shoes. Hunger drew him to the food line, which snaked around three sides of the large, single-story building. His reward after an hour's wait was a metal bowl half filled with chunks of potato and slivers of an unidentifiable meat floating in a tea-colored broth. He also received a thick slice of dark bread spread with a thin layer of reddish jam.

He tucked his possessions under his arm so he could carry his meal. He settled down in the first spot he could find among the hundreds of others sitting and lying around him and devoured the welcome food. When he was done, he licked the bowl and spoon before tucking them into his bundle.

The clothing line was considerably shorter than the one for food. He only had to wait a half an hour before he reached the distribution point. The woman standing there offered him a stained pair of *Wehrmacht* uniform pants, a torn shirt, and a heavy, lined leather trench coat.

"You give me Nazi clothes?" He spit the words in Polish.

The middle-aged woman, wearing a white headpiece and a jacket with a Red Cross patch, looked at him. Her lips and eyes thinned with animosity. "You Jews," she said with a heavy accent, making the word "Jews" sound like an obscenity. "You don't realize how lucky you are we even give you clothes. They're clean. No? They're warm. Right? If you don't want them, move along. The next person in line will be glad to get them."

Mendel—mirroring her sneer—took the clothing, gave a quick nod, and walked off, the garments hanging off his arm. He hated where they had come from, but the woman was right. Winter would be here soon enough. He would need whatever clothing he could get.

As the blue sky turned indigo, Mendel went up to another woman wearing a white armband with the Red Cross emblem. "Where are we supposed to sleep?"

The woman shook her head, letting him know she didn't understand Polish.

Rather than going through a litany of languages to find a common tongue, he pantomimed sleep by laying his head on the palm of his hand and closing his eyes.

The woman nodded and led him through the throngs into a large room filled with row after row of narrow army cots. A few empty ones sat tucked into a corner near the door leading down to the basement. In an instant, he realized why they were still vacant. The basement housed the latrines, and it smelled as though they'd never been cleaned.

He retched, his stomach threatening to riot against the offending stench. That night, he slept under the stars with the shirt and *Wehrmacht* pants as his mattress, his pack as his pillow, and the coat as his blanket.

During the next two days, the group waited in the hot sun for their papers. They sat and paced and slept fitfully with others who slept, sat, and paced anxiously waiting for news about family and friends and the necessary papers to move on. They hungrily waited, hoping for something other than the same soup meal after meal.

"Do they ever serve anything but soup?" he asked a fellow survivor, this one wearing wood clogs.

"I don't think the world has any other food left in it," another replied. "At least this soup is more than water and powdered potatoes."

The morning of the third day, Velvel met the group with news. "Your papers have arrived. Listen carefully. This is how our border crossing will work. It is imperative you obey these orders."

An electric charge ran through the group. People strained to hear Velvel's every word.

"We will leave for the train station on foot in about an hour. Later today we'll reach the Czech border. Your papers present you all as Greek nationals returning home. The *parol*—the paper I have to show the border guards on both sides—gives the exact number of our group and our final destination, Salonika, Greece."

"I don't want to go to Salonika."

"You promised us Palestine."

"Greece isn't *Eretz Israel*."

Velvel waved the papers to quiet the group. "We aren't going to Greece. This is just how we're going to cross into Czechoslovakia. The Russians are limiting the movement of Polish nationals, especially Jews. Once we are near the crossing, you must not speak anything but Hebrew. Success depends on this. No Polish. No Yiddish. No Russian. The guards don't recognize Hebrew and believe it to be Greek."

"I only speak Polish and German," a woman named Eva said.

"Do you remember any Hebrew prayers?" Velvel asked.

The woman nodded. "I know the *Shema*. Even in the camps, I said it every day."

"Then recite that. Use the lines from the prayer as though you are having a conversation. A conversation with God can only help, right?" Velvel tried to suppress a small smile. "Also, give me anything you have with Polish or Russian writing on it. If I can manage to smuggle them across the border, I'll return them to you after we're a safe distance from the guards. But I won't endanger our success for a few mementos."

No murmur here. People shouted. "My photos are all I have." "This is my father's prayer book. I have nothing left of him but this."

"I'm sorry. This is how it must be. I'll collect all the forbidden items now."

While others reluctantly removed photographs and prayer books from their pockets and bundles, Mendel walked a short distance away and removed two photographs—one of each of his parents—from his bundle. On the back of each one was a stamp with the name of the photographer and the date they were taken written in Polish. Taking the leather coat, he teased open a section of the lining's seams and pushed the photos between the layers. No way would he gamble with the loss of his precious portraits.

When Mendel rejoined the group, Velvel was busy assigning people their new identities. As each person received their new name, the group laughed. Every name was a play on a Hebrew prayer, a Jewish holiday, or a Yiddish expression. Adamos Yomkipporos. Iva Misheberach. Mendel's temporary name would be Moyses Nebbachos.

Velvel's group had transformed over their few days at the transit camp. Food, clothing, shoes, and a connection to the *bricha* organization had revitalized them. Women's faces filled out. Men stood taller. Mendel felt fortified. His stomach growled, a sign the soup—in spite of its monotony—had helped his digestive system function again.

"Today, we will travel by train to the Czech border. There, we'll rendezvous with Ben, the representative who will guide you through Czechoslovakia."

Sala, the woman Velvel had helped back at the Radegast station in Lodz, cried. "You've been so good to me. Can't you stay with us until we reach Palestine?"

"Sala, you'll be fine. Look at you now. Such a beautiful, strong pioneer. You say I've been good to you. Now I must go back and be good to the next group, and the next, until we've rescued all of the remnant left in Europe. You will help us liberate Palestine. We will all help each other, yes? Meanwhile, you still have me for quite a while. The border might seem close, but things creep along very slowly in this new world of ours."

Their new train was better than the previous one. The group found themselves in a real passenger car filled with hundreds of other people heading south. Three or four people squeezed onto seats meant for two. On this train, the smells of waste and loss seemed to have abated, replaced by the smell of garlic and smoked meat making stomachs growl with anticipation.

Mendel wanted to sing the songs of hope as they had on the other train. But this was not the time to attract attention. Instead, he sat quietly, rehearsing anticipated answers in Hebrew, a language he hadn't used in a very long time.

True to Velvel's word, this train moved as sluggishly as the earlier one, stopping every fifteen or twenty minutes to let other trains pass. The group shared the bread given to them by the Red Cross. Some rubbed it with garlic they'd managed to barter for at the transit camp. Others enjoyed the small pieces of salami they'd managed to save for this leg of the journey.

The train stopped at Czieszyn, and the group got off. Velvel signaled for everyone to wait silently as he entered a nearby building. He emerged a few minutes later with a dark-haired young man.

"This is Ben. He will be your guide from here to Bratislava. I now bid you farewell and wish you a safe journey."

There would be no drawn out farewells. Velvel gave the slightest of bows and walked away from the group and into the building from which he and Ben had emerged only a minute or so earlier.

Ben addressed everyone in Hebrew. Those who understood helped translate for those who didn't.

Mendel noted their new guide spoke flawlessly with no accent at all.

"This is where you leave your previous lives behind. Until I tell you otherwise, you are Greek nationals, even though we'll be speaking Hebrew." He gave a wink. "Remember, you must maintain this bluff until we're a good distance from the Russian guards at the border."

The group welcomed the two-and-a-half-kilometer walk. It felt good to stretch their legs after the days in the cramped transit camp followed by the long, equally cramped train ride. After about half an hour, Mendel heard a buzzing ahead. Bees? As they walked over the crest of a hill, the source of the buzzing became apparent. The area by the border station was swarming with hundreds of people sitting on the grass or pacing in the hot sun. It seemed even more crowded than the transit camp they'd just left.

Mendel looked over at Ben, who signaled for the group to follow him down to the mob scene at the foot of the hill.

Obeying another signal, the group sat down at the fringe of the crowd, while Ben walked over to one of the uniformed officials. Mendel watched as their new *bricha* leader pulled out a paper with an official-looking red seal. The guard shook his head. Ben waved the paper and said something. The guard shrugged. Ben gestured again, this time more adamantly. The guard turned, and Ben followed. They disappeared into the crowd.

Mendel unwrapped his growing bundle and removed the coat. He opened it and moved his fingers along the lining to make sure his precious photographs were still safe. Feeling his parents' images comforted him. He took stock of the other things in his bundle. He still had the metal bowl and spoon, along with his old, dirty clothes. Then, he rolled everything back into a compact package and retied the string that held it all together.

Mendel lay down with the bundle under his head. Others in his group napped or sat nearby. Nobody spoke. Nobody dared take the chance of being identified as anything other than Greek. The sun beat down on them. Sweat soaked their clothing. Ben finally returned as the heat of the afternoon dulled and a breeze cooled the group.

Mendel shot up.

Ben spoke Hebrew. "We will spend the night here and report to the border first thing in the morning, where they will consider our situation."

Sala gasped.

"Don't worry. I have the necessary currency to get all of you across."

"Not what papers for?" Mendel asked, struggling to remember his Hebrew. "To cross?"

"We've had an arrangement with the Russians for a while. They allow us to bring what they believe to be Greek nationals across as long as we pay them with one pack of cigarettes per person."

"And the Czechs? What must give?"

Ben smiled. "Let me worry about that. Find a comfortable spot and try to get some sleep. I give you my word. Tomorrow we will cross into Czechoslovakia. Then, on to Bratislava!"

CHAPTER THIRTEEN

FASTING ON YOM KIPPUR

"Religious obligation." Those two words echoed in my head, interrupted work on my dissertation, and kept me awake at night. What had Saba expected?

He'd been so proud during my Bar Mitzvah—that day I'd fulfilled what I understood to be my obligation. His new suit. The blue tie with his gold star of David clip holding it in place. All the men wearing Savta's hand-crocheted *kippot* on their heads.

I'd sung my Torah portion and given my commentary, the completion of the ancient rite of passage, my initiation into ritual adulthood. From that day on, I would be counted as part of a *minyan*, the quorum required for public worship. But what did it all have to do with the coat? Why did Saba choose that particular weekend to show it to me?

"You're awfully quiet." Amelia's voice pierced the buzz of conversations in the coffee house.

I looked up from my latte. A pause—that nuance residing in my genes.

A hand waved in my face. "Hey, you. Earth to Seth."

"Sorry. Just lost in my thoughts."

"I'll say. Need a penny?"

"Nothing important. Only my ongoing obsession about the coat."

"Want to talk about it?"

"I just don't know what the hell he expected me to do with it."

"He who? Your grandfather? Why not wear it? Remember when you tried it on for me? You looked great."

"The damned thing belonged to a Nazi."

"And then it belonged to your grandfather. Didn't he ever wear it?"

Did he? He must have worn it sometime. Otherwise, why would he even own it? I shrugged. "I guess. But I never saw it on him."

A sip of coffee. A long period of silence. Amelia waited.

The lapse in conversation became uncomfortable enough that I remedied the situation by changing the subject. "Let's go. I want to grab some dinner before the beginning of *Yom Kippur*."

"Are you going to services at the University Hillel?"

"No. But I am going to fast, so I want to get something substantial in my stomach before sundown."

Amelia nodded. She'd gotten used to my peculiar Jewish-atheist approach to life which had begun during *Machon*, my weekly Hebrew high school.

I thought back to the middle of tenth grade, when I'd challenged Rabbi Shafler, one of my teachers. "I don't think God really exists," I said. "Because, if he does, how could he have allowed the people in Europe to murder so many Jews?"

Rabbi Shafler didn't miss a beat. It seemed he'd confronted this sort of question before. "You're talking about something called theodicy. It's been debated throughout Jewish history. Rabbi Akiva spoke of it when he said, 'All is foreseen, yet free will is given.' It's been said God wept alongside the victims as He saw how evil His creations could be. Back in the Garden of Eden we wanted free will. He gave it to us when He banished Adam and Eve. It wasn't God who allowed the Holocaust to happen, Seth. It was mankind."

That pissed me off. The answer seemed rehearsed, so unsatisfactory when I considered the magnitude of the tragedy. That day, as I walked away from Rabbi Shafler, I began my journey away from the divine.

Saba wasn't happy when he asked how I was enjoying USY, our temple's United Synagogue Youth group, and I told him I was thinking of quitting.

"It's important, this youth group of yours." His tone surprised me. I'd never heard him raise his voice before. "You must have some type of place where you can go and be Jewish."

"Why do I need USY to be Jewish?" I challenged, jutting my chin forward. A moment of shame at my defiance brought a sudden wave of nausea, but I couldn't help myself. In spite of a burning feeling that I should stop, my stubborn fourteen-year-old self kept going. "I'm tired of having it shoved down my throat. Isn't it enough I go to Hebrew high school every Sunday morning?"

All of a sudden, my face grew hot. I felt like Jake Frankel during our trip to the Holocaust museum. I looked down, away from Saba's face. I didn't want to see any of the hurt in his eyes.

"I loved my group of *chaverim* back in Poland," he said, his voice back to its normal quiet tone.

"There was a USY back then?"

Saba chuckled. "No. I belonged to a group called *Tvuna*."

I'd never thought about Saba before the war. I didn't even know how to picture him with anything but white hair and sad eyes. "What sorts of things did you do?"

"We were preparing for *aliyah* to Israel. Everything we did was to that purpose. We became like family. In my troop—I was about twelve—we did exercises to make us strong. We ran. We marched. We played soccer. The older members gave me a few chickens, so I should learn about taking care of them.

"In my next level, I was fourteen like you. We had political discussions and did a lot of reading in addition to the exercises and farming lessons. That's how I learned Hebrew. You want to learn Hebrew, right?"

"USY doesn't actually teach us any Hebrew."

Saba's eyebrows shot up. "No? What do you do?"

"Mostly social stuff. We stay after Hebrew school and hang out or go to *shul* and hang out. There are plenty of other things I could be doing that are more interesting and more—" I searched for a good word to garner Saba's approval. "—productive."

"You can be productive after. You should, as you say, 'hang out' with other Jewish children. I want you should feed your Jewish *neshama*."

Feed my Jewish *neshama*, my Jewish soul, my spirit. I didn't understand what that meant back then. I only partly understand what it means today. Sometimes, when I'm in a poetic mood, I wonder if Saba saw the leather garment as a protective coat for his own *neshama*, later hoping it would help mine blossom.

My next question popped out before I had a chance to censor myself. "Did any of your *Tvuna* friends survive the Holocaust?"

"At least one of them did. You know him. My friend Motek. He was older and went off with my brothers to fight with the Polish partisans."

Motek. A partisan. He was one of Saba and Savta's best friends, one of the people who'd come to my Bar Mitzvah, and we always sat with him during High Holiday services at Saba's *shul*.

Saba's voice again, controlled and definite. "Seth, I want you should stay in your youth group. They must do something you like."

There was one thing. "We do get to miss school on all the Jewish holidays so we can go to services."

Saba smiled. His eyes nearly crinkling at the corners as he clapped me on the shoulder. "This is good. Do you participate?"

"Well, we sing the prayers. Sometimes one of us gets asked up to do something, open the ark or read a prayer. They never pick me, though." I didn't tell Saba they didn't pick me because I usually hung out in the entrance hall outside the sanctuary.

He nodded. "Stay in your group." He pulled out his wallet. "Here—I'll give you twenty dollars for every year you're a member."

Twenty dollars, Saba's reward for everything. He'd give us a crisp bill every time we visited, did well in school, or had a birthday. Now it would be a bribe for me to stay in youth group. The rebel in me retreated. The money didn't matter. What mattered was making Saba happy.

"I promise. I'll stay in USY."

The downside: There would be no chickens. The upside: excused absences from school—lots of them. Days off to attend holiday services and weekend trips to other groups' cities.

For a year and a half after my talk with Rabbi Shafler and my confrontation with Saba, I went through the motions on *Shabbat*, during the holidays, and at my youth group activities, all meaningless embezzlers of my time and energy—a sacrifice I was willing to make for Saba and Savta. I might not have accepted all the underlayments of faith, but I understood my long-suffering grandparents. My feelings of guilt were the initial result of their silence about the past, gradually growing into consideration and forgiveness, slowly blooming into compassion, and ultimately transforming into *chesed*—kindness.

Saba wanted me to feed my soul. I wasn't sure what that meant back when I decided to stay in USY to make him happy. Over the years, I came to understand what it meant when I decided how to express my Jewish atheism. I could deny theodicy but couldn't bring myself to turn my back on the centuries of culture that forged my family's traditions.

I choose to live a Jewish life outside the concept of an all-powerful deity. I go through the physical motions of ritual, hoping to maintain a meaningful connection to my heritage. I fast on *Yom Kippur* and *Tisha B'Av* as an exercise in reflection and introspection. I light the candles on Chanukah and fry potato *latkes* in oil. I eat *matzah* instead of bread during Passover and discuss the difference between slavery and freedom at my makeshift *seders*. Instead of practicing an orthodox Judaism, I choose to practice a Jew-ish type of worship, in which contemplation replaces faith as I move through the seasons in a dance of liturgy.

CHAPTER FOURTEEN

IN WHICH THE COAT IS A REWARD FOR A JOB WELL BEGUN

1945

The journey had been unremarkable. Once over the border into Czechoslovakia, Ben destroyed their Greek identities. Covert connections—combined with innumerable cartons of cigarettes—resulted in new papers, these identifying the bedraggled group as Czech workers.

They traveled from city to town, transit camp to transit camp. Searing sun. Thunderstorm deluges. Constant hunger. Wooden benches in the backs of rattling trucks. Overcrowded trains, each car with a single tiny, waterless latrine. Interminable exhaustion. The gradual wearing away of their precious shoes with one step, then another. Then another.

As their latest train approached Bratislava, they peered at the city's onion-shaped church towers rising out of the dawn's mist.

"Welcome to Bratislava," Ben's voice boomed out. "Our accommodations here will be at the glorious pearl called the Hotel Jelen, more popularly known as Hotel *La Wanz*."

Mendel laughed along with the others in his group. *Wanz* was Yiddish for "louse," a creature they'd all become intimately familiar with, in spite of the liberal spraying of their bodies with DDT at every transit camp they passed through. Lice. Filth. Hunger. All part of their daily reality. At least tonight promised a roof over their heads and something resembling a bed—even if just a wooden pallet.

The following day, Mendel emerged from Hotel Jelen to greet the long shadows of the early morning. Fresh air filled his lungs as his fingers caressed the building's outer wall, like so many other walls, filled with the written names of survivors or people they still hoped to find. He searched through the spider webs of Polish, Yiddish, German, Czech, Hebrew. Different hieroglyphs, all containing the same dew drops of hope. Mendel added his strand. His name. His place of birth. An affirmation of survival and continuance, no matter what it took.

The anticipated single day in Bratislava stretched into three. More refugees traveling along the *bricha* route arrived, packing the already overcrowded building. Three days became a week. They ate soup. Sipped endless cups of weak tea. Lived in rooms elbow to elbow. Latrines backed up. The stink of garbage, body odor, and defecation permeated every space inside the building.

One week became two. Then three. Then four. Food portions shrank, while new names appeared on the wall, spreading, reaching around the corner, rising as high as the tallest person could reach then, somehow, even higher.

A month and three days passed. Ben gathered his group early in the morning, the thick clouds obscuring the rising sun's light. "Good news. We have finally received the necessary permission to cross over into Austria."

A cheer. Perhaps they would celebrate Passover in Palestine. This year's *seder* in Jerusalem. Would it possibly be more than a dream?

"Where are we headed now?" Sala asked.

"Vienna. To be more precise, the old Rothschild Hospital on Waehringerguertel Ring Road. If any of you spent time in that city, I'm sure you know of it. Even though it is in the Russian zone, the Americans run the transit camp there."

"And from there?"

"One step at a time. One step at a time." Ben walked over to a short, clean-shaven stranger standing off to the side and put his arm around the man's shoulder. The stranger removed a dangling cigarette from his mouth and threw it to the ground, crushing it under the sole of his boot.

"This is Asher," Ben said. "He will be your guide on this next leg of your journey."

So this was how it would be, a different guide for each segment.

Asher nodded, his dark eyes studying each of the group's members as though establishing their identities—memorizing the details of their faces, their clothing, and their builds. Then he raised his hand, getting the group's attention. "We leave tomorrow afternoon. Please gather your things and meet me in this spot at two o'clock."

By three, they were at the border. Once again, only Hebrew was spoken. Once again, cigarettes purchased the group's passage. Once again, after crossing the bridge into Austria, their assigned identities were destroyed and new papers distributed.

When they arrived at the Rothschild Hospital Transit Camp, a woman in a Red Cross uniform handed each person a card to fill out. No longer a hospital, in spite of the name carved into the impressive stone facade, it was simply one more in a series of stops during a never-ending journey.

Mendel picked up a pencil and began filling in the requested information. Name: *Mendel Feinberg.* Date of Birth: *24.12.1921.* Place of Birth: *Lodz, Poland.* Nationality: Mendel froze, his pen hovering over the blank space on the form.

Mendel and his fellow group members had heard the recent news. Who hadn't? On July fourth, forty-two Jews had returned to Kielce, Poland, their home before the Holocaust, only to be accused unjustly of kidnapping a Polish child and ultimately to be slaughtered by their neighbors. Over the summer, more Jews were beaten or killed across Poland for nothing more than returning to their villages and knocking on the doors of their one-time homes.

Nationality. Mendel pondered the only possible answer. Nationality: *Jewish.* No other choice existed.

After registration another woman ushered Mendel into the medical line. He'd passed through lines exactly like this at previous camps, the routine now a familiar one. A precursory exam. An x-ray to check for tuberculosis. A spraying of DDT to temper the interminable infestations of lice. A vaccination against typhus, the disease carried by those bloodsucking vermin.

On to the line for fresh clothing. Assignment to yet another overcrowded room with bunk beds lined up row after row after row.

With processing finished, Mendel joined the end of the food line which snaked around the room and out the door into the hallway. The reward for his patience: The overly familiar menu of soup and coffee along with something new—bright green peas.

"Courtesy of the Russians," said the woman, spooning the small, round legumes onto the small tin plates.

Once seated on one of the long benches at an even-longer table, it didn't take more than a few minutes for Mendel to devour the food. He scanned the room. Hip bones still jutted. Collarbones still bulged. There didn't seem to be enough food in the world to soften the sharp angles of the survivors' bodies.

On the way to his assigned bunk room, Mendel passed the now-familiar sight of handwritten names crowding a white wall. Hope had thinned over these past months. But the compulsion to read the scrawls had become an addiction. Mendel walked over to this—the newest in the long series—and traced the writing like a blind man feeling bumps on a page and understanding them as words, then sentences, then entire stories. *Ewa Meller, Tarnopol. Israel Gebert, Krosno. Sofia Siminauskis, Bialystok. Avram Feinberg, Lodz.*

Mendel froze, his finger on the name he thought he'd never see. *Avram Feinberg, Lodz.* His brother's name. His brother's handwriting. Their city. Was it even possible? Still alive? Here? He ran to a camp nurse walking nearby.

"*Potrzebuje pomocy,*" he pleaded.

The nurse shook her head.

Mendel repeated the appeal in Yiddish. In Hebrew. In Russian. The nurse continued to shake her head. Finally, she took his hand, walked him to an office, and knocked on the door.

"Yes? Enter," came heavily accented English from inside.

Mendel nodded his thanks and entered the office.

The man standing behind the desk looked haggard, his graying hair a halo against the light streaming through the window behind him. His deep-set, dark brown eyes contrasted with a pasty complexion, as though he'd been hidden away from the sunlight forever. Mendel wondered if this man had spent months, possibly years, in a *bunker* as well.

"Good afternoon. I am Benzion Teichholz," the man said in perfect Yiddish. "What may I do for you?"

"Mr. Teichholz, I found my brother's name on the wall of survivors. I must find him. Is he here? His name is Avram Feinberg. Do you know where he is?" Mendel couldn't stop speaking. A negative answer more than he could bear.

Teichholz pointed to a chair. "Please, sit down. You are?"

"Mendel Feinberg."

"Mr. Feinberg, we try to keep records of our guests here—where they come from, where they intend to go when they leave. Of course, with so many people passing through here over so many months, finding one individual's information might take a while. Did you arrive here on your own or with a group?"

Why was he asking? What did it matter? Mendel needed the information before Avram moved on and disappeared again.

Teichholz spoke again. "First of all, I'm also part of the *Sh'erit ha-Pletah*, the surviving remnant, as it were. But I can only help you if you help me. Let's start again." He pulled out a piece of paper and licked the pointed tip of a pencil. "Your name is Mendel Feinberg. You are from what village?"

"Not village. City. Lodz."

Teichholz wrote. "And the name of the person whose name you saw?"

"Not a person. My brother, Avram. Avram Feinberg. Also from Lodz."

"Very good. And, I ask again because you didn't answer me before: Did you arrive here on your own, or with a group?"

"I came with a group. Ben was our leader. He never told us a last name."

Teichholz's face broke into a smile. "Ah! You are with our *bricha* movement headed to Palestine. You are in luck. I am a member of the movement."

Mendel didn't care. He only cared about the man's current authority. "Can you find my brother's information?"

"Mr. Feinberg, I promise I will have someone try to find your brother's information as quickly as possible. Unfortunately, we are grossly understaffed. Fortunately, our *bricha* guests are here from a week to a month, depending on their group's movement and capacity to obtain necessary papers. I am hopeful I can get the information you need before you move on, if we have it."

Mendel sighed, his lips pressed into a thin line. "Please, Mr. Teichholz. I must find my brother. Years. It's been years since we've..." His loss. His suffering. His grief. A sob escaped through his effort to hold back the flood of emotion. Another sob. His shoulders shook as suppressed grief flooded out of him.

Teichholz walked around his desk and held Mendel's head against his body, tears wetting Teichholz's jacket's wool fabric—one man comforting another, each anguishing over the destruction of the world they'd once known.

After a short while, Mendel composed himself, and Teichholz returned to his seat. "We have hundreds—no, thousands of registrations from people who have passed through here. We are only a transit camp so our guests do not stay long. You have my promise, we will do everything we can to find your brother's information. Before you move on, please come to me with your next anticipated stop. Usually, when people leave here, they go to one of several displaced person's camps in the U.S. zone, especially if they are traveling on one of the *bricha* routes."

"My apologies for my breakdown. It's just…" Mendel's voice trailed off. He needed to be strong. Allowing emotion to overcome purpose only served to cloud the mind. Better to think, speak, and act deliberately— create a ritual. A pause before any rash action would be the key to control, giving him time to reconsider, shift over to a less emotional view of things. It was the only way to get through these times. "Again, I am sorry. I'll return to my quarters now. How will I know if you've found anything?"

"I'll see if I can find a volunteer to go through our active file and will be sure to let you know if we do or don't find anything."

Mendel thanked Teichholz, left the office, and walked across the hospital's courtyard. His mind searched through a labyrinth of possible ways to find his brother. That was his name written on the wall. It was unmistakable. He had survived. Was Avram traveling alone or was he with Shmuel? Was he here or had he already left? Did he have Ida with him?

His mind raced like a madman. Slow down. Pause. Breathe. Use logic.

When Mendel was young, his *Tvuna* youth group leaders always preached the value of action. Teichholz had papers. It was only a matter of finding the right one—one with his brother's name and destination.

Mendel headed back to Teichholz's office with a proposal. "Mr. Teichholz. You have hundreds of papers, I have thousands of minutes. Perhaps we can pool our resources. I will take your papers and organize them. Hopefully, during that process, I can find the one I'm looking for."

Teichholz's smile didn't take long to appear. His teeth were yellow. Cigarettes? Coffee? "I believe we have a deal. Come with me. I'll take you to the office where we keep our registrations."

With that, Mendel spent every free moment in that office. Registration cards filled boxes and drawers and sat in piles on every surface. The cards were banded together, loosely organized by date of arrival. There was no possible way to find an individual's card if you didn't know that date and, even then, finding the cards from a specific date could take hours. He might never find Avram, let alone organize the thousands of cards into any order that made sense.

He needed to think. What information would someone search for first? Name. Second? Place of birth. Third? Date of birth. This was how to create lists. It would take too long to alphabetize things in the limited time he would be here. But if he could make a start, get things going, perhaps others could continue the work. No. He had to find Avram. What if he didn't? Maybe Teichholz could get the information to him through his *bricha* contacts. At any rate, sitting at a desk and logging the living would be a *mitzvah* to counterbalance the losses suffered by every person each card represented.

He opened the desk's drawers. The first drawer held a box of unsharpened pencils and a small metal device marked *Norola* that Mendel assumed was to sharpen them. In the deepest drawer, the one on the bottom right, he found several boxes containing lined paper. Three pencils sharpened, a fresh sheet of paper for every letter of the alphabet, he began his work.

Alter, Joseph - Bodzentyn, Poland - 8.12.1920
Weinberg, Jacob - Berlin, Germany - 7.8.1913
Baum, Frida - Budapest, Hungary - 5.3.1932

Minute by minute. Hour by hour. Name by name. When he ran out of paper, he asked Teichholz for more. He stopped eating in the dining room. Instead, he carried his meals to what was now *his* office, eating while he worked. Every day the new transit papers were delayed was another day gifted to his cause.

On the sixth day, he came across a card holding a familiar name. *Gitla Kober, Lodz.* Could this be their friend, Gitla? The one they'd worked with in the factory? Was she still here? The date showed she'd come through Rothschild Hospital three months ago. His eyes dropped down to the lower right-hand corner of the card with the printed word *Destination*. Blank! Was this to be his fate? A *Gehenna* of searching but never finding? He pressed his fingers against closed eyelids. He needed a break. He stepped outside into the crowded courtyard.

It was a beautiful day. People sat on the ground, leaning against the walls of the building, smoking contraband cigarettes or strolling in pairs and small groups. Mendel knew the conversations in these groups without needing to hear them. "Where are you from?" "Do you know…?"

As he stood there, breathing in air that didn't smell of ink and paper, Sala ran up to him.

"Did you hear? Our papers have come through. We'll be leaving in a day or two."

A hitch in his breathing. A long breath in. "Did they say where we would be going?"

"Asher didn't say the exact place. Just that it would be in the American Zone. We'll receive training there for our arrival in Palestine." Sala smiled broadly. Her face had filled out over their time in the different camps, and her hair was coming in nicely as well, the dark waves almost reaching her chin.

An angst of conflicting desires overwhelmed him. He needed to speak with Teichholz. Avram was alive somewhere. So was Gitla. What about Shmuel? And Ida? Who else might be out there? And how to find them?

He ran over to the administration building and knocked on the familiar office's door.

"Yes? Enter."

As always, Teichholz sat behind a desk filled with disorganized papers, evidence of the flotsam and jetsam called refugees, displaced persons, The *Sh'erit ha-Pletah.*

Mendel entered. "I've received word my group will be leaving in the next couple of days."

Teichholz nodded. "*Mazel tov,*" he said. "Another step closer to your destination. Did they say where you would be going?"

"Not yet. I hope they tell us, so we can add that information to my card before I leave."

"I know. Unfortunately, since the *bricha* is an illegal movement, a great deal of the information is communicated on a need-to-know basis. The British are intractable. They do whatever they can to prevent our people from reaching Palestine's shores. But we will continue exerting pressure on them. The world cannot, must not allow us to be homeless forever. Until then, we will continue to do what needs to be done."

"We?"

"Yes. Before taking over the administration here I worked with the partisan-run *bricha* movement."

Mendel stood silently, reverently, hopefully. "So, you are a hero."

"All the real heroes are dead."

"Do you think I'll ever find my brother?"

"I can only hope all surviving families and friends will find each other. Were you able to learn anything?"

"I found the card of an old acquaintance from the Lodz ghetto. But there was no destination written on it."

"I see. I'd like you to show me what you've done. Perhaps we can find other volunteers to continue the work you began."

Mendel walked with Teichholz to the nearby office and showed him the banded cards grouped by date followed by sheet after sheet of lists he'd parsed into alphabetical groupings.

With a hand clasping Mendel's shoulder, Teichholz nodded. "You've made an excellent start, and your system will eventually make it easier to locate names. I'm sorry you didn't find the one you were looking for. I'm also sorry we've been unable to reward you for all your work."

Mendel had never considered payment. Being of use was much better than waiting for the next unknown step. "Perhaps you can avail on our group's leader to at least tell you our destinations, so those who are looking for us have some clue on how we might be found."

"I'll speak with Asher about it. But I don't believe the *bricha* would endanger their mission by divulging such information, even to a fellow Jew."

So Teichholz already knew which group Mendel was with, who their leader was. "Thank you."

"I would like to give you something for your trouble. No matter where you go, fall and winter will come sooner than later. Come with me."

Mendel accompanied Teichholz to the staff quarters and up to his small apartment. He waited in the sparse front parlor while Teichholz left the room.

A few minutes later, Teichholz emerged, a full-length brown leather coat in his hands. "I would like you to have this. Many of the German prisoners of war were kept here immediately after the war. When they were moved elsewhere their possessions remained. I was hoping to keep this specimen for myself, but I think you've earned an honorarium. The person who wore this officer's coat worked at tearing our people apart. You've spent your time here trying to bring them together. I would like you to have it as my agent of organization, and a friend."

"What did I do except organize a few papers?"

"It isn't what you did, or why you did it. It's that you didn't give up. That's the spirit we need in Palestine. Perhaps, in the future, when we finally meet there, you can return the coat to me. Until then, use it in good health. Now, before your group takes its leave, let's go back to my office for some schnapps and a *L'Chaim*."

CHAPTER FIFTEEN

IT'S NOT ABOUT THE OIL AT ALL

Chanukah. Again. It would be Amelia's and my second time celebrating the holiday together. This time she came prepared. After we lit the candles for the first night, she lit into me. "Did you know most of what you believe about Chanukah is a lie?"

"Huh? What are you talking about?"

"I went to the source, the actual *Book of Maccabees One and Two*. Not an easy read, that tome." When I didn't react, she continued. "Hello. The Maccabees? Did you ever read the actual story?"

"Should I have?"

"Well, considering you light the candles every year…According to the translation I read, at least from what I can tell, the story about the oil as the foundation for the holiday isn't true."

"Of course it isn't. God didn't make one day of oil last for eight days and eight nights, because there is no God."

Amelia rolled her eyes. "It has nothing to do with God at all. It has to do with the revolt, the victory, and celebrating the rededication of the Temple."

I could tell this was going to be more than a before-dinner discussion, and I had too many exams to grade that evening. "Let's put this discussion off until the weekend, when I have more time for a world history lesson. Okay?"

We did. A few days later Amelia and I sat across the table from each other at Rollerback's, a nearby cheap eats place. Over a couple of beers, and Seattle's famous hot dogs slathered with melted cream cheese, we continued our discussion. This time, I was the one who came prepared. I had no intention of being one-upped by someone who hadn't spent thirteen years attending Hebrew school. "I did a little research myself. You're right. The story about the oil is exactly that—a story. It seems the whole eight days' celebration had to do with all those victorious Maccabees celebrating an after-the-fact *Sukkot,* since they'd missed it during their battles with the Greeks."

"I read about *Sukkot.* Meant to ask you about it."

"I guess I've never shared the pleasure of that particular holiday with you. In English, it's called the Feast of Booths, commemorating the Jews being forced to wander in the desert for forty years."

"And what foods are associated with this new-to-me holiday? I hope there's something with chocolate in it."

"*Sukkot* isn't so much about what we eat. It's about where we eat. We're supposed to build an outdoor structure, a *sukkah*, and you have to be able to see the sky through the covering that makes up the roof—corn stalks, bamboo, or palm fronds, depending on where you live. It's pretty cool, except in the fall, up north, when it can get downright cold."

Amelia leaned forward in her seat and smiled broadly. "Sounds like fun. Did you and your family build one every year?"

"No. We always went to the *sukkah* parties at our *shul* or someone else's house."

"It seems like the Jews did an awful lot of camping out."

I could usually follow Amelia's thought processes. But she lost me with this one. "What do you mean?"

"Your people wandered around quite a bit. Joseph going down into Egypt then, a few generations later, leaving Egypt and wandering in the desert for forty years. Then there was running from the Crusades, the Inquisition, and so on and so forth. Until, finally," she pointed at me, "the diaspora."

"And even then…" my voice trailed off as the coat crept its way into my thoughts. The unforgiving leather. The implied warmth of its lining. The contradictions built into its physical and existential reality. What was I about to say? Something about the diaspora. "Never mind."

I bit into my hot dog and chewed, the mouthful of food an excuse not to speak.

Amelia rescued me from the silence. "How about your Saba and Savta? Did they celebrate *Sukkot*?"

I'd never considered this. "Now that you made me think about it, I don't think they did. At least I don't ever remember it. But we were almost always there for *Yom Kippur* and just after it ended would have been when they would have put up the *sukkah.*"

It seemed odd. I assumed Saba and Savta observed everything. Savta kept her *Siddur*, her prayer book, under her pillow and always read the *Kriat Shema al Hamitah* prayer, kissing the bottom of the page before she closed the book and shut the light. I know this because Ilana and I watched *The Golden Girls* with them every night whenever we'd visit. The end of that show signaled their bedtime. We'd kiss them goodnight and head downstairs just as Savta pulled out her *Siddur* and opened it to the page stained with the remnants of different colored lipsticks.

I ran through the major holidays in my head. Were there other holidays Saba ignored? I needed more information. When I got home, I called my father.

"Hello?"

"Hey, Dad. I have a weird question for you. Did Saba ever celebrate *Sukkot?*"

"That's an odd question."

"Did he?"

I heard my mother in the background. "Is that Seth? What does he want? Is everything okay?"

"He's fine. He's just asking a question about my father."

My mother's voice again. "Be sure to give him my love."

"Sorry about that, Seth. So, did my father ever celebrate *Sukkot?* Actually, I don't ever recall us celebrating it, not even at other people's houses or in *shul.*"

"Do you know why not?"

The pause. "Saba had his own approach to Judaism. When I was young, I don't remember him being religious at all, except for his religious fervor around the High Holidays—*Rosh Hashana* and *Yom Kippur.* In fact, back then, he and Savta worked on Saturdays and most of the holidays."

"What about Chanukah? And Passover?"

"Well, yes. Passover. I guess that was always Saba's opportunity to shine."

"What do you mean?" Another pause, this one a long one. Maybe the call got dropped. "Dad, are you still there?"

"I'm still here. I'm just trying to figure out how to tell it. Look, your Saba and Savta had very hard lives. They had to struggle and scramble for everything they had. But your Saba had a strong religious background. In fact, Avram once told me your Saba trained to be a cantor. But history had other plans. The High Holidays and Passover gave him the chance to role-play, be the cantor he always wanted to be."

Dad was right. During the High Holiday services, I always heard Saba's voice above the other members of the congregation. He had no compunction about correcting the rabbi or the cantor, so familiar was he with the liturgy and its various melodies. Perhaps the importance of these holidays to him had nothing to do with God or faith.

Maybe these were the times Saba reclaimed something he'd lost along the road of life. Empowerment. A path to leave behind the anguish of watching family members ripped away. Was this the avenue to make up for the years wasted in hiding so he could avoid the terror of the barrel of a gun pressed against his head? The guilt from not having stood naked in a room with a thousand other people, knowing what's been promised, but having absolutely no idea what is actually to come? His way to prove, in spite of things that had gone terribly wrong, there was some form of salvation to be found?

"Thanks, Dad. Sorry to bother you."

"No bother. It's always great to hear from you. Mom sends her love."

"I know. I heard." A kiss.

CHAPTER SIXTEEN

IN WHICH THE COAT
IS PART OF A RUSE

1945

As Mendel's *bricha* group walked along yet another muddy road, they heard a new convoy in a never-ending series of convoys coming up behind them. Russians? Brits? Americans? His group stepped to the side. As the vehicles got closer, They heard singing. Hebrew lyrics. The voices were singing *Hatikvah*!

Asher smiled and waved both arms at the vehicles. A jeep and a truck pulled up, slowed, and stopped. The letters T.T.G. were stenciled in black on the front fenders. Stamped on the doors at eye level were large yellow stars of David.

Mendel studied both vehicles. There was no possible way the star of David would be on military vehicles like these in a place like this. Might he have died without knowing it? Did an afterlife exist? A closer inspection revealed writing covered the metal surface of the truck. Names. Again. *Ruchel Fantich. Aleksander Ayzikowitz.* Places. *Pochayev. Grodno.* Messages. *I am alive. I have survived.*

Asher walked around to the rear of the truck and spoke to a swarthy young man with curly black hair and a thick mustache that hung over his top lip. After a short conversation, the man jumped out of the truck and he and Asher came over to the group.

"This is where I leave you," Asher said. "These young men will take good care of you and get you to your next stop." Without even a wave, Asher walked away and got into the jeep which ground into gear and continued up the road. Another change. How many would there be before they finally reached Palestine?

"*Shalom, chaverim!*" the new leader called, his baritone voice booming. "M*edaberim Ivrit?*"

Mendel wondered if this was some sort of trick. Of course he knew Hebrew. He'd had to study it all through his youth. His family had hoped he would become a cantor for the local *shul*.

When there was no reply, a man leaning out the passenger window of the truck's cab spoke. This one a little older, thinner, with a receding shock of red hair and a big, toothy smile. "*Vy govorite po-russki?*"

The group didn't react, their interest focused on the scrawled names. Instead of fighting through the crowd, Mendel stared at the men in the truck, too confused to reply. Who were these people?

A third man spoke. "*Czy mówisz po polsku?*"

Mendel didn't look at this one's face, his attention drawn instead to the patch on his uniform's upper sleeve—a yellow star of David. This wasn't at all like the ones he'd had to wear in the ghetto. This one stood against a field of blue and white embroidery.

Hebrew. Then Russian. Then Polish. A star of David. Mendel slowly nodded. Smiles broke out as others in his group joined his response. Many reached up to the uniformed men wearing the stars.

The Polish-speaking soldier—at least he appeared to be a soldier— continued speaking, putting out his hand. "Climb on board, *chaverim*. You are with us now. We will take you to a safer place."

The balding man and the man with the mustache jumped out of the truck and helped Mendel and the other members of his group climb into the open bed of the military vehicle.

"I'm sorry we don't have a comfortable seat for you after your long walk. There will be too many of us to drop the benches. But we can invite you to sing. Of course, you all know *Hatikvah*. No?"

As the soldiers sang, Mendel looked from person to person. In addition to the tanned, healthy soldiers, he saw ghosts like himself. Many were barefoot. All wore tattered garments which hung off their bodies as if on stick figures. Several wore striped pajama-like uniforms still emblazoned with the more familiar yellow stars reading *Jude*. Shaved heads and sunken eyes hinted at their recent past. A few sang softly. Others mouthed the words. The rest stood silently, looking down or watching the countryside and towns pass by.

"What is this? Who are you?" Mendel asked the older, balding soldier.

"I will answer your questions in reverse." The man grinned. "I am Adin Talbar, a member of the Second Battalion of the Palestine Regiment. This mustachioed fellow next to me is Israel Tal and my friend sitting in the front is Haim Laskov. You'll meet everyone else in time."

"How shall I address you?"

"By our names. Adin, Israel, and Haim, of course."

Mendel needed to sit, but there was no way among the group of soldiers and survivors. "And what are you?" he asked.

"We are known as the Jewish Brigade. During the war, we fought in the British army. Now, we're here to help you and your fellow survivors come to Palestine."

The rocking and bouncing of the truck along the road became meditative. Smells changed with the scenery. Smells associated with colors unknown in camps, ghettos, or tunnels dug under the floors of basements. The green smell of springtime fields. The brown smell of pastured cows. The blue smell of winding streams.

Every so often, they would stop as the convoy picked up another emaciated wanderer; more surviving remnants of humanity. The trucks rapidly filled as they traveled through the evening and into the night.

Mendel looked up at the infinite universe, the waxing moon the same as the one a few nights before his escape from the ghetto, when there had been no moon at all. Now the stars shone with a new freedom, a new hope—*Hatikvah*.

Hours after the stars had come out, the trucks finally pulled up to what seemed to be a farmhouse. "Adin, what time is it?" Mendel asked.

Adin looked down at his watch. "It is 2:30 in the morning."

Several men approached the trucks. A few wore uniforms. Others wore shirts with their sleeves rolled up, cigarettes dangling, barely holding on to their lips. Mendel and his fellow survivors were helped off the trucks and escorted into a room set up with long wooden tables. What sat on the tables registered with Mendel's nose. Potato soup and coffee, smells promising this meal might be richer than their recent meals of watery soups and weak teas.

"Sit," Adin said. "Eat. Those of you new to food, please eat slowly, and not too much; otherwise, you will become dangerously ill. We will ease you back to the world of food carefully—put some *fleisch* on those bones."

Fleisch. So, Adin spoke at least a little Yiddish as well. Mendel smiled. The possibility of life approaching something familiar filtered into his consciousness.

That night, Mendel slept with his fellow survivors on wooden-slatted bunk beds. They slept barely at the edge of consciousness, their instincts still filled with memories of all they'd endured. A woman cried out. A man mumbled. A teenage girl sobbed. Morning came.

A new group of Brigade soldiers came into the sleeping room, a multilingual wake-up call. "Good morning, friends. It is time to get up and welcome the new day. There is bread and soup and coffee waiting for you in the dining hall. Afterward, another day of travel in our luxurious vehicles before we reach our destination—the American camp in Landsberg. That is where you will be assigned to *kibbutzim* to receive your training in preparation for your settlements in *Eretz Israel*."

Was there no direct route anywhere? Did everything have to be convoluted and twisted? Would they ever leave Europe?

"Unfortunately, the Americans have tried closing their zone to us, so we need a small deception to get you across their checkpoint. When I call your name, please go with Tuviah, the man standing by the door."

The anticipatory silence was immediate and overpowering.

"Ferenc Kurcz. Jozsef Aladar. Aron Sandor. Mendel Feinberg…"

With the roll complete, the explanation came. "We will be smuggling you across the border into the American zone as German POW's. Ironically, the Americans are willing to house Nazi prisoners but no longer welcome Jewish survivors. We will employ their preferences to achieve our goal."

Tuviah took the group upstairs into a room filled with piles of German uniforms. "We borrowed these from a deserted *Wehrmacht* storeroom. I apologize if you are not happy with your assigned rank. It has more to do with fit than merit."

When Mendel's turn came, Tuviah handed him a pair of gray wool pants and a full-length leather coat to wear over the worn shirt he'd received from the *bricha* back in Lodz.

Dressed in their new uniforms, the group followed Tuviah back downstairs and to a waiting three-tonner. Unlike before, this one had benches and a canvas-covered back.

Tuviah spoke. "It's time for you to meet your new leaders for this leg of your journey. Your driver is David, accompanied by Amichai."

The two men standing by the front of the truck casually saluted.

"The fellow in the back with the friendly looking rifle is Yossel. He will be your guard. You are soldiers now—but your uniforms belie your allegiance. You are fighting for the liberation of Palestine and the re-establishment of a homeland for yourselves and your people. We will show the world there is no carpet under which they can sweep the *Sherit HaPletah*. Safe journey." With a curt nod, Tuviah was gone.

Amichai took charge. "*Shalom, chaverim.* David, Yossel, and I will be with you for more than just this leg of the journey. We've been assigned to work with one of the *hachsharot* units once we get to the American camp at Landsberg. Now, climb on board."

Mendel knew *hachshara* was Hebrew for preparation. As the truck rattled along, he thought about his new situation. He'd been in a *hachshara* during his time as a member of his Zionist youth group. How many years ago was that? Six—a lifetime. Now the world was a different place. He looked over at Yossel. "What type of training will our *hachshara* offer?"

Yossel gave a wink as everyone on the benches leaned in to hear over the three-tonner's drone. "Skills you will need to reestablish a Jewish state. Exercise to strengthen your bodies. Farming to feed our people. Building to establish settlements. Self defense so that nothing like these many recent years can happen again."

Several men applauded. One of the women said softly, "Amen."

Renewed anticipation galvanized the group and conversations about hopes for the future filled the air. Relatives they still hoped to find. Activities they'd probably be assigned once they reached Israel. Conversations halted as the engine's gears ground and the truck slowed.

Yossel spoke in a harsh whisper. "Be silent and look miserable. Remember, you are my prisoners. After all, you've lost everything and, to make it even worse, we *Judenscheisse* are now your captors. We will be through the checkpoint in short order."

As the truck stopped, so did all movement in the back of the truck. Would the guards notice their dark hair? What about the women? Maybe luck would continue to be with them. They all strained to hear the exchange outside the protective canvas cover.

"Papers?"

"Here you are. We are transporting German prisoners of war."

"These papers say your unit is the T.T.G. What does that stand for?"

"You mean you don't know?" David yelled to the back. "Hey, Yossel! He doesn't know what T.T.G. stands for. Do you believe that?"

Amichai's voice. "I'll bet his commanding officer would love to hear how ignorant he is of his own army's divisions."

Laughter. A door slamming. A pause that seemed like eternity. A door slamming again. A sudden jerk as the truck began to move.

Mendel looked over to Yossel and whispered, "What *does* T.T.G. mean? And why didn't the British official know?"

More laughter. "*Chaver*. T.T.G. is the Brigade's 'special' unit. It stands for *tilchas tizig gesheften*. We combined a little bit of Arabic with Yiddish and named our unit 'Kiss My Ass Business.' We make sure to embarrass them when they don't know what it is. Then, if they still don't let us pass, we threaten to tell their higher-ups. It works every time."

Mendel joined in the new round of laughter filling the truck. The release felt good. As the truck continued forward, the men's voices broke out into song.

"Never say this is the final road for you, though leaden skies may cover over days of blue.

As the hour that we longed for is so near, our step beats out the message: We are here!"

Yossel lit up a cigarette and offered to share the bounty with his fake POW's. Everyone on the truck wanted one and patiently waited while Yossel handed out one cigarette each, lighting each one and watching each recipient inhale the gift.

As the compartment quieted, Mendel leaned over. "Why do you do this? You must have family back home. Don't you miss them?"

"I do this because you are my people. I do this because there is no other choice. I do this because the only way to a free Palestine is to show the world why."

A long drag. The cigarette's paper crackled delicately. An exhalation of fragrant white smoke. A repetition of their mission. "We're taking you to a displaced persons camp run by the Americans. While you're there, we'll place you into a *hachshara* and train you for your new agricultural lives in *Eretz Israel*."

"So this is why you take us to Germany?"

A wisp of a woman in an oversized German infantry uniform spoke. "No. I hear something different. I hear we're being used." She sat in the darkness of the farthest corner, likely placed there to obscure her gender. In the low light, with her thin frame and short curly hair, one might have mistaken her for a young boy.

Yossel looked up, the cigarette drooping from his lips. "There are all sorts of rumors about all sorts of things."

"I believe the one I heard, the one that says you're using us to exert pressure on the British foreign minister." the woman replied.

Yossel's angry voice thundered over the sound of the truck. "What do you expect us to do? Magic? Britain is recalcitrant. Antisemitism didn't disappear when Germany was defeated. The British prefer to align with the Arabs and work against us. We need the Americans to see and understand. We'll fill their damned camps beyond capacity so they'll see how many refugees there really are and exert pressure on Bevin, the British Foreign Secretary, to discontinue the quota for immigration to Palestine. Then, maybe, our brothers and sisters can come home where they belong."

"So you lie?" Mendel asked.

Yossel threw the stub of a cigarette to the floor and crushed it under his foot. "When the time is right, we'll smuggle you in groups to Italy. We have ships there that will take you down the Adriatic and across the Mediterranean to Palestine. Now, *chaverim*, let's sing." Yossel began one of the now-familiar songs, and the group joined in.

Hours later, the truck stopped. "We are here," David called from the cab.

The canvas opened, and the three Brigade soldiers helped their charges down from the truck and escorted them inside the gate of the Landsberg Displaced Persons Camp. Throngs of fellow survivors swarmed around them. Faces scanned faces.

Suddenly, out of the buzz of inquiries, a voice screamed out. "Mendel Feinberg! Mendel! Mendel!"

Mendel's head jerked around, searching for the source of this sound. The voice was unmistakable. He and Avram had found each other at last.

CHAPTER SEVENTEEN

THE BEST OF
ALL POSSIBLE WORLDS

"I have the stories in my head. Each one of them makes sense, but when I try to write them down the words won't translate onto the page."

Amelia stood over me. I'd asked her to bring me a glass of ice water, wanting the warmth of her near me more than I wanted anything to drink. Now, I sat with her standing next to me and my computer, and I didn't want to be near either one.

"The words look wrong, or they sound wrong, or they don't express what I'm trying to say."

Amelia handed me the glass, the ice already making it sweat cold drops of condensation. She continued to listen. I continued to vent. "Sometimes it takes me an hour to write a single paragraph."

She put her hand, still cool from the glass, on my arm. "That must be frustrating."

I looked up at her, my discouragement spilling over. "Don't patronize me."

Her hand fell away. The slight sensation of coolness remained, as did the ghost of her touch. "I'm not patronizing you. I'm trying to understand. I've seen you work on your academic papers. With those, your body language reads differently than when you work on your family stories."

I didn't want to give in to the dark cloud moving between us. But there it was. Palpable. Threatening. I leaned away. She took a step back.

"Maybe it's too close. The compulsion to write is there, but so is the fear of getting too intimate with the truth."

"What truth? You're writing about your grandparents' survival. They lived through the horrors and came through to the other side."

"Amelia, everything I read about the other side mimics what went before. Hunger. Suffering. Life with barbed wire and guards, even if they belong to the benevolent Americans rather than the evil Germans. You know what the great General Patton said about the Jews in the displaced persons camps?"

"I assume, with that lead-in, nothing good."

"Let me look up the exact quote. I want to be sure I get it right." After a few seconds, I read the quote off the screen. "'Harrison and his ilk believe the displaced person is a human being, which he is not, and this applies particularly to the Jews who are lower than animals.' This from the man overseeing the displaced persons camps operations across Europe. Can you imagine?"

Amelia's now-warm hand returned. "Let's think about some of the positives in their post-war lives."

"Like what?"

"You."

"You're just saying that because I take you to the finest cheap eats joints in Seattle."

"I say that because I couldn't love anyone who was less than the best."

The dark cloud above us dissipated. I pushed the chair back from the computer and pulled Amelia into my lap. "The positives, you say?"

"Sure. Every situation has them. The first positive—you." Her finger poked my chest.

I paused. Was I a positive or an inevitable? Were my father, my aunt, my entire extended family on that side meant to be the building block replacements for all the other generations that had been lost, or were we part of a more visceral begetting? It's amazing that survivors—after all the deprivation and suffering—were able to procreate as quickly as they had. Perhaps the bigger surprise for me was, after all their losses, how they were able to consider procreation at all. "Well, my being a positive is probably the last item on the short list, since I came decades after the Holocaust."

Amelia took one of my untamable curls and twisted it around her finger, giving it a little tug. "Then name something positive. Whatever it is, I want—no, demand that your next story be about that."

I ran through the chronology of the stories I'd already finished. The common thread of survival against the odds seemed a bit played out. I pulled her hand away from my head and held it in her lap while I thought out loud. "They're stuck in the displaced persons camp. I guess the best thing that happened there was how Jews began to organize and become themselves."

"Become themselves? Is that a Sethism?"

"Might be. Let me try to work through it a little better. Up to that point the survivors had been at the mercy of the fates. The oppression of the Nazi regime and its collaborators. The *bricha* movement transporting their hapless disciples here and there. Constantly changing routes and destinations. Then...the DP camps with their fences and guards—the oppressors believing they were being altruistic when they were, in fact, imprisoning thousands who'd known nothing else for almost a decade."

"I thought we were trying to come up with the positives."

I squeezed Amelia's hand. "I'm getting there."

"Well then?"

"It was in those DP camps, especially the largest ones like Landsberg, where the surviving Jews started to move toward independent nationhood, an ingathering, as it were. They set up independent camp governments, held elections, appointed camp police, and even had a court that offered jurisdiction over minor internal disputes."

I took a sip of the water, the ice now melted, then continued. "They organized schools, where they educated themselves and a new generation of children. Finally, they created *kibbutzes* so they'd be ready to join existing ones or build new ones when they finally arrived in Israel."

"See? Maybe not so much oppression. Maybe some optimism."

"I guess you could call it that."

Amelia looked at her watch. "Speaking of optimism, I predict we can get the dishes done before bedtime."

She got up from my lap. I held on to her hand. "You sit. I'll do them tonight."

I didn't really want to do the dishes, but I needed the monotonous action of washing them so I could continue to think about the possibilities for my next story. Amelia was right. I needed to see if I was capable of writing optimism. Optimism, even if it was guarded, must have been what kept so many from committing suicide or going crazy. Optimism had to be what allowed survivors to continue believing in their God in spite of His betrayal. Optimism must have existed with each paltry celebration of *Rosh Hashana*, *Yom Kippur*, and Passover, even if the rituals were carried out minus the necessary trappings.

I stood by the sink, my hands moving mechanically. Optimism. Savta had never completely recovered from her losses. I thought about her whiny sadness whenever our visit ended, her expression wrinkling downward, her entire face a frown. Saba had never completely come to terms with his past, either, refusing to share anything, changing the subject or claiming he was tired. How was I to write about optimism if I couldn't parse it in the survivors who'd been closest to me?

Yet optimism must have existed. Was so much suffering necessary to bring Europe's Jewish population together to work toward the same cause? Even after all the evil, even under the conditions of the displaced persons camps, they'd married and had children. If nothing else, those events must be proof of some humanistic equation.

When did optimism peek through the clouds of despair? When people found surviving family or friends? With the promise of three meals a day, even if those meals were small and unfamiliar? Perhaps the *bricha* bolstered hope when they promised a rising up, a collective movement, an *aliyah:* Israel. Perhaps this was what finally allowed the *She'rit ha-Pletah* to move forward and take destiny into their own hands.

CHAPTER EIGHTEEN

THE COAT COMES OUT
OF A STOREROOM

1946

Mendel sat at a long table in the dimly lit dining hall and stared at the strange food on his tray. The bread looked bleached as though the overly soft slices had been buried with him in his *bunker*. The yellow globules pretending to be eggs seemed as though they'd sat too long in one of the many puddles he'd wandered through on his way to nowhere. A sip of strong coffee. A poke of the oversized spoon into the tangle of watery yellow blobs.

"You should eat." The voice next to him spoke a heavily accented Yiddish. A Russian, maybe? "You can't expect to grow strong on nothing."

"Is it safe?"

"Did you ask that same question while you were in the camps?"

A wave of shame crashed over Mendel. People he'd met since emerging from his private *bunker* had told him stories; the types of stories that would haunt him for the rest of his life. Compared to them, he'd had it good—escaping from the ghetto, being allowed to hide. The only thing he shared with so many of these other survivors was a burning desire for a return to a normal life. No. Even this desire had been taken away from so many—the ones who haunted the roads with dead eyes and scarred souls.

"You're right, friend." Mendel tentatively spooned the yellow curds into his mouth. The acceptable taste helped mitigate the unpleasant texture. Mendel finished the eggs and the anemic bread and licked his spoon and plate clean.

The man slapped Mendel on the back. "Now we can formally introduce ourselves to each other. I am Yuri Narokov from Odessa. You?"

Mendel paused to study the young man seated next to him. Dark hair, neatly combed back from a broad forehead. Dark eyes that burned, much like Menachem's had back in Lodz. Finally, he spoke. "Mendel Feinberg from Lodz."

"Any family survive?"

"So far, only a brother. But we still have hope. You?"

"Me? It seems I alone survived. Happily I have found a new family here."

"A new family?"

"My *chaverim* at the *kibbutz*. There we work and play planning our final *bricha* to Israel so we can rebuild our homeland."

"Your *kibbutz*. Is it called *Tvuna*?"

"Ah! You were a member before the Germans invaded?"

"Yes." It seemed so long ago. So many of the memories he'd carried with him during the eternal hours in the *bunker* had faded. "Does it still exist here?"

"No. Our *kibbutz* is not *Tvuna*. But it is something just like it. Come. Let me take you over and introduce you to my brothers and sisters there. We welcome everyone willing to work with us. Do you like farming?"

Mendel paused for a beat before answering. "Who can remember such things?"

They walked from the dining room to a nearby Jeep with Jewish Brigade emblems on the doors and hood. A short drive later, they passed under an arch with hand-painted Hebrew letters spelling out *Blessed Are Those Who Come.*

Mendel wondered if he'd entered paradise. Fit, tan young men and women rode tractors, hoed fields, and tended livestock. The relaxed nature of their movements and their broad smiles as they sang or shouted back and forth produced a vitality missing back at the DP camp.

"This is quite something," Mendel said.

"A triumph," Yuri replied. "During the war, this property was a rest camp for SS officers. After the war, the Americans appropriated it and allowed us to claim it as an agricultural training annex to their DP camp. We've become a strong collective, preparing for the day we will arrive in *Eretz Israel.*"

"Does everyone travel back and forth to Landsberg every day?"

"No. We have our own quarters and facilities here. We even have a school for children and adults run by Jacob Olejski. We don't only train bodies; we also train minds. But a few of us travel to Landsberg every day to find new *chalutzim* who are ready to join us." Jacob put his arm around Mendel's shoulders. "Let me show you our gymnasium and dormitories."

Mendel returned to the Landsberg camp with renewed purpose and immediately sought out Avram. "I've decided to join a *kibbutz* that exists up the road." He continued, describing what he'd seen that afternoon, urging Avram and his new wife, Tova, to join him.

"I'm glad you've been able to find some purpose," Avram said. "Me? I'm tired. Fighting with the Partisans and then the Russians gave me enough purpose for a lifetime. Tova has family in a place called Cleveland who are willing to sponsor us so we can get the necessary papers to travel to America. Israel is a pipe dream, America a reality."

Mendel's stomach dropped. "Please, Avram. We've only just found each other." His voice pleading, even while he presaged the answer.

Avram grabbed his brother's hands and squeezed them. "Wait for us to send for you. Then you can come to America as well." The same pleading. The same foreknowledge.

Mendel thought about his life—past, present, and future. Everyone around him had different stories, all tainted by the same losses of family, friends, dignity, and hope. Now Avram, wanting him to wait in this purgatory until…when? No. Yuri had offered a better way. Mendel hadn't fought before. He wouldn't be able to live with himself if he didn't fight now. "I must believe Israel is more than a pipe dream. I must become someone who works to make it a reality. I've come to realize we can only be free when we have our own land, populated and governed by our own people. Who knows? Maybe you and Tova will be the ones I sponsor once Israel becomes a reality."

Avram continued to hold his younger brother's hands. "Then you must follow your destiny. We won't be parted just yet. After all, *Moshiach* might arrive before our papers." A wink.

Mendel laughed. If he didn't laugh he might cry, and he was done showing weakness. He squeezed back. "Will you at least come and help me pack?"

The next day, Yuri glanced at the small suitcase wrapped with a leather belt so worn it threatened to break if one breathed on it. "I see you haven't managed to accumulate much during your transits."

"I left some of my clothing and my second pair of shoes with my brother. He and his wife are hoping to go to America soon."

"A shame. We can use strong young couples. America is an unfortunate dream for many." Mendel climbed into one side of the Jeep, Yuri into the other. "No matter. As for your lack of clothing, we'll find you some appropriate garments once we get to the *kibbutz*."

During the short drive, Mendel closed his eyes. As they distanced themselves from the DP camp, the air around him felt lighter. Gone were the DP camp's overused latrines and its atmosphere of bereavement and despair. The freedom of hope lay ahead—he imagined freshly cut hay from the fields he would till, manure from the cows he would milk, and the soil turned by the tractors he would learn to operate.

Mendel opened his eyes when he felt the jeep slowing.

Yuri parked the vehicle in front of a long brick building dotted with windows. "Come, *chalutz*. We'll get you registered and requisition clothes more fitting for your work here."

Mendel smiled. *Chalutz*. A wonderful new title. So much better than "dirty Jew" or "filthy swine."

A new form to fill out. Name. Date of birth. Father's name. Mother's name. Skills. No line for place of birth or nationality.

"Many of us take new names here—Hebrew names to reflect our rebirth. But that is your choice."

A new name. A new start. Mendel Feinberg. Mendel Something else. He shook his head. "I still have hope others in my family or from my city might have survived. A new name would make it harder for them to find me. I will keep the one I have."

"Fine. Then let's get you some clothing. I'd say you're about one-and-a-half meters tall? You're pretty thin now. But you'll get healthier with our good food and exercise. Wait here."

Yuri disappeared into another room and came back with an armful of clothing. "The storeroom here remained untouched after the Allies arrived and took over. It's our good luck this place was a vacation spot for German officers. When we got here, we found clothes for all seasons. Then The Joint—"

"The Join?"

Yuri laughed. "No. 'The Joint,' what we call the American Joint Distribution Committee. They help by sending donated food, clothing, and money from America. They are our silent allies in our fight against the British. Now, speaking of clothing." Yuri placed items on the table as he ticked them off. "Two pairs of shorts and one belt. I guarantee your waistline will change after a couple of weeks with us. Two short-sleeve shirts. A bandanna, handy on hot summer days, and a bit of protection from the cold once winter comes. And speaking of winter…"

More clothing moved from Yuri's arm onto the table. "One pair of long pants. A sweater—sorry it's a little ragged. Some of the items from America were a little more than used."

"That's fine. I kept one of my own sweaters." As Mendel spoke, his eyes caressed the single item that remained draped over Yuri's arm, a full-length brown leather coat, the kind German officers wore and half-naked Jews coveted during Poland's brutal winters.

Yuri placed this final item on the table, the coat gilding the gift of more garments than the cumulative total Mendel had owned over these past six years. Six years that had seemed like an eternity.

"*Nu,* Mendel? *Bruchim habayim!* Welcome home! Come, let's get you to your dormitory where you will meet your new brothers and sisters. As for your first job as a new *kibbutznik*, what do you know about chickens?"

CHAPTER NINETEEN

HALLOWEEN HITLER

Every year, my friend, Prakash, and his girlfriend, Liz, along with their three housemates, threw a Halloween party. Being from India, the novelty of such an idea enchanted Prakash. He embraced it the way many fellow Hindus embrace the twinkle and tinsel of Christmas. Amelia and I always attended these parties because she's great at thinking up couples costumes and I'm less uncomfortable with pagan/Celtic dress-up than I am with pagan/Christian symbology. After all, I'm pretty sure the Celts never committed wholesale slaughter of the Jews.

This particular year, Amelia and I dressed up as *Fifty Shades of Grey*. She'd gone to a hardware store and asked if she could have fifty paint chips in different hues of gray, explaining how they were for a Halloween costume. The employee, thinking it was a great idea, gave her a fistful of tricolored sample cards. Amelia took them home, cut them apart, and basted the pieces onto two t-shirts.

As was our custom, Amelia, and I began the evening by doing a few legs of the annual Halloween Pub Crawl, lubricating ourselves to a pleasant buzz before taking a bus over to Prakash's house in the Fremont neighborhood of Seattle.

By the time we arrived, the party was a mob scene. Clusters of costumed guests stood shoulder to shoulder around the combined living and dining room. Prakash and his roommates had pushed the couch and chairs against the walls and added a couple of cheap plastic folding tables to supplement the small four-top they used for studying. A few people sat on the beat-up couch, plates on their laps, the drinks on the scuffed wood floor adding to the collection of water rings from generations of students who'd done the same.

"Great costumes!" Prakash said, coming over to greet us. Instead of his usual jeans and t-shirt, he wore a traditional Indian *kurta*. Gold embroidery around a maroon top's neckline complemented a pair of gold pants visible from his knees down to his ankles.

"Drinks are over there." He pointed to a punch bowl filled with an amber liquid, bloodshot eyeballs floating on the surface. Several of the earlier arrivals flanked the concoction. Antony and Cleopatra stood nearby. Disney's Elsa handed me the ladle she'd just used.

"Those floating eyeballs look pretty gross," Amelia said.

Prakash laughed. "Liz found those somewhere. You pop them in the freezer. They don't dilute the booze like regular ice. Anyway, she's in the kitchen playing mad scientist. You should go in and say hi."

We served ourselves a couple of drinks and peeked into the kitchen, now dressed up as a laboratory with peeled grape eyeballs, spaghetti innards, and gelatin brains on plates along the countertop's limited space. Liz, dressed in a white lab coat from her job in the University's genetics research department, escorted a blindfolded "subject" on a tactile tour of her haunted lab.

Amelia backed out of the doorway and wrinkled her nose. "It's a little too cheesy for me."

I pointed at the food sitting in chipped, mismatched bowls and on paper plates along a folding table in the living room. "Nah. I think the cheese is over there."

We walked over to the finger-food buffet, joining a few people from my department. Together, we passed judgment on different costume choices around the room. Peanut butter and jelly: Tasteful. A bottle of glue: Tacky. A bag labeled *Eminem's*: Very punny.

Amelia and I made the rounds, visiting with people we knew and exchanging niceties with others we didn't.

Then Hitler goosestepped into the room.

Obviously, it wasn't Hitler in the flesh. It was, however, a highly effective costume. A long black vinyl version of my leather coat. A red armband with a black swastika painted inside a white circle. Dark hair slicked across a broad forehead. A greasepaint toothbrush-mustache smeared above narrow lips. The newcomer clicked his booted heels together, raised up his arm, and shouted, "Heil, Halloween!" loudly enough that the room quieted. He made his way around the room with a low goosestep, jostling the guests, occasionally swaying from side to side, then regaining his balance and marching on.

Who the fuck was this guy? Certainly not a part of the Seattle culture I was a part of. My crowd—and Prakash and Liz's—was all about political correctness and sensitivity. Was Hitler trying to be offensive? Provocative? Shocking? I couldn't think of anyone we could possibly know who would dress up like this, even as a joke. He had to be a party-crasher.

A few uncomfortable giggles broke the silence. Most of us, however, weren't quite sure how to react. *Sotto voce* comments buzzed around the room.

Hitler strode over to the punch bowl and, oblivious to Antony, began entertaining Cleopatra and Elsa—leaning in a little too close, touching their shoulders, then fondling a strand of Elsa's hair.

Amelia and I watched as he filled a glass with punch and whispered something into the Ice Queen's ear. Amelia nodded in his direction, her head close to mine. "What an asshole." Her unabashed comment apparently louder than she thought.

"Hey!" shouted our invading Nazi. "At least I put some work into my costume. Yours looks like it took all of ten seconds." Several of his esses were slurred.

I wondered how long he'd spent on his own pub crawl before deciding to stop in here. Had he invaded other house parties before this one?

I stood, drink in hand, trying to think of a pithy response. Several people nearby leaned in, hoping to have something to tell their friends in the coming days.

Amelia put her drink down on the table and took my hand. I heard the suppressed anger in her voice—a controlled wavering in a tone half an octave lower than usual. "I know we just got here. But I'd like to leave."

Hitler swayed, steadied himself on the punch table, then walked over. He winked at Amelia, the wink surrendering to a blink. "Don't be that way. I mean, I got the idea from Prince Harry. Pretty funny. You know, 'heil Halloween' instead of 'heil Hitler.' It's just a thing, dudette. Chill out." A shrug and a big smile revealing a mouthful of unnaturally white teeth. The smile unmasked how young he really was. I put him at about fifteen or sixteen years old.

Amelia would not be placated. "Well, for the record, not funny. Prince Harry—not cool. You? Even less than not cool."

A slight whine from the chastised dictator. "Hey. C'mon. Like, I really spent a lot of money on this."

Amelia was—on the cool scale—absolutely the coolest. "Now you can spend time figuring out why it might not have been the best of ideas." She looked at me, I guess to see how I was feeling.

I tried to give a weak grin. It came out more as a grimace. My initial stomach-turning reaction surrendered to common sense. The intent mattered, not the costume. The guy didn't have a clue. He fancied himself a comedian. This was Seattle three generations removed from World War II and the Holocaust. "C'mon," I said. "I'm okay. Let me get you a fresh drink."

Amelia shook her head. "No, really. I'd rather leave. All the fun's gone out of this party."

We walked over to Prakash, but he was busy debating the efficacy of different biopesticides. In the kitchen, Liz was still engrossed in her mad scientist laboratory tours.

Amelia pulled on my arm. "Let's go. We'll catch up with him and Liz another time. They won't even notice we've left."

We stepped out into an unusually warm and clear night for the end of October, a night with the rare combination of nice weather, clear views, and amusing costumes. The full moon illuminated Mount Ranier's rarely seen snow-covered peak. We decided to walk the few miles home rather taking the bus.

While we ambled down the steep incline of Prakash's street, Amelia linked her arm in mine. "Do you think I overreacted?"

I was surprised there weren't more people on the street. What time was it, anyway? "Would you have confronted him the same way if you'd taken a sec to think about it first?" I asked.

The click of Amelia's heels sounded against the sidewalk. "Probably. I was thinking of you more than anything else. I didn't want you to be hurt by that sort of idiocy."

I snorted.

"What's so funny?"

"Not laughing at you," I said, "I'm just thinking about our tipsy Adolph. I'm sure he only thought he was being funny. We might just have ruined his night."

Amelia and I walked from Greenwood Avenue along North 36th Street. At the junction of 36th and Fremont Place, we took a break and sat down on the steps leading up to Seattle's enormous statue of Lenin. The sixteen-foot high statue was a popular tourist attraction, partly due to its impressive artistry, but mostly due to its odd presence in a large, American city.

Our conversation turned to the statue looming over us. "I wonder if we'd have been as upset if someone walked into the party dressed as Lenin?" I asked, gesturing up at the revolutionary dictator.

"Or, even worse, Stalin," Amelia suggested.

"Genghis Khan."

"Mao."

"Pol Pot. Or Idi Amin. Would we have reacted the same way with any of those tyrants?" I asked.

"I guess that depends on who was responsible for the murder of the most people."

I pulled out my phone and did a quick search. "Wow!"

Amelia grabbed the phone out of my hand and scrolled through the information I'd pulled up regarding murderous regimes. "So Hitler isn't number one."

"Can you believe it? He comes in third. Mao was responsible for sixty million and Stalin for forty."

"Hitler's not too shabby. He adds thirty million to those inconceivable numbers, a trifecta of evil."

"You have the phone. Is our host Lenin on that list?"

Amelia scrolled down. "He's a lightweight. Only responsible for the murder of an estimated four million."

We turned and looked up at the dictator at whose feet we rested. Sometime during the previous few weeks, someone had painted his hands with red paint, the bloodlike tinge visible even under the dim street lighting.

I glanced down at the time. "Hey, it's almost two-thirty, and we still have to walk a couple more miles."

We walked on in a *façade* of silence, the streets mostly empty. It was a weeknight, after all, and people had things to do in the morning. I wondered how many of them would go to work after doses of acetaminophen and multiple cups of coffee. Meanwhile, the pleasant buzz from the earlier alcohol had transformed into a cataclysm of thoughts, all focused on the topic of offensive costumes.

Was our Halloween Hitler simply a youthful *faux pas*? After all, he did look a lot younger than the rest of us. Or was his choice of costume a continuation of the barber joke, with its negative stereotyping of rabbis and its peculiar manner of desensitization? And who was I to throw stones? As a kid, I always wore my Cleveland Indians baseball cap, the one prominently displaying the offensive image of Chief Wahoo. When I was nine, I dressed up as Tatanka, the WWF's Lakota, my own ignorant case of cultural appropriation way before cultural appropriation became "a thing."

Amelia gave my hand an "are you all right?" squeeze.

I smiled—and lied—with a nod. I wasn't all right. I wouldn't be able to sleep. I'd tell Amelia I needed to work on a paper that was due in a couple of weeks. I'd really sit in front of the computer doing research on costumes—specifically Hitler costumes. When did dressing up as Hitler become "a thing?"

At exactly 3:47 a.m., I found out.

CHAPTER TWENTY

IN WHICH THE COAT
SERVES AS A SATIRICAL PROP

1946

Tombstones with Hitler's name written on them dotted the courtyards around the Landsberg Displaced Persons Camp. Posters, slogans, and caricatures plastered building walls, reminding everyone of the victory over the recent German incarnation of ancient Persia's evil advisor, Haman. It was Purim, the holiday celebrating the vanquishing of Haman's plan to slaughter all the Jews. That afternoon's parade and the carnival following it promised a wonderful celebration.

Leah strolled around the camp with Shoshana and a couple of other Stopnica survivors. Almost seventeen years old, she felt all grown up in her narrow gray wool skirt and soft pink blouse, both gifts from a Red Cross volunteer. Another volunteer—this one from the organization she only knew as ORT—had given her a pair of low-heeled pumps which Leah had saved for a special occasion. Although a bit worn and scuffed, their soles were intact and, when she didn't think anyone else was watching, Leah angled her legs to admire the shoes' feminine profile.

Since the end of the war and the establishment of several Jewish DP camps, the entire *She'rit ha-Pletah* searched for ways to live again, to throw off the mantle of worry and fear and continue on as normally as possible within the limits of a continually abnormal existence—to have made it through the labor and death camps only to be confined behind barbed wire yet again.

Leah, like others, suffered through her memories with nightmares in the dark—when she would wake up screaming for her lost parents—and restlessness during the day, when fits of despair would push her to the ground weeping. Others complained of lost memories and an inability to concentrate on the simplest of tasks. Everyone fought against these abnormalities with the most human of solutions. Connect. Marry. Make a family.

Her section had celebrated seven weddings over the past two days. She'd attended most of them, as had hundreds of others. The ceremonies offered an opportunity to celebrate continuance with new beginnings. In a few days, Shoshana would be marrying Yitzchak, a short, skinny redhead from Vilna. Leah longed for a husband of her own, someone to start her own life with and have children whom she would name after her dear mother and father.

"We have a few hours before the parade," Shoshana said, grabbing Leah's hand. "Let's go to Minna's to help with the alterations on the wedding dress."

Leah saw her darling sister was excited. Shoshana would be the next in line to wear the much-shared white dress. The camp had no stores and, besides, most people had no money, so the few wedding dresses that somehow had appeared in camp became communal property, traveling from one bride to another.

"That tiny room will be crowded with brides," Leah said. "I think I'll find a quieter spot and enjoy today's weather."

Shoshana frowned.

Leah knew her sister hated not being with her. But there were always so many people around. A dormitory with wall-to-wall beds. Elbow-to-elbow seating at every meal. She desperately wanted to find a place in the sunlight for a few moments of solitude.

"I'll be fine, Shoshana. What can happen? Everyone is busy preparing for weddings and parades." Leah gave her sister a hug. "Go help Minna. Maybe she'll let you try on the dress so you can see how beautiful you'll look when your turn comes."

Shoshana kissed her sister. "We'll meet you at our usual table in the dining hall for lunch. Don't be late. You know I worry."

Leah stopped to pick up a copy of that day's camp newspaper, *Jiddische Landsberger Cajtung*. Then she found a relatively quiet spot in a grassy area near a picket fence. Shrubs and young trees obscured the slats of wood, beckoning her to the peaceful setting. The newspaper's date read

March 24, 1946. The front page held the schedule for the day's events. A parade with costumes and floats. A carnival. The reading of The *Megillah*. She read a section of an article on the second page.

> Hitler hangs in many variants and in many poses: A big Hitler, a fat Hitler, a small Hitler, with medals and without medals. Jews will hang him by his head, by his feet, or by his belly. Or: A painter's ladder with a pail and brush, near a tombstone with the inscription: 'P.N.' (*po nikbar*) here lies Hitler, may his name be blotted out.

A movement nearby drew her attention away from her reading. A tall young man casually leaned against a nearby building wearing one of the day's many costumes—a German officer's brown leather coat. The stub of a cigarette hung from his mouth as he gazed upward at a flock of pigeons wheeling across the sky.

Had he been there this whole time? Leah found herself staring at him. She couldn't help it. There was an ease about his posture, an ease missing from so many of the men she'd met during her weeks at the camp. Most were either too shy or too pushy. Leah hated the limp handkerchief hands even more than she hated the aggressive groping ones.

The man at the wall looked away from the sky and met her glance. She averted her eyes, her face growing warm with embarrassment. But the pull was irresistible. She looked up again and saw him walking toward her, removing the stub from his mouth and tossing it onto the dusty ground. He moved easily, with long, careless strides, arms swinging in a gentle counterpoint to each step.

A lifetime ago, Leah would have panicked. A lifetime ago, this young man would have spoken to her father before ever daring to approach her. Her eyes locked on his. Something tightened in her throat, moving down to her chest and then her stomach. All sound disappeared, except for her heartbeat pulsating in her ears.

A smile played around the young man's lips, even as the camp's universal sadness remained in his eyes—a reflection of the losses impossible to forget. A breeze pushed a dark curl down onto his forehead as he approached. She longed to touch it, hold it between her fingers.

He squatted down in front of her, arms resting on his knees, and cleared his throat. A pause. Then: "Hello. I don't think we've met. I am Mendel Feinberg from Lodz. And you are?"

A lifetime ago, she would have looked away. This was now. She forced her eyes to remain locked on his. "I am Leah Kalman from Stopnica."

Mendel grinned. "Kalman from Stopnica. I think I know your sister. Is her name Shoshana? There's a Shoshana Kalman in my Hebrew class."

He knew Shoshana. Did he think her sister was pretty? Did he know Shoshana was going to be married? Leah's hand touched her own short hair as she looked at the handsome man standing over her. If only they'd met when she'd had her long, luxurious braid. If only they'd met when she was still plump and attractive and wore nice clothes. The years in the labor camp had dulled her hair and taken several of her teeth. And Mendel. So strong. So attractive. "I think I've seen you before."

He rescued her, filling in the conversational gap. "Where is your sister? From what she's told us in class, you two are pretty much inseparable."

Leah put the newspaper aside and stood up. Even at her full height, she still had to look up to maintain eye contact with him. "I came here to wait for her. She's with a group of her friends preparing for a wedding."

"Hers?"

"Well, hers soon enough."

"And you? Have you found yourself a husband yet?" He smiled now, revealing a few of his own missing teeth.

Had the loss resulted from the years between a lifetime ago and the present? What stories had his own interval held? She might never be able to take a deep breath again. Unable to speak, she shook her head.

"Well then, why don't we meet again at tomorrow's soccer match? I play on the *Ichud* team here at the camp. I'm one of the wingbacks."

"Is that an important position?"

Mendel stood up, straightening to his full six feet. "The most. You should come around three. That way you can find a good place to watch the game."

Leah beamed. "I know where the soccer field is. I'll try to be there."

How quickly the *neshama* can recover. To remember how to smile, let alone to smile at someone and have that smile returned. Even when the eyes remain sad, just the simple act of the mouth forming a crescent—catching and holding the moment of happiness—is the awakening of something positive, an invisible synapse between two people, a spark of optimism in the future.

At lunch, she told Shoshana about the young man she'd met.

"Mendel?" Shoshana asked. "He's quite the celebrity. He's the best player on our soccer team."

"He told me he's the team's wingback. Does he have...you know...a...a..." Leah's voice trailed off.

Shoshana laughed. The sound embarrassed her sister. "A girlfriend? I think he's too busy testing out the goods to decide what he wants to buy. He likes the tall, willowy ones, from what I can see."

Tall and willowy, the opposite of Leah. Her cheeks felt like they'd been branded. Humiliation? Shame? No. Anger. Anger at herself for acting like a silly schoolgirl. Anger at that man for having led her on so shamelessly.

Shoshana reached out and took her sister's hand. "Your face is really red. He didn't behave improperly, did he?"

Leah shook her head. "He invited me to his ridiculous soccer match tomorrow afternoon. That's all."

"What did you tell him?"

"I told him I'd go."

"Do you still want to go? I didn't mean to—"

"What do you think?"

Shoshana thought for a second while she smeared jam on her thin slice of bread. "I've been meaning to go see our team play, but I didn't want to go alone, and you were never that interested in sports. It seems like things have changed. Why don't we go together?"

They both smiled, glad for a seemingly simple solution; a pair of sisters supporting their team. And having Shoshana with her would signal that Leah wasn't just another piece of merchandise for Mendel to sample. A lifetime ago, she came from a good family. A lifetime ago...

"Come on, then," Shoshana said. "The Purim parade starts soon and I want to get a good view."

Leah took a last sip of her coffee. Maybe she would see Mendel at the parade. Maybe he would see her, too. She wiped the thoughts from her head, angry she'd considered those things at all.

Outside, it seemed as though the entire Jewish population of Eastern Europe had come to the parade. Shoshana and Leah made their way to a hillock just as the parade began.

The camp's older children—orphans all—led the procession wearing more traditional Purim hero costumes, Queen Esther for the girls and Mordechai for the boys. The men followed, riding military trucks festooned with Zionist slogans.

Rise up and go to the land of Israel.
People of Israel, live!

An epidemic of Jewish Hitlers and Gestapo paraded by in all manner of Nazi uniforms, making fun of the more recent enemy who'd almost succeeded where Haman failed. Other men riding the same trucks wore their own striped concentration camp garb, a testament to the difficult struggle of shedding the second skin of near annihilation.

Purim, 1946, proved Haman's defeat was Hitler's defeat, and the afternoon was for celebrating. Leah and Shoshana stood watching and cheering, arms linked, enjoying the afternoon's acerbic humor.

After the parade, after the carnival with children's games and adult satire, thousands of displaced Jews gathered for the reading of the *Megillah*—the tale of Esther and the salvation of the Persian Jews. Instead of a *bima*, someone had constructed a platform and decorated it with greenery. Instead of a rabbi, fellow survivor Reuven Jamnik stood by the microphone wearing his concentration camp uniform, a flat cap, and a pair of wire-rimmed glasses. Instead of a beautifully decorated *Megillah* scroll, he held a single piece of paper in his hands.

Leah leaned her head against Shoshana as Reuven began. "The beast is conquered. Not only for us but for all humanity. A year ago today, in the concentration camps, we did not imagine that the prophecy of the Prophet Ezekiel would be fulfilled: 'dry bones' again become a living people. We must build our lives from the ground up and build our own home."

Leah shivered, goose flesh rising under the thin fabric of her pink blouse as the chill of the early evening settled against her skin. She startled as the weight of a coat, warm from someone else's body, was placed over her shoulders. The shock of the unexpected sensation both disquieted and comforted her.

Behind her the clearing of a throat. She knew who it was even as she turned.

Mendel grinned down at the two sisters, crinkling the corners of his eyes, his imperfect smile still the nicest Leah had ever seen. He leaned in and spoke to her in a rough whisper, "Remember. Tomorrow at three. You can return the coat to me then."

She beamed back at him; a big, toothy smile. Life shimmered in her eyes and brightened her heart. The constriction plaguing her chest all afternoon disappeared. This was the man with whom she would build her future.

CHAPTER TWENTY-ONE

HIKING THE CASCADES

Amelia and I had decided to hike the Thornton Lakes trail a little over two hours from home. I needed a break from my schoolwork and Amelia wanted to enjoy an unusually nice, sunny day.

We started the hike on an old logging road. Sunlight speckles glimmering through the tall hemlock and fir trees covered our bodies as we marched along the trail. After about a half-hour, we reached a forested slope with plenty of switchbacks, crossing a cut log bridge over a quickly moving stream. We reached an open meadow with a beautiful view of the Cascades around noon and enjoyed our lunch of PBJ's and apples.

"Do we take the scramble trail for the view, or go up the one to Thornton Lake?" I asked, as we packed up.

Amelia frowned. "Maybe we should consider going back down. Those clouds look a little sketchy."

"I thought we were stalwart Washington State residents," I countered. "Surely we can survive a little rain along the way."

I was optimistic. The forecast hadn't predicted any rain. But we never reached the lesser ridge, with its famous view of Thornton Lake. The rain, a virtual deluge, started about twenty minutes later.

"Fuck!" Amelia's curse echoed back at us off a nearby ridge.

"Do you want to turn around?" I asked.

"No shit, Sherlock," Amelia answered, her hair already soaked and dripping rain down her back. "We should have turned back after lunch. I told you it didn't look good."

I had no answer.

"Goddammit, Seth! We have to hike in this. Did you even think to bring plastic bags for our cell phones?

I reminded her about the sandwich bags. Luckily, we always followed the "carry in, carry out" philosophy of hiking.

"So glad you thought ahead." An acid accusation.

"Hey, I'm not the only one who was going on this hike. You could have thought of it too."

"I was busy making lunch and filling water bottles while you were playing on the damned computer."

"Working. I was working."

"You always use that as an excuse for things you don't get done. The burden of everything always falls on me. Not fair, Seth. Not fucking fair."

We needed a distraction. I forced my voice into a calmer register. "Did I ever tell you about my Saba's friend, Motek?"

"Are you trying to change the subject?"

"You just answered a question with a question. Very good. You're learning."

Amelia sneered at my weak attempt at a joke as the downpour continued. Water flowed down the now-boggy trail as we moved to the side, trying to avoid the growing stream.

"Well, whether you want to hear it or not, he was one of Saba's friends from Europe. I guess they grew up together and refound each other after liberation, got separated again then—many years later—discovered they lived in the same U.S. city."

Motek. His nickname was Hebrew for sweetheart, a word that described him perfectly. There's a great deal of truth to the expression "opposites attract," because Motek was the antithesis of Saba. Whenever he visited, he always offered me a smile, a joke, a story, or a piece of cellophane-wrapped sucking candy pulled out of a linty pants pocket.

Dad told me he'd driven from Cleveland to New York City with Saba and Savta for my *bris*. He'd also come to Rochester for my Bar Mitzvah, telling Mom he wouldn't have missed it for the world.

"Was he one of the greeners?" Amelia asked.

"He was the only one I ever spent any time with. Saba and Motek used to play poker together when they wintered in Florida. You know how I told you my grandparents never spoke about the Holocaust? Motek did."

The rain continued to pelt us. Drenched clothing stuck to our skin. We should have planned better and put ponchos in our day packs. Rivulets now coursed down the path. There was no way to avoid the water splashing up with each step. It filled our hiking boots and soaked our socks.

I continued talking. "I was fourteen, and we were in Cleveland, waiting to break *Yom Kippur's* twenty-five-hour fast. I remember Motek and me sitting alone on the green sofa in the living room before dinner. Savta and Ewa, Motek's wife, must have been in the kitchen preparing Savta's usual break-the-fast meal—bagels, cream cheese, smoked fish, and pickled herring. Mom hated the pickled herring but, for some reason, Savta thought she loved it. There was always a funny routine with that. Savta putting a bunch of it on a plate for Mom and Mom smiling, then turning at us and wrinkling her nose."

"Did she eat the fish?"

"She used to nibble at it. I guess she didn't want to offend Savta."

Amelia wiped the rain off her face with her hands, a useless gesture.

"Anyway, we sat on that sofa and he talked while I listened. I've never forgotten what he told me that day as we sat there." I imitated his Eastern European accent. "'We survivors, your Saba and Savta, me, the entire *Sh'erit ha-Pletah*; we were like drops of rain. After the war, some of us appeared as a drizzle, wandering out of our hiding places or leaving the forest where we'd fought as partisans. More often, we were a downpour, skeletons with a sheath of skin stretched tight, waiting at the gates for our liberators to come.'

"I didn't respond. I wanted to hear what he had to tell. He was a talker, so I let him talk. At that point, Motek leaned closer to me. I distinctly remember him leaning his elbow on the carved wood that framed the sofa's green velvet upholstery. I also remember his smell. He and Saba wore the same cologne—Brut in the glass bottle, never the plastic one. They also combed their hair the same way, that same straight-back-from-the-forehead-and-temples style you see in so many post-war photographs. But, while Saba had let his hair turn silver, Motek colored his a dark brown, the curls often refusing to be completely tamed by pomade."

I wiped the rain off my own face, another useless gesture.

"He kept talking. I kept listening. I remember wishing I had a notebook so I could jot things down. Instead, I tried to memorize what he was saying." Back to the accent. "'We individuals, we drops of rain, converged into rivers traveling along the roads, fluid in our movement. We didn't decide where to go. Instead, we were directed by others, controlled by politics. Do you understand what I'm telling you?'"

"Did you?" Amelia asked.

"I understood some of it. I loved history, but the school year always ended before we could study World War Two. I could name all the presidents, talk for hours about the Constitution, and discuss the Civil War. But the second world war?

"So I told him I got most of it, but that I wasn't sure what he meant about politics. 'That *mamzer* Bevin,' he said"

"Who was Bevin? And what's a *mamzer*?"

"I knew *mamzer*. It's Yiddish for bastard. As for Bevin, Motek must have seen my confusion, 'cause he told me about him. He said Bevin was the foreign secretary for Britain after the war. He told me the Jews wanted to go…no…needed to go to Palestine, which belonged to the British, who refused to let them in. Instead, the Jews were forced from camp to camp, each one only slightly better than those run by the Nazis. The Americans tried to help, but couldn't adequately accommodate the multitudes. The floodgates had opened. Two hundred and fifty thousand Jews converged on camps set up to house a few thousand each. The *yishuv*—the Jewish government in Palestine—hoped the overwhelming numbers would force the Americans to put pressure on Bevin. No such luck.

"I pointed out how they had wound up in Israel after all. Motek smiled and ruffled my hair. He said, 'I guess our stories have a happy ending after all. Right, *yingele*?'

"At that point, Savta called us into the dining room."

Amelia and I reached the lower part of the mountain, where hemlocks and firs offered partial protection from the chilling rain.

Amelia grabbed my shoulder. "Can we take a water break?"

"Aren't we already in the middle of a water break?"

Now she punched my shoulder. "Not funny."

"C'mon. A little funny."

"Not even a little."

We sat down on a nearby log. I couldn't even feel the wetness of the wood through the wetness of my jeans.

Amelia took a sip of water and offered me the bottle. "Did Motek tell you anything else? Fill in any details?"

"Just one more thing. He said, 'They used us, you know.' Those were his exact words. I'll never forget them. I'm not sure when in the evening he said them. It might have been after dinner, before he left for home."

"What did he mean?"

"I didn't understand back then. Now I understand completely. He meant that the different governments after the war, especially the Jewish government under the British mandate of Palestine, understood Holocaust survivors would be the perfect pawns in the post-war political chess game. They strategically moved them around Europe to pressure Britain's foreign minister to allow 100,000 Jewish refugees into Palestine, the religiously and politically promised homeland. He never did."

"Politically?"

"When we get home, look up Balfour Declaration of 1917. Too much to explain right now."

The rain stopped. Amelia and I resumed our downward trek, soaked to the skin, water squishing in our boots with every step.

"So," Amelia said, as we pushed on. "I guess things aren't as black and white as history paints them."

"Things never are," I answered.

We hiked down the last part of the trail in silence, our only goal to reach our car at the road's turnout. The rhythm of our footsteps fell into sync.

I didn't know what Amelia was thinking about, but my brain was racing. I thought about how we speak in absolutes. I thought about "I never," "You always," "They were the bad guys," "We saved the world." I thought about how life can't be described simplistically. Evil often wins while good loses. History shifts with time, softening criminals into antiheroes and demonizing the innocent victims on both sides of any conflict. I thought about the arc of a story and the hearts of its characters. Who wears white and who wears black? Is it possible for a hero to become villainous, and can a villain ever become heroic? I wish I knew.

CHAPTER TWENTY-TWO

IN WHICH THE COAT
ALMOST BECOMES A SHROUD

1947

"We leave in two days."

The announcement—made over lunch—shot like a bolt of electricity through the *kibbutz*. The rumor mill generated snippets of information about where they would go, how they would travel, what they would be allowed to bring. The answers came soon enough. Italy. Truck, on foot, then by ship. And, as for their possessions, as few as possible.

A distraught Leah ran to her new husband. "Mendel, we are to leave so soon? How will Shoshana know where to contact me when she gets to Israel if we leave now? I need more time."

"Time is something we lost years ago." He gathered Leah in his arms, still delighted by her newness. The softness of her body's curves. The smell of her hair, her skin, and her breath. He, like Leah, wanted their lives to be settled. Others in the camp already had children. He'd hoped to have at least one before leaving for Palestine. But to have a first child born in Jerusalem. What a blessing that would be. "The sooner we arrive in Israel, the sooner we can truly begin our lives together. I'm sure we'll be able to locate Shoshana and Yitzchak when we get there. Just think of it, Leah; a chance to have a real life in a real homeland."

She sighed and rested her head against his chest. If he was so sure of these things they must be true.

He held her for another moment then gently pushed her away from him, simultaneously pushing away the stirrings he felt having her body so close against his own. "Two days doesn't give us much time. Come. We need to consider what we will bring with us. The Alps lie between Landsberg and Italy. I believe wearing layers rather than packing bags will make the most sense."

Mendel turned to his friend standing nearby. "Ho! What do you say Motek?"

The tall, thin man nodded and winked. The loose curls on his head trembled with the movement as he smiled. "Much better than traveling naked."

"Motek, don't tease so." The short, red-headed woman with Motek was Ewa, his wife.

The two couples had married in the same shared ceremony, the short break between each one just enough for each of the brides to trade off the communal wedding dress, which most of the married women had worn at one time or another. Back then, Leah had envied Ewa's looks—her fair complexion, red hair, and blue eyes—all traits that had helped her survive by hiding in plain sight among the Catholics in Warsaw. Over the months since then, Leah and Ewa had become good friends, practicing Hebrew together while they learned to repair farm equipment or milked the cows they'd tied to makeshift wood fences.

"Come, Leah," Ewa said, taking the younger woman's hand. "Let's go see what we want to take with us."

The two women, arms linked, left the dining hall. Living with so little for so long made them determined to take as much as they could on the long journey to Italy.

The scene of the group's journey away from the camp was all too familiar. Over a hundred Jews crowded together to face their fate with one major difference: purpose. This time the decision to move had been theirs. This time they were determined to reach a known destination.

Two evenings, one morning, one train, and a convoy of trucks later, the large group of Jews found themselves in the middle of a field lit only by moonlight at two in the morning. Little time was wasted between the marriage ceremonies and the seeding of a new generation. So many of the couples had young children with them. Babies were in arms or placed in makeshift carriages. Toddlers were shepherded between their parents or rode happily on their fathers' shoulders.

The many layers of clothing each person wore made the group look like a collection of rotund Petrushka dolls with bundles tied over their backs or the handles of small leather suitcases clenched tight in their hands.

The fire Mendel had seen in Menachem Smulovitz's eyes back in Lodz now burned in the eyes of each member of this collective. The air buzzed electric with their voices.

Leah's eyes shone as she looked up at her husband. She grabbed his hand as the group prepared for the beginning of their long climb across the Alps, trusting this journey would end at their new home: Palestine.

Szulim, the *bricha* guide, whom everyone hoped would be their last, quieted the group. *"Chaverim,"* he said quietly while gesturing for the group's attention. "We have a long climb ahead of us. It will not be easy. We must travel in silence so as not to alert the British to our presence. I realize this will be a challenge with the children, but this is how it must be."

Parents looked at their young ones, then at each other.

Leah leaned closer to Ewa. "Five hours is a long time to keep a child quiet."

Szulim, standing nearby, walked over to the two women and rested his hands on their shoulders, while he continued to speak to the group. "All my groups have managed with their children. One of our advantages is the fact that we hike up late at night, when the youngest sleep. The older ones somehow understand the circumstances. Because the adults are quiet, they remain quiet." He stepped away and moved over to a tall, blond, blue-eyed man in a long-sleeved shirt, leather shorts, and a heavy pair of Alpine hiking socks rolled down to just below his knees. "Now, I would like to introduce you to a very important man in our lives over these next few days. This is Viktor. Every few days, he helps groups like ours traverse this climb up to the Tauernhaus, where we will eat and rest before continuing on. Please give him your attention."

The group buzzed again. Viktor motioned for silence. "Good evening," the Austrian said. "I have three rules for this journey we will take together. 'Get out quietly. Leave no traces. Go as if nobody had ever been there.' Do not worry about the Austrians living nearby. The police chief sleeps knowingly, and the locals sleep in ignorance. I will lead the group, and Szulim will bring up the rear. Some of you will be good climbers and others not so good. This is not a problem. Even with the poorest of climbers we have always reached the Tauernhaus in Krimml by around seven in the morning. Now, let us go. Time is short."

They climbed the well-worn path in darkness, the only sounds those of footsteps crossing makeshift bridges over waterfalls—structures built by others who'd gone before. How many hundreds, thousands of the *Sh'erit ha-Pletah* had come this way, tread this very path?

They passed the murky impression of a cow field and trekked up a narrower footpath through difficult terrain with more and more rocks to trip over in the blackness of the night.

They climbed in darkness, suppressing coughs from the tightness threatening their lungs. It grew harder and harder to catch their breaths as they climbed even higher.

"I must rest," a thin man in front of Mendel said.

Mendel didn't recognize the man. Had they been in the same *kibbutz* at Landsberg, or had he joined them from elsewhere?

Mendel grabbed the man's arm as he stumbled to the side of the trail and sat down on a large rock. He experienced a momentary pang of envy when his fingers touched the leather coat the man wore. How had he come to own something this precious? Pushing away the unwanted cloud of emotion, Mendel cradled the man in his arms and took one of his bony hands. "What is your name?"

The man panted. No answer.

Mendel looked up at Motek, who'd joined them. "His heart is awfully fast. I can feel it through his fingers."

The man's breath crackled while Motek put a hand to his forehead. "He's sweating. It feels like he has a fever." Darkness swallowed everything except the three men off to the side of the trail. He squatted down next to the man. "Open your coat so I can listen to your heart."

The crackling became a gurgling. "You must help me get to the bunkhouse," the man said.

Motek looked at Mendel and shook his head. "He's delirious."

Leah and Ewa joined their husbands. Leah pulled on Mendel's sweater sleeve. "We must go on. We can't risk falling behind."

"You two go on ahead," Mendel said. "Motek and I should stay here until Szulim can tell us what he thinks we should do."

"I can't," Leah said, her eyes wide with fear. "When they separated me from my parents, I never saw them again. Then Shoshana went away with her husband. You're all I have. I can't lose you, too."

Mendel stood up and held Leah's chin. "Don't worry Leah. There's nowhere to go but up this path. I know where you'll be. I promise you'll see me soon enough."

Ewa put her arm around her friend's shoulder. "Come, Leah. Mendel knows how you worry. He'll catch up with us as soon as Szulim comes and takes over."

The two women returned to the footpath and disappeared into the darkness.

By now, the man could barely catch his breath. His chest heaved. "I must lay down," he said "My bed. It is somewhere nearby. Please help me find it. I must get back to the bunks before the *kapos* realize I'm not there."

The rest of the group hiked silently upward, one after another, their footsteps on the rocky path and the man's desperate struggle to pull air into his steadily weakening lungs the only sounds in the inky blackness.

"What is your name?" Motek asked.

"I...75267. I am...75267. Enough. I have had...enough." The man sobbed, sucking air, shoulders shaking, the plumes of moisture from each exhale growing thinner and smaller.

Mendel continued holding the stranger's hand, kneading the cold fingers, counting every heartbeat, suffering through every faltering breath. "His heart is skipping now. I feel it. Motek, what can we do?" Mendel felt as though his own heart wanted to escape his chest as he answered his own question. "We must help him say the *Shema*."

"You think he is dying."

"I am sure of it."

People continued climbing past them in the darkness. Viktor had told them there was no time to waste. Viktor had told them the climb would be difficult. Viktor had not told them of the possibility of death, even though death was a constant companion, peeking from behind different curtains. How cruel, to peek from the curtain of darkness when salvation seemed so near.

Szulim's voice pierced the air, cold and emotionless. "Tell me the situation."

"We must say the *Shema*."

The small group of people climbing past them in the darkness, upon hearing the name of the prayer said before death, stopped and stood. Some came over to see what would happen. Bodies tensed as the question of what to do hung over the small group. The miasma of what history had wrought colored the decision now standing before them as the man took his final breath.

Mendel released the cold hand, the fading heartbeat now gone. He looked into the darkness and quietly sang, "*Shema Yisrael Adonai Eloheinu Adonai echad.*" He didn't care about the danger of the British hearing. He didn't care about the others by his side, reciting the rest of the prayer in unison. He only cared about the prayer, unsaid for so many. This would not be the case for this one soul.

The prayer finished, people stood quietly, unsure of what to do. Szulim broke through the stillness. "We must continue on so we can reach the Tauernhaus by sunrise. We've already lost enough time. To hike in the light of day is to beg for the British to find us." He motioned to Mendel and Motek. "You two, do what you can to move him a decent distance from the trail. We don't want the patrols to discover his body anytime soon. And give him some sort of burial. The ground is still frozen, so it would probably be easiest to lay him against a large boulder and cover him with whatever you can find. We must not let the British discover we've passed through here."

"Mendel and I will take care of it," Motek said. "We'll catch up with you shortly."

Motek grabbed the legs of the body, while Mendel reached under the shoulders. As they lifted the body, they were surprised at the weight and thickness of the leather coat the man wore. A short distance from the trail, they found a large boulder with a crevice on one side. They lay the body down and Motek examined the coat and shoes, while Mendel ran his hand through his own hair, pushing back the strands that had fallen onto his forehead. "*Nu?*" he asked, looking at Motek.

"The coat is too large for me. You should take it. I'll be content with his shoes."

Mendel calculated the value of a coat and a pair of shoes in the currency of survival. They would no longer be of any use to this man. Motek was right. The choice was clear. No *chevra kadisha* to prepare the body. No white shroud. No rabbi. No *kaddish* would be said. No *shiva* observed. What did anything matter? The world had gone mad long ago.

They removed the coat and shoes. "What about the rest of the clothes?" Mendel asked.

Motek thought for a minute. "I think the coat and shoes are enough. That suit is beyond use. Let it serve as his shroud. Now, let's get to work so we can rejoin the others."

In the yellow light of the predawn, Motek and Mendel finished the task of gathering and piling rocks until the body had disappeared between the boulder and a mound of rubble. By the time they were done, they fought for breath in the thin air.

"We should say something," Mendel wheezed, the coat at his feet, his eyes on the improvised sepulcher.

"To have survived everything else, only to die now." Motek murmured, the shoes tied together and hanging around his neck.

The two men stood looking at the improvised grave. The footsteps of their group had long ago faded into the distance, replaced by the predawn songs and calls of Alpine birds.

"Do you remember any Psalms?" Motek asked. "We can do *Tehillim*."

Mendel nodded. "The first one. Do you remember the first one?"

They bowed their heads and drew on their memories to piece together the words of the first Psalm.

"Happy is the man that has not walked in the counsel of the wicked, nor stood in the way of sinners, nor sat in the seat of the scornful. But his delight is in the law of *Adonai*, and in His law does he meditate day and night. And he shall be like a tree planted by streams of water, that brings forth its fruit in its season, and whose leaf does not wither; and in whatsoever he does he shall prosper. Not so the wicked; but they are like the chaff which the wind drives away. Therefore the wicked shall not stand in the judgment, nor sinners in the congregation of the righteous. For *Adonai* regards the way of the righteous; but the way of the wicked shall perish."

The two men lifted their heads and walked as quickly as they could to rejoin their wives.

CHAPTER TWENTY-THREE

BIRTHRIGHT

As graduate school dragged on, I desperately needed a break. My schedule of research, teaching, and writing—interspersed with meetings with students, professors, and visiting lecturers—had ground me down. Finally, gifted with an upcoming summer free from responsibilities, I filled out the application for a free ten-day trip to Israel sponsored by the organization known as Birthright. A few weeks later, I received a response. My application had been processed, and I'd be on El Al's flight 28 out of Newark leaving on June 24th.

"You know," my mother said, "Ilana extended her trip while she was there and stayed an extra month. You should extend yours and visit with our family there."

I didn't even know this family. Never met them. Never spoke with them. I was in it for the free trip. I had to answer without answering. "I'll see how things go once I get there."

"Well, let me give you their email addresses and phone numbers."

"Fine."

At three in the afternoon, on June 25th, thirty-nine other Birthrightniks and I arrived at Ben Gurion Airport after a rowdy ten-hour flight. We'd spent most of that time playing musical chairs with our seating while consuming tiny airline bottles of whiskey, vodka, and tequila. We were well on our way to forming our trip-long cliques.

I'd become especially friendly with two of my fellow travelers, Leslie Frankel and Yoni Kohn. The three of us commandeered a row of seats and bonded over a dinner of vodka and chicken. Excitement kept us awake the entire flight. We all desperately needed a nap in a real bed.

We deplaned, got our passports stamped, picked up our luggage, and passed through customs. As we exited the terminal, the first thing we saw was a brightly painted tour bus idling at the curb. A slender, tan young woman with long hair almost as curly as my own stood in front of its open door.

"*Shalom!*" she hollered. "My name is Lital. I see you all have your luggage. Let's get going. We have a long drive up north. Our bus is number 640—*shesh, arba, efes*. Get your ID tags from me, get on board, get settled, and we'll be off."

There would be no nap, no real bed. Our bags loaded into the belly of the bus, we climbed aboard. Yoni grabbed the seat next to mine while Leslie sat in the row behind us. Her seatmate, Katie Feldbauer, a very petite, very quiet blonde, kept trying to sleep by curling up in her seat and wrapping a sweater around her head.

"*Shalom, chaverim.*" The speakers boomed as though the amplifier was turned up to eleven. "That means 'hello, friends' in Hebrew." When Lital only got a few weak replies, she shouted into the mike. "I said, *shalom, chaverim!*"

If anyone had managed to actually fall asleep, the shrill feedback accompanying her shout was a sharp wakeup call. "*Shalom,*" we all answered back, though our enthusiasm was admittedly quite a bit less than our guide's.

"That's better. Once again, in case you missed it, my name is Lital, and I'm going to accompany you on your Birthright trip through Israel. I promise you the most amazing experience of your life."

She outlined the rules of our trip. Respect for the staff and each other. Respect for the country of Israel. Everyone laughed when Lital told us there would be designated drinking times at pubs, clubs, or during our free evening time. The laughter abated when she told us we were absolutely, positively forbidden to leave the group.

A girl in the back raised her hand. "I have family in Jerusalem. I won't be able to visit them?"

"There will be available time for them to visit you. If you want to go to their home, you can extend your trip and visit with them then. See me if you want more information or help with an extension."

Three hours later, we stood in a *kibbutz* dining hall. Once we'd been well-fed, exhaustion became desperation. Instead of the sleep we craved, we played getting-to-know-you games, followed by trust-fall ice breakers.

At nine p.m., Lital finally allowed us to collapse into our beds. I quickly fell into a dreamless sleep.

Most of our days followed similar schedules. Wake up. Wash up. Breakfast. Onto the bus. Visit an ancient site in ruins because of the Assyrians, or the Babylonians, or the Persians, or the Romans, or the Arabs. Lunch. Rappel or kayak or hike. Visit a "strategic area" to understand how small Israel really is. Back to the *kibbutz* for dinner. Exhaustion. Dinner. Drink. Sleep. Repeat.

We bonded over Israel's beauty, Israel's history, Israel's identity— which, we came to realize, was our history and our identity as well.

On day four, we were joined by Galit and Yoav, a couple of soldiers in the Israeli military. Leslie and Katie abandoned their usual seats behind Yoni and me to settle in near Yoav, with his perfect tan and Sephardic swagger. He shared his dimpled smile with the girls, cultivating a growing pack of Bus 640 groupies.

Galit was more serious. While we drove to Jerusalem she walked around the bus, talking to us about how wonderful it was to live in Israel. "It's such an amazing place for young people with its beaches, and clubs, and fabulous restaurants."

"What about safety?" someone asked.

"What about it? Look what's happening in other places now. France, for example. And is your home, the United States so safe these days? Israel is still the best place for us."

"Never again!" a boy's voice from behind me shouted as we pulled up to the entrance of the *Yad Vashem* complex, Jerusalem's Holocaust Memorial and Museum.

We stopped at the visitor center's security desk, checked our backpacks, walked through the metal detectors, then met Pnina, our guide for the day, in the large plaza surrounded by the complex's many buildings and structures.

Pnina led us through the main museum's exhibits on either side of a long passageway. Unlike the Holocaust Museum in Washington, *Yad Vashem's* atmosphere, though dark, was less gut-wrenching, more historical. Television monitors Played survivors' testimonies befitting the subject matter of each exhibit arm. I searched each face for some familiar feature. Dad's chin or thin lips. Ilana's almond-shaped eyes with their thick dark lashes. My high forehead or tightly curled hair. Was it possible any of these televised faces was that of a lost relative? Would any of the many exhibits hold a photograph of murdered family members? If so, how would I even recognize them?

Yoni examined photographs as well. "Are you doing what I'm doing?" I asked.

"You mean looking for possible relatives?" he replied. "Two sets of grandparents and their entire families. You?"

"My Dad's parents and most of theirs."

Toward the end of our two-hour tour, we entered an exhibit about the *Haganah* ships that had tried to smuggle Jews into Mandatory Palestine before, during, and after the war. I froze while looking at the next-to-last photograph. Among those faces, the hundreds of faces in the exhibit's dozens of photographs, I recognized two—a man with my forehead and Dad's long face standing next to a woman who looked back at him with Ilana's almond eyes. I strained to make sense of what I was seeing. The voices from the monitors around the room disappeared. All I could hear was Motek's voice saying, "They used us, you know."

An entire museum. Hundreds, maybe thousands of photos. Screens filled with strangers and their videotaped testimonies. Until now, I'd been able to distance myself, make all of it nothing more than an abstract notion. In an instant, the abstraction had become real. These were my grandparents in that old photograph. Sure, they were much younger and much thinner. But there was no mistaking the couple preparing to board the ship. They were my Saba and Savta, and that must have been their ship—the *Mordei Hagetaot*.

My group moved to the next exhibit. I was carried along with them. I vaguely listened to Pnina speak about the founding of Israel. I failed to hear where we would be heading next. I only drifted with the wave of my group to the far end of the central corridor where we stepped out into Jerusalem's searingly hot, dry afternoon air.

I stood on the building's cantilevered terrace and gazed out at the distant white buildings with orange roofs dotting the surrounding pine-tree-covered hills. I desperately needed to touch someone. I walked over to Leslie and grabbed her hand. She squeezed it and leaned into me as we stood there, looking out at the land my family had seen as their only possibility after the Holocaust.

That evening, when the bus pulled up to our hotel, Lital grabbed the microphone. Her bright voice grated against my mood. "Clean up and be downstairs at seven to welcome in *Shabbat*. If you'd like to light candles, we'll have them in the lobby. Please wear white. *L'hitraot.*"

I wanted to sleep, but I knew someone would come to drag me down to the group activity, so I put on my khaki shorts and a white button-down shirt.

We welcomed *Shabbat* with *kiddush*. We stood in a circle. A few of the girls teared up. I closed my eyes to hold back my own threatening wetness. The *Shabbat* ritual was our tradition, our heritage, and we were celebrating in Israel, the land of our ancestors and my family—my Saba, Savta, aunt, and father.

A relaxing *Shabbat* and an insanely busy next few days helped compartmentalize what I'd experienced at *Yad Vashem*. Camel rides to a Bedouin tent, where we ate dinner and spent the night, brought the group back up to its previous level of partying. Yoni played a drum called the *tarbouka* and Lital played guitar while we sang *Billboard* top-40 hits with our soldiers, who knew the lyrics better than we did. An early morning hike to to the top of Masada to watch the sun rise and hear that historic site's story inspired us. A relaxing afternoon float in the Dead Sea reminded me what the afternoon sun can do without enough sunscreen.

Tuesday night, at our usual evening briefing, Lital filled us in on the plans for our last full day in Israel. "Tomorrow, we'll return to Jerusalem for a tour of the Old City, called The Cardo. There are quite a few nice shops there, so it will be a good chance for you to buy any last-minute gifts or souvenirs. After lunch—you do want more falafel and shawarma, *nachon*?—we'll visit the *Kotel*, what some call the Western or the Wailing Wall, the last remnant of the great temple built by King Solomon over 3,000 years ago. Remember, everyone, breakfast is at eight and the bus leaves at nine. *Laila tov*."

Morning. Jerusalem. Afternoon. the *Kotel*—the epicenter of Judaism, the pinnacle of holiness.

At the area leading to the Wall's plaza, three orthodox Jews dressed in black offered to help the guys put on *tfillin*, two leather boxes with prayers inside, binding one box to the forehead and the other to one arm with long leather straps. Then they led us in the related prayers before taking back their loaner *tfillin* and slapping our backs with a congratulatory "*Yasher koach!*"

While the guys went through the mechanics of Jewish prayer, the girls listened to another pair of orthodox Jews, these wearing jeans and t-shirts with long curls hanging in front of their ears, while they played guitars and sang Hebrew songs. A little ways down the street, we all bought red strings with eye-like beads on them from a young boy for a *shekel* each—Kabbalistic talismen against the evil eye—tying them on to each other's wrists. Then we passed through security with its bag checks and metal detectors and entered the massive open plaza in front of the Kotel.

The wall stood before me, an overwhelming symbol of struggle, triumph, and loss. I no longer felt the heat of the summer sun against my sunburned back. I could only stare at the enormous blocks of stone. At the lower part of the wall, the spaces between the blocks were stuffed with thousands of folded slips of paper holding visitors' prayers. High above our head, rooted plants flourished in similar spaces.

A crowd of men filled the horizontal area at the base of the wall. Some wore black. Others, like me, wore shorts and t-shirts. Locals and tourists. Young and old. Religious and...and...me. I didn't believe, but I was still drawn to this place where people believe God resides.

I took it all in. Tourists read about the temple's construction, destruction, reconstruction, and renewed destruction in their guidebooks. Many people held prayer books and rocked back and forth while they prayed. Others planted their own *Dear G-d* notes between the stones. Then there was me, in khaki pants and a wrinkled blue shirt, wondering how so many of these people were able to decipher so much from this remnant of King Solomon's temple.

As I looked at the wall and its congregation, I noticed a dark horizon of a line stretching at eye level along the length of the large, limestone blocks—particles of DNA from the thousands who touched the wall every day with their fingers, their arms, their foreheads, and their lips.

I went and stood near a man who melted into a dark area of the stone, as though communing with a lover. I reached out to touch the wall. My fingers moved over the stone, hot from the afternoon sun, appreciating its roughness, wondering at its age, its meaning. The image of Saba and Savta standing in front of the *Mordei Hagetaot* returned to me. They'd left Israel and moved to the United States in 1958. Did they ever mourn the fact they'd never been allowed to visit the *Kotel*? My being there would have meant so much to them.

Suddenly, all I could think about was *Kaddish*, the prayer for the dead. I needed to say *Kaddish* at the *Kotel* for my grandparents. I grabbed a prayer book with a blue cover and a black satin *kippah* from one of the numerous tables around the plaza.

Back at the wall, I put the *kippah* on my head and opened the book to the appropriate page. "*Yitgadal v'yitgadash shmei rabah…*" I swallowed hard as something welled up from the depths of my soul. I was too exhausted to fight it. Decades after the Holocaust, years after their funerals, I stood at the Wailing Wall in Jerusalem weeping for my grandparents' lives and deaths.

CHAPTER TWENTY-FOUR

IN WHICH THE COAT MORPHS FROM SPOILS OF WAR

1947

One couldn't describe the Orietta as a rustbucket. There was little on the three-masted barkentine that could rust.

The first time Leah laid eyes on the ancient looking wooden ship, all optimism and hope deteriorated. "Mendel, this ship doesn't look like it can stay afloat long enough to get us to Israel."

A *sotto voce* from their side. "Don't worry. She sailed here from France. She'll make it across the Adriatic."

Mendel put a protective arm around his pregnant wife's shoulders. "You. Who are you?"

In the absence of any light other than the waning quarter moon, all they could make out was a man's silhouette. "My name is Shuli Oren, your second-in-command on this trip and, in case you need more assurances, this isn't my first time on one of these missions. I was also the second-in-command on the *Kaf Gimel Yordei Hasira* last year. "

In spite of Shuli's baritone reassurance, Leah shivered. Even though it was mid-May, the dampness off the water chilled her face, hands, and legs. Somewhere between the Alps and Bari, they'd lost their satchel along with the sweater she'd worn over her thin layers of clothing.

Mendel pulled her closer as they boarded the Orietta, joining the other souls sailing for their homeland.

The scene on the main deck was mayhem. Mendel heard a man a few feet away shouting in Hebrew. "Who on board speaks Polish? Yiddish? Hebrew? We need someone who can help us communicate."

Mendel waved his free arm in the air. "I speak all three, as well as a little Italian."

"Good. Good," the man said, coming up to Mendel and shaking his hand. "I am Shalom Burstein, the *gideoni* for the Orietta."

Leah peered at the man but could only make out a head covered with dark curls atop a slim figure wearing the type of coat German officers wore during her time in the labor camp.

"*Gideoni*?" Mendel asked. "I'm not familiar with that word."

"Communications officer. I run the radio transmitter, along with other improvised duties. We're a very small crew, so we all wear multiple hats."

"*Nu*, Mr. Burstein, what do you want from me?"

"Shalom. Call me Shalom. We've rigged up a public address system on the upper deck and below. Once everyone gets situated I would like you to help me with announcements."

Mendel nodded.

"Come, Mendel," Leah said, tugging against the arm still resting around her shoulder. "We must claim our place before we wind up without a bed or—worse—sleeping near the latrine."

"It seems your wife has other plans for now. Let's meet after this magnificent vessel sets sail."

Mendel agreed and husband and wife walked through the throngs, around the tall masts, and down a ladder into a dimly lit area.

Leah gasped. The few naked light bulbs strung on overhead wires cast long, moving shadows. The deep, three-tiered shelves of wooden bunks were almost identical to the sleeping arrangements she'd known at the labor camp. The unwelcome flashback wrung a whine from her throat.

Only Mendel heard her, the sound otherwise lost in the din of the hundreds upon hundreds of people crowding the murky space. He took her chin between his thumb and forefinger, turned her face up toward his, and stroked her hair. "Sha, sha, Leah. It will be okay. This only looks like the camps. The people in charge are our people, our saviors, not our enemy."

Leah shook her head away from Mendel's fingers and cried out. "Shoshana. I want my sister. Why is she not here with us?"

Three women responded to her cry, rushing over, clucking reassurances.

"It's only for a few days."

"I had the same reaction when I first came down here. But this is a good thing."

"I have a few sugar cubes in my pocket. Would you like one?"

The offer of sweetness in the moment's bitter fear worked. Leah nodded. The short woman wearing a man's jacket and pants pulled a few cubes from her pocket, and the four women shared the sweetness.

Feeling his wife was in good company, Mendel checked around for a sleeping shelf. He found one that offered fresh air from the open hatch but seemed to be out of any direct breezes. He took off his jacket and tossed it on to the shelf, hoping it would be enough to indicate the space had been taken. Then, he made his way through the throngs of people claiming their own bunks back to where the four women still stood.

"Leah, I'm going back up to meet with Shalom. You'll be all right down here?"

The tallest of the women put a protective arm around her new friend. "Don't worry husband. We'll take care of her."

Mendel gave Leah's hand a quick squeeze before he disappeared up the ladder.

"Leah," said the tall woman. "It won't be hard to change that name to your new one when we reach Palestine."

"What do you mean?" Leah asked.

A second woman, this one Leah's height, with a raised scar under her right eye, answered, . "A Hebrew name. I used to be Gitl Krasnovsky. I changed my name to Gila Or. I wanted a Hebrew name. A rabbi back in the DP camp suggested it. He told me Gila means joy and Or means light."

"Have the two of you changed your names as well?"

"Not me," said the tall woman. "Mine's already Hebrew. Chaya. I can even write it in Hebrew. Our *bricha* leader taught me."

"And you?" Leah asked the last woman, the one who'd offered up the precious gift of sugar cubes.

"My name is Perla, but my husband used to call me 'Zissel,' so that is the name I'll be taking. But I refuse to change my last name, since that's all I have left of him."

Suddenly, Mendel's voice came over the horn speakers. Hearing his voice broadcast with the crackle of improvised wiring startled Leah.

First Yiddish. "Attention. Welcome aboard the Orietta. For your information, our commander is Mr. Armon, assisted by Mr. Cooperman. Our second-in-command is Mr. Oren, and our communications officer is

Mr. Burstein. We will be setting sail as soon as we've finished taking on food and water. Right now there are 1,457 *ma'apilim* aboard."

Gitl/Gila leaned over and said, "*Ma'apilim* is the Hebrew word for immigrants. That's what they're calling us. Farewell to that awful term, *She'rit ha-Pletah!*"

Mendel's voice continued. "In a few days, we will rendezvous with another ship, the *Yehuda Ha'Levi*, to take aboard 400 more m*a'apilim*. For now, it is imperative you obey any orders given by our crew. The British are watching every ship in these waters so, if we make an announcement that you must go below deck, you must do so in a quick but orderly fashion. For now, please settle in and remain below. We will make another announcement when we believe it is safe for you to come up on the deck for fresh air and food. Thank you."

The announcement was repeated—first in Polish, then Hebrew. People had been quiet during the Yiddish announcement, but their voices multiplied through the Polish one, making the final Hebrew iteration inaudible.

"More people? Where will they fit?"

"We're already so crowded."

"Why do we have to stay down here when there's so much room up top?"

Perla motioned her group over to a lower bunk. "This is mine and Chaya's. Let's squeeze in here so we're not shoulder-to-shoulder with the entire population of the ship."

The four women climbed into the tight space where they shared their stories, their hopes, and their expectations when they would finally reach Israel.

Mendel returned to a wife with bright eyes focused on what lay at the other end of the voyage. "Chaya told me in Israel we won't be hungry. She said the *kibbutzim* there grow oranges and olives, and the cows provide plenty of milk and cheese. She'll be joining her sister in Kfar Saba, a *kibbutz* in the north."

The ship lurched. The voices around them grew louder.

"The ship is moving," Mendel said, stating the obvious.

A few people began the Traveler's Prayer. Others joined in. Those who didn't pray became silent, allowing the supplication for a voyage filled with health, joy, and peace to rise through the dark opening of the hatch.

When the prayer was over, Leah and Mendel climbed onto the paper sheets of their bunk and wrapped their arms around each other. In spite of the loud voices and crying children, in spite of the lack of fresh air, in spite of their unknown future, they fell into the deepest sleep since before the Germans invaded their lives.

They awoke to *Hatikvah* playing over the speakers and dust-filled light filtering down through the open hatch. They smiled at the song, which had become the anthem for their survival and their determination to reach the Jewish homeland.

"How long did we sleep?" Leah asked, raising herself up onto her elbows, instinctively stopping short so she wouldn't hit her head against the wood of the upper bunk.

The sounds of people walking on the deck above them beckoned. Had they missed breakfast? An early morning announcement? The anticipation of fresh air and the possibility of food lured them out of their quarters. But first, the latrine.

As they approached, the stench of urine mixed with feces made Leah heave. She would have vomited had there been something in her stomach. Instead, she held her nose and breathed through her mouth, rushing away from the area as soon as she was done.

"Those poor people who wound up too close to the latrines," she said to Mendel when he joined her on the upper deck.

"It will get even worse when the seasickness starts."

Leah was grateful her early pregnancy hadn't caused the morning sickness she'd seen in many of the women at the DP camp.

An announcement over the loudspeaker. "Mendel Feinberg, report to the *gideoni*. Mendel Feinberg to the *gideoni*."

A quick hug and kiss and Mendel headed off. Leah heard his voice a few minutes later.

"Good morning, *chaverim*. You are no longer on board the Orietta. That's a terrible name for such a beautiful ship. We've renamed her. From now on, your home on the water will be known as the *Mordei Hagetaot*."

Simultaneously, an enormous banner unfurled between two of the masts. It was emblazoned with the ship's new name in large, Hebrew letters.

Those who understood cheered. *Mordei Hagetaot* meant Fighters of the Ghetto. The inspiration was clear. They, too, would be fighters. They would fight their way across the waters to their new home. The cheer became a battle cry, then it transformed into the melody and words of the song that had played only a short while before—*Hatikvah*.

The rendezvous with the *Yehuda Ha'Levi* to pick up the additional four hundred *ma'apilim* happened quickly and smoothly. The transition to the increased numbers wasn't as simple. Down in the sleeping quarters, it seemed as though there was no air at all, and the heat during midday became almost unbearable.

In the days that followed, the movement of the ship combined with the below deck's overpopulation, stagnant air, constant engine vibration, and fetid smells soured Leah's stomach and sent her to the railing.

Mendel tried sleeping with her above deck to avoid the foulness below, but the damp chill coming off the water had Leah shivering against his body, her teeth chattering.

Perla offered her extra portions of bread. Gitl/Gila tried back rubs. Chaya prayed, reciting the *Mi Sheberach*. Nothing helped. Leah paled, and it became increasingly difficult for her to climb up and down the ladder between the decks.

Mendel consulted with Shalom. "You've been on these voyages before. Surely you have some sort of solution."

"Seasickness? No solution other than making sure she drinks plenty of liquids."

"Not seasickness alone. Leah is pregnant—three months, I think."

"So seasickness and morning sickness combined."

"Except it is morning, afternoon, evening, and night sickness. She seems to do better in the fresh air on the deck, but it's so cold at night. Then, when we go below, the odors overpower her."

Shalom pulled at his earlobe. "Wait here." He returned ten minutes later carrying the coat he'd been wearing the night they'd boarded the ship. "My coat's quite heavy, and its lining is wool. This should help keep her warm at night so you can sleep up on deck. Did you need something as well? I can ask around."

Mendel, embarrassed to ask for anything more, shook his head. "This is more than enough. I promise we'll return this coat when we reach our destination."

"I have no doubts."

Limiting their time below improved Leah's situation. Extra portions of bread or soup and strong cups of boiled coffee shored up her strength. Fresh sea air offset the trips down to the latrine to relieve herself. And the embracing warmth of Shalom's coat made it comfortable for her during the cold nights on the upper deck.

Ten days had passed when people heard a buzzing overhead. They looked up to see a British plane. An announcement in Hebrew over the loudspeaker—no time for additional translations.

"Everyone below-deck. Everyone below deck."

Mendel knew it was too late. The plane had plenty of time to see the ship's living cargo. Instead of taking Leah below, he rushed with her to the *gideoni* where frantic communications passed over the radio between Shalom and the *Haganah* officials in Palestine.

When Shalom saw his interpreter and friend, he gestured for him to get on the microphone. "People are just milling about. Tell everyone to go below deck. We can only hope the plane didn't see them, though I doubt that's true. Tell them, if the British ships come—and be sure to use the word 'if' to keep their hopes alive—we must live up to our ship's name and become fighters for our freedom and our right to return to our true homeland."

Leah stood off to the side. To fight against—no, they would be fighting for something. She blurted out, "It's too late. We need to prepare ourselves. We need something to fight with, things we can use."

"You're right," said Shalom, turning to the young woman. "On my two previous ships people used cans of food as weapons. You'd be surprised how effective they can be when thrown full force at an enemy."

"Did it work?" Leah asked, unsure a tin can filled with a few vegetables could protect anyone from anything.

Mendel had no interest in the answer. "How long before the British arrive?"

"Probably an hour. Two, if we're lucky."

"Let me help," Leah said.

The men looked at the young woman, her dark eyes focused on Shalom as she waited for his reply.

"Both of you, go and get others to help you. Don't forget the kitchen's utensils, especially the knives."

"I'm going to leave the coat here. It's heavy and restricts my movements. We're going to need to move quickly."

Shalom took the coat from her and laid it under the radio equipment table. "It will be here for you after the battle has been won."

On the main deck, others had seen the plane as well. News quickly spread. By the time Leah and Mendel emerged from the *gideoni's* hut, people crowded the railing, scanning the horizon on all sides of the ship, watching for British warships.

"Faster. Why aren't we going faster?" a man asked Mendel, grabbing his arm. "You work for the *gideoni*. What are they doing to protect us from the British pigs?"

Leah handed the man two cans of peas from the box Mendel carried, forcing the man to release her husband and take a step back. "Aim these at their British heads. If enough of us fight back, they'll think better of trying to stop us."

The man stood a little taller. "Ho! Fight against the British Mandate?"

"I'm ready to stop allowing others to write my history, aren't you?"

The man glanced down at the cans in his hands, then back at Leah. "Let's go," he said.

Within an hour, Mendel and Leah had rallied a group to help distribute all the cans, potatoes, and tools they could find until every man and woman on-board had something with which they could fight if and when the British tried to take the *Mordei Hagetaot*.

Mendel turned to Leah. "Come with me to the *gideoni*. I don't want us to be separated when things get crazy."

"No. I've spent too many years not fighting back. I have to do my job, and you have to do yours—for us, for our child."

The tone of her voice, the firmness in her posture, told Mendel how useless it would be to protest any further. "It's going to get chilly this late in the day and who knows when the British will come. Maybe you should get the coat and put it on."

"It's too heavy. I'll come up and get it after we've won the battle."

Mendel kissed her. "Then we'll see each other soon. Take care of our child."

Leah's hand massaged her still-flat belly. "Of course I will."

Another kiss and Mendel headed toward the *gideoni's* room. "Shalom, what happens now?"

Shalom sighed deeply, knowing he needed to be honest but not wanting to shatter his friend's dreams. "You're aware the British have probably spotted us from the air. They'll have radioed their nearby Naval vessels, which will approach us, but they won't do more than shadow us until we reach Israel's waters. At that point, Shuli will try to outrun them and get everyone to shore as quickly as possible. A few of our ships have succeeded."

"A few." Mendel pondered the word. "So we have a chance?"

Shalom nodded. "A very slim one, but, yes, a chance."

"If we fail?"

"There is a British detention camp at Atlit. You will probably be detained there. That's what's happened in the past."

"At least we'll be in Palestine."

"At least that much."

Shouts came through the *gideoni* hut's small window.

Two destroyers had appeared in the distance. People stood and watched. The ships flying the British flag sped closer, only slowing when they were close enough that people standing along the railing could clearly see their numbers: L79 and L75. They shadowed the *Mordei Hagetaot* the way a barracuda shadows its prey before attacking.

Leah looked up. Eight days spent on cold, misty waters. Why had this ninth day cursed them with clear weather and a cloudless sky? A sudden shudder under her feet as the crew pressed the barkentine's engines for greater power. A woman somewhere among the crush of people on-deck screamed. Voices shouted. Children cried.

The gap between the destroyers and the barkentine grew slowly as the *Mordei Hagetaot's* engines throbbed with the effort, but the distance was short-lived.

Time seemed to slow as Leah held on to a rope hanging down from one of the masts with one hand, a can of peas in the other. Soon, the ships were close enough that she could see the faces of the British marines as they lined up on the battleships' landing platforms.

"Are they going to shoot at us?" a woman next to Leah asked, pressing a can of beans to her chest as if to stave off a heart attack.

Leah didn't answer. She wished she were at the front of the ship so she could gauge the distance to Palestine's shore, but there was no easy way to get there through the forest of people.

Some continued to hold the cans, tools, and potatoes they'd been given. Others dropped theirs, the objects rolling among the legs rooted to the deck. People clung to their spouses or their friends. Mothers held their children close. Men closed their eyes and swayed in prayer.

As the British ships separated to flank both sides of the barkentine, a beautiful tenor voice came over the loudspeakers singing the opening lines of *Hatikvah*. Mendel!

Leah joined in. One by one, ten by ten, a hundred by a hundred, over one thousand voices rose from the main deck.

Closer. Louder. A shudder as one ship collided into the starboard side of the *Mordei Hagetaot*. People screamed and pushed against each other to get away from the railing. Parents picked up their children. Nobody ran. There was nowhere to go.

A second shudder as the second ship struck the port side.

Leah dropped her can and scrambled against the frozen crowd as they watched the British sailors make their way onto the deck of the *Mordei Hagetaot*. She needed to get to the *gideoni's* hut. Mendel was there. He would take her in his arms and they would be together when the British took them or the ship sank.

A voice from the British ships' loudspeakers boomed. "Royal." "Atlit." "Camp." What were they saying?

Mendel's voice anew. First in Hebrew. Then Yiddish. Then Polish. "The British announce they have disabled our ship and will tow us to Atlit, where we will be housed in their detention camp until we have been processed. Then they will move us to a more permanent facility."

A woman's voice pierced the sonant buzz. "They are taking us to Atlit. We're going to *Eretz Israel*!"

The opening strains of *Hatikvah* yet again. Its lyrics rose from the deck in a defiant chorus.

Leah wove her way through the singing congregation, finally arriving in the small radio room. Mendel stood there—alone.

"Where is Shalom?"

"Hiding. He knows too much, and he didn't want to learn how the British would extract that information from him."

Leah reached under the table and picked up the coat. "He forgot this." She fingered the buttons, aware the garment was now Shalom's gift. "What will happen when the British find us?"

Mendel wrapped the coat around his wife's shoulders and gently pulled her to him. The harsh sound of whistles along with shouts and screams. "Who knows? What I do know is I won't let them separate us. Perhaps, someday, we will live under our own rule in a country of our own making. This isn't yet that time."

CHAPTER TWENTY-FIVE

HUNGER

Sometimes what we are, what we become, isn't our fault. I learned this during my Applied Evolutionary Anthropology course when we read about The Dutch Famine Birth Cohort Study, colloquially referred to as The Dutch Hunger Study. Its researchers traced the prenatal and maternity records of babies born at the Wilhelmina Gasthuis hospital in Amsterdam between November, 1943 and February, 1947 and found they were statistically more susceptible than the rest of the Dutch population to diabetes, obesity, cardiovascular disease, and other health problems.

During his lecture on the subject, Professor Thomas Ingleton said, "The study concluded there are, indeed, relationships between adverse conditions during fetal development and the resulting health of that adult. According to the study, the living conditions of the mother and father during conception and pregnancy provide a mechanism to explain the link."

The whole idea was pretty heady stuff and, even though the study made no mention of European Jews, I could only picture the photographs I'd seen of the skeletal bodies troops encountered when they liberated the numerous labor and concentration camps toward the end of the war. I thought about the continuing scarcity of desperately needed calories during the many years following liberation. I needed to learn more. I made an appointment to meet with Ingleton in his office later that week.

After the usual niceties—him asking how my academic year was going and me telling him how much I was enjoying his course—I asked him if the Hunger Study might have any application to Holocaust survivors.

In his aloof, academic dialect, he answered, "Seth, the study acknowledged there are things out of our control in life that affect the unborn. Starvation. Stress. By extension, this would apply to someone surviving a years-long cycle of the Holocaust's imprisonment, deprivation, and insecurity."

Over the next hour we discussed what I had learned about the Jews after liberation including the conditions in the DP camps, the *Haganah* ships, and this wandering population's subsequent internment by the British.

As I left Ingleton's office, my phone vibrated with a message from Amelia. *Can you stop at the supermarket on your way home?* followed by a short list of our usual staples: skim milk, whole grain bread, organic peanut butter.

The supermarket, with its abundance of food. Dozens of displays holding rainbows of produce. Refrigeration units filled with beef, chicken, turkey, pork, and fish. Dairy cases offering milk, cream, yogurt, and cheese. Shelves filled with boxes of cereal. White, brown, turbinado sugar, and all its substitutes. Bags upon bags of bread. Soups of every imaginable type.

I thought about living in a world without supermarkets or easily accessible food. I thought about how I felt toward the end of the Yom Kippur fast, knowing I needed to get through the final prayer service, waiting for the last blowing of the *shofar* before I could take a sip of water and eat a light supper. I thought about what real starvation must feel like—stomach clenching, muscles wasting, organs failing—the type that turns civilized men and women into animals who then turn on one another for an extra sliver of potato in their soup, the real starvation Saba and Savta must have suffered.

I thought back to Ilana's video with Savta talking about how hunger traveled with them from camp to camp. Savta's pregnancy took place during that continuous cycle of calorie deprivation. My aunt Sarah was born of it. Both Savta and Sarah became stereotypical Jewish mothers: anxiety a way of life, guilt-tripping an elevated art. Overweight and diabetic, Sarah's life is focused on worrying about everything, interfering in her grown children's lives, and professing nothing in life can ever go right.

However, contrary to Shakespeare's belief, our fate doesn't lie in our stars. Sarah's fate was chiseled into the sandstone of her epigenetics from the moment Savta became pregnant. Years of starvation in the ghetto. Years of starvation in a labor camp. Years of starvation in a *bunker* under a Polish peasant's floorboards. Years of starvation on the road, in a DP camp, over the Alps, on a barkentine, and in Cyprus. How could all that history not take its toll? How could that history not have worked its way into the nucleotidal fibers of existence, corrupting the spiral chain of life and, through that genetic highway, become part of my Aunt Sarah's essence?

Spiritually, the hypothesis made sense. Biologically, empirically, science had proven it to be correct. It wasn't just my grandparents and their generation who suffered at the hand of the Germans and the war. The suffering wasn't limited to that starved and brutalized generation, the one who became homeless, living as citizens of nowhere. If starvation passed on epigenetic alterations to following generations, what might trauma have bequeathed?

Weeks passed. Classes—both ones I took and the one I helped with as a teaching assistant—kept me busy. Then the quarter ended, and I found myself with some free time. I returned to the Hunger Study.

Other journals presented newer research on the topic, and more recent evidence suggested the effects of one generation's suffering might well be visited on the generations that followed. Not only were my grandparents survivors, so were my sister, my cousins, and I. My cousins, doubly "blessed" with survivor grandparents on both sides, are all overweight and pre-Diabetic.

The coincidences of my birth might have spared Ilana and me, at least when I consider the tenuous safety net of my parents' genes. My father was born on a *kibbutz* years after Saba and Savta had settled in Israel when living conditions, though still not perfect, had improved exponentially. My mother's side of the family, the side that left just before the tsar's pogroms in Russia, only suffered poverty—meals with cheap cuts of meat and lots of potatoes, long hours in underpaid sweatshops, and overcrowded, vermin-filled living conditions. All of that might have had their emotional effects, but that comparatively milder environment might have spared their delicate strands of DNA.

In spite of the many roots on my mother's side—the ones that experienced deep-seated antisemitism rather than industrial extermination—the branches of her family tree never multiplied the way my father's did. It seemed as if damaged-gene fecundity was the obligation of Holocaust survivors—new relatives filling the void of those they lost.

Often, when I find myself discussing the Holocaust with others, I hear them say things like, "Your grandparents must have been strong" or "Your grandparents must have had a positive attitude to have survived where others didn't" or "They must have been smart and figured out how to stay alive."

Not so. My Saba and Savta survived because of dumb luck. Saba's luck that he didn't get caught when he cut his way out of the ghetto, and even more luck when he met a Polish Catholic willing to risk his life to save another's. Savta's survival was merely the result of happenstance and the luck of having a dedicated sister.

One afternoon, in the middle of reading a paper on Dr. Ancel Keys' Great Starvation Experiment, I took a break. I went into the bedroom, pulled the coat out of the closet, and put it on.

I stared at myself in the mirror and wondered about the person who'd worn the *Ledermantel* before it came into my family through some unknown event. Who was this person? What color were his eyes? How straight was his hair? Had he also emerged from the other side of conflict with an altered genetic code? Could Alan Turing have deciphered that code's enigma—why some people turn to evil while others become its victims?

I imagined the coat's original owner also lived under the umbrella of luck. The luck to be born a heterosexual white Christian in a society that decided to exorcise anyone who wasn't all those things. The luck to be born into a family of some means, allowing him to become an officer rather than a foot soldier. How long did his luck hold out? Long enough to lose his conscience to a mob mentality of genetic superiority? Long enough to see the allies discover the infection of evil let loose by his country, contaminating others with moral immunosuppression? Long enough to make it through to the other side of the war unscathed, except for losing his coat to a Jew? Long enough to see Germany divided up by its conquerors? Long enough to see it reunited?

The more I thought about the Dutch Hunger Study and epigenetics, the angrier I got. Was anger my grandfather's intent when he gave me the coat?

I needed to talk. Amelia? No, she wouldn't understand the deeper nuances of my feelings. Dr. Ingleton? He was almost a stranger. I didn't want to talk about the coat with someone I barely knew. It had to be Dad. Even though he would be at work, I hoped he'd find a few minutes to talk with me.

The phone only rang twice.

"Seth, is everything okay?"

"Yeah, Dad. Do you have a minute?"

"I do. My patient was a no-show, so I have about twenty minutes to spare. What's up?"

"I wanted to talk to you about Saba and Savta."

A pause. "You sure we can fit this into twenty minutes?"

"We can try. Have you ever read about the Dutch Hunger Study?"

Dad and I spoke—about the study, about Saba and Savta, Sarah, my cousins, and Ilana and me. Our conversation cut through the mess of ideas swirling in my brain and helped distill them.

"You know," I said. "I put the coat on for a bit this afternoon, just before I called you."

"How did it feel?"

"Heavy." The weight of history. The weight of knowledge.

"I know. I put it on once as well."

My turn to pause. "Why didn't you ever tell me?"

"About what?"

"About everything."

"Because Saba and I wanted you to reach your own conclusions."

"So did you know all along how Saba got the coat?"

"No. It was the same with me and Sarah as it was with you and Ilana. He never spoke about anything, other than mentioning how he cut his way out of the ghetto."

"What do you think I should do?"

"About what?"

"About the damned coat."

"Well, other than heavy, how did you feel wearing it?"

"Angry."

"About?"

"A lot of things. Angry about what was done to our family. Angry about not knowing if there's some insidious flaw hidden in my genes. Angry about hating the bastard who wore the coat but, at the same time, finding myself trying to make him human."

"He was human. I think you're realizing there's no solution to be found in hatred and revenge."

"No solution. But no deliverance either. What do you think I should do?"

"About the coat?"

"About my life. About my inheritance. About my responsibility?"

"I think you've finally arrived at the root of Saba's Bar Mitzvah gift."

"Responsibility?"

No answer.

"Dad?"

"*Tikkun olam.* Do what you can to help repair the world."

CHAPTER TWENTY-SIX

IN WHICH THE COAT
IS OFFERED AS SWADDLING

1947

The pangs of early labor woke Leah in the cold darkness of the December morning. For a brief, disoriented moment she forgot where she was. Then she smelled the garbage, sweat, and despair of reality. Not Israel. Not Haifa. Cyprus. Detention Camp 55, a prison camp surrounded by barbed wire and uniformed guards. The previous month, when her belly had grown large enough to be visible at a distance, the British had offered her the opportunity to give birth at a hospital in Haifa. That she would have to leave Mendel behind in Cyprus made her decision to stay in Cyprus an easy one.

Now, as she lay on her back, tears rolled down her face. No mother or sister to hold or guide her. A new life, her child, entering this capricious world in an overcrowded canvas tent with no running water and no privacy.

The sixteen other people sharing the unlined canvas tent slept on. Their snoring and occasional cries from fitful nightmares eliminated any possibility of peace.

As the intensity of her contractions increased, Leah got up from her cot—a length of canvas stretched over a rigid wood frame—and padded over to Mendel, sleeping on a cot identical to her own.

"Mendel," she whispered, gently shaking his shoulder, her breath coalescing into a small cloud.

He shot up. "What's wrong? What's happening?"

Leah's hands instinctively cradled her belly, way too small for a full-term pregnancy. "I think it's my time."

Mendel swung his legs over the edge of the bed and slipped his feet into a pair of stretched-out shoes, laces long gone, soles barely attached by worn stitching. "What should I do?"

Her own calmness surprised Leah as she focused on reassuring her husband. "There's nothing to be done. Nature will take its own course."

Their conversation caused others in the tent to stir, Chaya, her friend from the *Mordei Hagetaot*, among them. "Nu, Leah? Is it happening? Is it your time?"

"I think so."

Chaya transformed into an animated mother hen, moving about the tent, gathering items from others—a thin, worn blanket, an old towel that had once been white, now the color of weak coffee, and as much water as she could glean from everyone's cans or buckets, promising to replace what she could after the water truck arrived sometime during the next few days. "Leah, walk around the tent. It will help move things along. Mendel, walk with her. Hold her arm."

Mendel took Leah by the elbow and turned to one of their tentmates. "Leibel, please tell Akiba I won't be able to attend *Haganah* military training today."

"With good reason," Leibel answered. "Don't worry. There's still plenty of time to turn you into a soldier who will fight for Palestine's independence—if we ever get out of this place."

Chaya wrapped her own shawl around Leah's shoulders. "Don't let her get a chill. I'll put a knife under the bed when the time comes. It will help cut the labor pains. Bring her back when the pains become so strong she can no longer walk around."

The promised pains didn't take long. Mendel stepped back and allowed Chaya and a couple of the other women in their tent take over. By the time the sun was high overhead, Leah held her new baby girl in her arms.

Before putting the tiny infant to her breast, Leah put her ear to her infant daughter's chest and listened to her heart. It fluttered like a bird's. She was perfect. But the damp winter air was so cold. What could she use to keep this fragile newborn warm?

Chaya spoke up. "I'm going outside to check the clotheslines. Maybe there will be something we can use against the cold." She returned empty-handed, reached under her cot, and took one of her own two dresses, swaddling the baby in it as best as she could. "Mendel," she pleaded, "you have to find something for the baby. It's so cold, and we have nothing to wrap her in to keep her warm."

Mendel ran to the office of Rivka Kahana, the social worker for the American Joint Distribution Committee. The AJDC provided camp internees with donated clothing and meager boxes of the most basic survival goods. "Da Joint" was what everyone at camp called it, most speaking the nickname with the same Polish/Yiddish/Hebrew cadence as Mendel and Leah. Rivka had helped other new mothers who needed things for their newborns. He knocked on the door, hoping she'd be in.

"Yes?" came the familiar voice.

Mendel stepped into the cramped office.

Rivka smiled broadly. "Is it Leah's time?"

How this young woman remembered everyone and their circumstances always impressed Mendel. "Yes. It's a girl. But it's so cold, and we don't have anything for her. We need a blanket, or something—anything to protect her from the cold."

"Come into the back room with me. We'll see if there's anything left. Donations come every week, but so many refugees come every day, everything is claimed before we can even sort through the boxes."

The next room, where months ago a mountain of clothing had been, only held a pair of shorts and a single shoe.

"Go back to your tent and take care of your family. I'm going to ask around and see if I can come up with anything. Will you be having a naming?"

"Of course," Mendel answered. "How can we not celebrate the *simcha* of a new generation?"

Walking back into his tent, Mendel saw Leah breastfeeding their new daughter, the child still swaddled in Chaya's dress. The sucking sounds coming from such a tiny creature made Mendel smile.

"Look at your daughter," Leah said. "She might be tiny, but she's got a strong mouth. I just hope I have enough milk."

"*Hashem* will provide," Chaya said. "And, Mendel, I've already sent Leibel for the British doctor and Rabbi Mendelbaum. One to weigh and register your daughter, and the other to name her. You've decided on a name, right?"

Leah nodded.

The doctor and his nurse arrived first. Tall and slim, Dr. Hawkins put his worn, black medical bag on a nearby cot. The much shorter nurse—wearing a starched white apron over a simple blue dress—placed the scale she'd been carrying on the tent's makeshift table. They made a fuss about listening to the baby's heart and lungs, smiling and nodding when she screamed at the disturbance, much to Leah's distress. Rather than unwrap the infant completely, the nurse placed her, still wrapped in the dress, on the scale.

"Her heart and lungs sound just fine," the doctor announced in clipped English. "Didn't even have to listen with the stethoscope. That cry of hers would have been enough. As to her weight, she's just under two kilos. Keep her to the breast. If you're short of milk, let us know and we'll see about getting some powdered formula. You can mix that with boiled water as a supplement."

The nurse smiled at Leah and translated what the doctor had said into poorly spoken Polish.

Mendel grunted. "Formula. We can go for days without a water truck and he promises powdered formula. Even if we can get enough water, even if we can find a bottle, how are we to keep it all clean?"

"*Sha*, Mendel," Leah said. She turned to the nurse. "Tell the doctor thank you."

The naming that afternoon was a crowded affair with Mendel, Leah, Chaya, Rabbi Mendelbaum, Rivka Kahana and, it seemed, everyone from the surrounding tents in attendance. The choice of names had been a simple one, Sarah Julia after the infant's grandmothers of blessed memory, grandmothers she would never meet.

The Rabbi spoke. "The one Who blessed our mothers, Sarah and Rivkah, Rachel and Leah, and the prophet Miriam and Abigail and Queen Esther, daughter of Avichayil—may He bless this beloved girl and let her name be Sarah Julia *bat* Mendel with good luck and in a blessed hour; and may she grow up with good health, peace and tranquility; and may her father and her mother merit to see her joy and her wedding, and male children, riches and honor; and may they be vigorous and fresh, fruitful into old age; and so may this be thy will, and let us say, Amen!"

His voice was barely audible over the intonations of the surrounding attendees. Nevertheless, after the "Amen" cries of "*Mazel tov!*" filled the air.

A bottle of ouzo appeared, and the Rabbi served *schnapps* as he explained, "A humanitarian snuck this over the fence one day. I save it for special occasions like this one."

Rivka hugged the new mother and peered into Sarah Julia's face. "*Mazel tov*," she said. "Sarah is just perfect. A sweet, perfect gift from God."

"Thank you," Leah said, beaming up at the social worker.

"And I have found a wonderful gift for your wonderful daughter. I didn't want to bring it here, with all these people. Come to my office later."

Leah frowned. "I heard the water truck is supposed to come to our area today. It didn't come by last week and, if we miss it…"

"Then, don't worry. I will bring the gift to you."

"Thank you, Rivka."

The afternoon passed with Leah, Mendel, and the baby huddled together on Mendel's single narrow cot, each drawing warmth from the others. By now, Chaya's dress had been put aside, soiled with Sarah's black meconium. Leah hoped diapers would be part of Rivka's morning gift.

Early evening brought gray clouds, blocking out any warmth the sun might have brought to the camp that afternoon. True to her word, Rivka arrived just as the sun was dropping below the stretch of tents obscuring the horizon.

"Leah!" she called from outside the tent.

Leah walked over to the flap masquerading as a door and pulled it aside. "Come in."

The social worker entered with a large bundle in her arms, its outside brown leather. She placed it on a cot and opened it up revealing a moth-eaten red shawl, several rolled pieces of linen, and a small collection of safety pins.

"A coat," Mendel and Leibel called out at the same time. The men picked up the brown leather garment, dumping the other items back onto the cot.

"Yes, a coat. A *Ledermantel*, to be precise." answered Rivka. "There's a German prisoner of war camp adjacent to this one. The British allow us to collect items the transferred Germans leave behind. This is one of the good ones. I thought you could cut the lining out and use it for a baby blanket or swaddling. Mendel, the coat looks like it might be your size. It would look quite dashing on you, even with the lining removed."

Leah hesitated and looked over at her husband.

Mendel scrutinized the coat lying on the narrow cot. Then he looked into the eyes of each of the men standing nearby to gauge their reactions. Each one, in turn, gave a small nod—an acquiescence to the gift.

After the men's silent vote, Leah let go of the breath she'd been holding and hugged the social worker. "Thank you, Rivka. These things are so much more than I expected. Thank you."

"You are quite welcome. By the way, I put a crochet hook into the roll of the linen squares. You know how to crochet, right? I figured you might be able to do something with that awful shawl."

Mendel knew his wife could milk cows, repair a thresher, and raise chickens. But crochet?

"Yes. My mother..." Leah swallowed hard, "She taught me back in Stopnica." She forced a smile.

"A good skill to have. A shame the Americans don't understand the situation here. Many of our donations are old, damaged, stained, or inappropriate. But you can certainly reuse the shawl's yarn to make something for Sarah. I'll see what else I can come up with. Meanwhile, use that coat's lining! It's good wool and in perfect condition."

Rivka went around the tent and spoke a few words with each person before leaving.

As soon as the tent flap closed, Chaya spoke. "You cannot destroy that coat!"

Chaya's tone shocked Leah. She'd never heard such resolute strength in her friend's voice.

Chaya continued, her voice maintaining its stridency, her hands gesticulating wildly. "People forget. History forgets. We must never allow that to happen. Part of keeping history's memory alive is physical evidence. Of course, many of us have numbers tattooed on our arms. But how long will we live? What will stand as evidence once we've turned to dust?" Her voice broke. Tears poured from Chaya's eyes. She gulped in a wavering breath and continued. "To pull the lining out of this coat is to rip away its value. It will become one more damaged piece of used clothing and will be thrown away. The memory will die. The world will forget. We must not allow that to happen! I'll give you all my clothes and go naked. Just don't destroy that coat."

The tent was silent except for Chaya's sobs.

Leah clutched Sarah in one arm as she ran over to the weeping woman and pulled her close with the other. "*Sha, sha*, Chaya. I understand. But to choose between protecting Sarah or protecting history. You have to understand."

"There's the shawl" Chaya whined.

"The shawl is filthy. I can't use it until we've washed it, and we can't wash it if there's barely enough water to drink."

"Please, Leah, I beg you. There must be some way you can save the coat..."

Mendel walked over to his wife and gently removed the infant from her arms. He'd removed his shirt and wrapped the tiny child in it. Dressed only in a worn, sleeveless undershirt, gooseflesh covered his arms as he held Sarah tightly against his chest. "*Kein briere iz oich a breire.* You cannot make a decision, so I will decide for you."

CHAPTER TWENTY-SEVEN

GOD BLESS YOU

"God bless you." The words escaped before I could think about them. "I mean, *Gesundheit*."

"Honestly," Amelia said, giving me a crooked smile. "You're the weirdest atheist I know."

"How many do you know?"

"Me. You. Your sister. Our friend Hal."

"Aren't we all weird?"

"Not me. I'm a straight-out, party-line atheist. But you. You say 'God bless you' and curse invoking Jesus Christ—and he's not even a blip on the big-screen of Jewish theology. Let's not even talk about all those holidays you pseudo-celebrate faithfully every year."

"So?"

"Why do you do all that?"

How could I define Jewish Atheism? The two words were antithetical, but a lifetime of indoctrination in empty words had created my automatic retort. "Isn't it interesting that American culture is the only one I know of which invokes God's name after a sneeze?"

"That still doesn't explain why you say it."

I needed to clear my head before jumping into this debate. A walk to the park would give me some time. "It's a beautiful day, and Greenlake Park beckons."

On our way to the park, we walked together down the narrow sidewalk, avoiding the many blossoming fruit trees' drooping branches. Maneuvering single-file through the maze of hanging vegetation put our conversation on hold until we reached the park and sat down on a bench overlooking the water.

Behind us, people ran alongside their dogs, and mothers jogged with babies in crossover strollers. In front of us, a few ducks hung around hoping we'd throw them some bread crumbs or cracked corn.

"So, Seth, putting aside the sneezes and the curses…"

"You want me to explain about the holidays." Maybe I could deflect long enough to figure out an adequate answer. "Because I like to cook big meals for large gatherings?"

Amelia play-pushed me. "C'mon Maimonides, you can do better than that. Let's start with *Yom Kippur*. Why do you fast, even though you don't even bother to take the day off from work?"

"Fasting does interesting things to your body and your mind. When I don't eat for a long period of time I think more and more about food, about when I'll be able to eat again. That draws attention to the fact I can't eat, which gets me focused on why I'm fasting in the first place."

"Well, that seems nice and simple."

"Give me a chance." The words came. "I fast because it helps me focus on things I've done over the past year that I'm sorry for—people I've hurt, mistakes I've made, things I can try to do better over the next year."

"A spiritual cleanse?"

"Now who's using theological terms?"

"Guilty as charged."

"Ha!"

"What term would you use?" she asked.

I ran through a mental thesaurus. Spiritual. Atonement. Absolution. Every word had some religious over- or undertone to it. "God damn it," I muttered.

Amelia snickered.

I sighed.

Thankfully, she allowed me to move on. "How about the Passover *seder* you love to hold every year? That's a crapload of work for a story you consider a fairy tale."

I corrected her. "An allegory. The story might not be true, but its deeper meaning can teach us lessons about life."

"There are plenty of ways to teach life lessons. Why do you always have to base them on something with overtly Jewish tones?"

She sounded so accusatory. My face got hot, and my voice came out a little louder than I wanted it to. "Because I'm Jewish"

"So," Amelia smiled and winked, an apparent effort at defusing my growing emotion. "Finally, a sign you're not all intellect where your Judaism is concerned. I'm relieved. There is an emotional connection in there after all."

"Relieved?"

"There's someone home other than the academic."

"Did you start all this to get a rise out of me?"

Amelia stood up. A breeze blew a strand of hair into her face. She brushed it away. "Let's take a turn around the lake. I think stretching our legs would do our brains some good."

Amelia set a brisk pace, one that didn't allow an opportunity to continue our conversation. During the walk, I calmed down. A smart girl, that one.

The path around the lake was crowded with people, making it difficult to remain side-by-side. I grabbed Amelia's hand to pull her closer and prevent others from walking, jogging, or rollerblading between us.

As we walked, I dissected the issues we'd been discussing. Why did I cling to an ancient religion with all sorts of rules that made no sense in the modern world? Sure, I didn't keep kosher, but I knew the rules well enough to comfortably hang with observant family and friends. I could read Hebrew competently, even if I didn't know what all the words meant. My Birthright trip to Israel had offered me a window into modern Jewish culture in our homeland—my homeland—the place my grandparents had struggled to reach, fought to build, and ultimately left, Saba tired of fighting in war after war, deciding to leave and reunite with Avram in the United States.

Then there was the coat. My inheritance. A single tangible piece of my family's history. The reminder of what my Jewish ancestors suffered under the Assyrians, the Babylonians, the Romans, the Inquisition, England's King Edward I, the Nazis and, more recently, in Iraq, Yemen, Syria, Ethiopia, Russia—centuries of my people forced from place to place, clinging to the two things they imagined they could never lose: their religious identity and their yearning to return to their homeland. The coat was my grandparents' proof of their survival against the world's odds, proof there was something about the Jewish people which allowed us to continue in spite of those odds.

I have no idea whether Saba believed in God or not. We never discussed his faith, except for his faith in the Cleveland Indians' Jim Thome or Kenny Lofton—the ritual that took place on the family room's television set while watching the Cleveland Municipal Stadium's broadcast. During those visits we ultimately celebrated religious rituals as well. Those times brought us together and created a bridge between cultures, continents, and generations.

I was ready to have the conversation I'd been parrying. I pulled Amelia over to a shady area on the nearby grass, and we sat down.

As she floated her fingers over the blades of grass, I spoke. "Thanks, Amelia, love of my life."

"Wow. What did I do to deserve that?"

"I think I finally understand why Saba gave me that coat."

Amelia wrapped her arms around her knees, hugging them to her chest while she waited.

"The coat is his concrete symbol for fasting."

"I don't follow."

"Okay. Remember I told you about how fasting focuses me on trying to become a better person?" I was amazed at how sharply defined my thoughts were becoming. "That's what the coat is for—to focus on my family's history. Not just my Saba and Savta's; farther back than that. Judaism is one of the oldest continuous religions in the world. That's got to count for something."

"I think you're getting there. Keep going."

I looked at the reflection of the sun glinting off the water. It was a beautiful, cloudless day. We could probably see Mt. Ranier if we turned the right way—its visage appearing to float in the atmospheric distance.

"The coat is the proverbial question wrapped in an enigma. I remember Rabbi Shafler's discussions in class about how the *Gemara* is the commentary on the oral tradition of Jewish law. *Gemara* began with questions. Those questions led to other questions, resulting in an eternal discussion regarding how we interpret the 613 laws found in the *Torah*."

I kept going. "Judaism is like oxygen. I'm not conscious of breathing it, but it nourishes every cell in my body, feeds my brain, reminds me to choose one path over another."

There was more. "Jewish life is layered with ambiguity. Answers to questions are debated in Yeshiva classrooms, rabbi's studies, letters to the editor, on the street, and at the *Shabbat* table. The need to question everything is in my education, my heritage, my genes."

Voices whispered. The conundrum echoed in my head. Saba, Savta, Ida, Avram, Shoshana, Motek—all gone, but still alive in me. Were they religious? Did they really believe in God? Is it possible to be only part of the equation? Is the answer hidden somewhere in that part?

I continued. "I'm not sure if my Saba was really religious or if he simply went through the motions, needing to belong, giving Savta a way for her to belong as well. Even if they lost their faith, they never lost their identity. No matter how hard I try I can never stop being a Jew. Something will always be there to remind me. The guy on the street I overhear saying 'I Jewed him down.' A newspaper article showing a splash of black or red paint spelling out *JEW* on somebody's wall. An antisemitic poster in a restaurant's window. An elbow and a wink with someone asking, 'C'mon. Can't you take a joke?'

"Sure. Right now they don't burn our homes or smash the windows of our businesses, but they rob us of our sense of safety and make us doubt whether we have a secure place in society. I'm always half waiting for another shoe to drop. My mother's mother always told me all Jews should have a current passport and cash on hand 'just in case.'"

Amelia let go of her knees and pulled the hair back off her face, fastening it into a ponytail with an elastic hair tie she had around her wrist. "Where does the Jewish God play into all this? Other religions believe God will protect them if they pray hard enough or believe in certain things in a certain way. Do the Jews ever think God betrayed them?"

I looked for a way to explain what I understood about the Jewish relationship with the God they breathed life into before claiming God breathed life into man. "Even though Judaism is a monotheistic religion, we aren't taught to depend on God to do things for us. Sure, God matters, but it's our behavior that matters the most. We aren't taught to do things because they make us feel good or because there's some heavenly reward for doing them after we die. We're supposed to do things because they're the right thing to do. We call that *tikkun olam*—repairing the world."

"And the coat? What does that have to do with everything?"

"I think the coat is the perfect symbol of all that. It symbolizes the evil that created it, as well as the victory over that evil. It reminds us the only way to fight against future evil is to always do the right thing."

CHAPTER TWENTY-EIGHT

THE COAT

"Tell me about your shoes."

"Whatchoo askin' 'bout that for, dude?" came the challenge from the back.

The classroom of teenagers, ranging from pale to black, from Aryan to African, looked at me, the curly-haired, brown-eyed Jewish special guest standing in front of a freshly-cleaned blackboard with a rolled-up projection screen up top.

"I'm asking about your shoes. What are you currently wearing on your feet?"

A few faces glanced down in response.

I pointed at a boy in the front row, his feet stretched out, claiming all the space his legs could reach beyond his desk. Gold-colored shoes prominently defined the boundary of his territory.

"Those are some good-looking shoes. What are they?"

Slouched in his seat, he lazily raised his eyes to meet mine. I relaxed when he answered, "Jordans. What the fuck do you care?"

The teacher made a move. I held up my hand to stop her. I didn't want anything to interrupt any possible momentum.

"And you?" This time I pointed to a young woman a few rows back.

She stood up and lifted the hem of her pants so we could all see the ankle boots on her feet. "Vince Camuto."

Another girl's voice piped up from the back of the room. "Nah. Them ain't Camutos. She prob'ly bought those at Walmart. And, if they are Camutos, I'm sure they Goodwill."

"Uh uh!" Ms. Boots replied. "They're Vince Camutos all right. My boyfriend bought them for me. New."

The classroom erupted into laughter, excluding me from some inside joke. The laughter quieted, but a few catcalls still echoed around the room. Raising my voice slightly, I said, "I gather what shoes you wear matters to most of you."

I engaged a few more of them and they proudly shared—Jordans, Dunks, Zigi Girl, and more. Several students now sat up straight, animatedly debating the merits of one brand over another. I had them.

I pulled down the screen, walked to the projector at back of the room, and asked the teacher to turn off the lights. A projected image of Budapest's Shoes on the Danube Bank appeared on the screen. Sixty pairs of rusted Holocaust-period shoes cast out of iron sit along the river commemorating the Jews forced to strip naked on the banks of that river, face the water, and be shot in the back of the head, falling in to be washed away by the current.

The next projection showed a post-liberation photo of the thousands of shoes Russian forces found stored in an Auschwitz warehouse.

The third showed the walls of shoes at the Najdanek Museum in Lublin, Poland.

"Do any of you know why I'm showing these slides?"

"Because you have a thing for shoes?" This question from the front. Laughter from the back.

I raised my voice to be heard over the sound. "These are just a small number of the shoes worn by Jewish Holocaust victims before the Germans murdered them."

I changed the photo on the screen to a pair of old Mary Jane shoes— the type young girls used to wear, the ones made of black or brown leather with a strap across the top.

"Those Jew shoes, too?" A voice from somewhere in the room. More laughter.

"No. This pair belonged to a young African-American girl who was murdered in 1963." The room quieted as I continued. "She died after white supremacists bombed the 16th Street Baptist Church in Birmingham, Alabama. She died for many of the same reasons the Jews were murdered by the Germans. She died because people's hatred made them believe she was less than human, that she didn't matter."

I changed the photo again. This one of a plaque from Washington D.C.'s Holocaust Museum.

We are the shoes, we are the last witnesses.
We are shoes from grandchildren and grandfathers
From Prague, Paris and Amsterdam
And because we are only made of fabric and leather
And not of blood and flesh, each one of us avoided the hellfire.
Yiddish Poet Moses Schulstein (1911 - 1961)

"Their shoes are important as evidence that the victims of hatred existed and a reminder that they died. The many piles of shoes are a tangible declaration that millions of Jews were murdered in the Holocaust, the single pair of shoes a tangible declaration that Addie Mae Collins and five other children died during—and immediately following—the 1963 bombing of that Birmingham church."

A girl sitting near me coughed gently. Everyone else in the room was silent.

I changed the image on the screen to the pair of ruby slippers at the Smithsonian.

"Shoes can sometimes be iconic. Dorothy's ruby slippers from *The Wizard of Oz* movie sit in a case at the Smithsonian Museum in Washington, DC."

I continued my presentation, talking to the class while alternating between photos of shoes and photos of survivors' faces. Each one stared back at the class.

German Jews.

"People think what happened during the Holocaust was an isolated event."

Polish Jews.

"It isn't.

Czech Jews.

"We continue to dehumanize groups of people using all types of propaganda, especially on social media."

Romani.

"There are increasing numbers of people who deny the Holocaust ever happened."

Achés.

"This is dangerous, not just to the persecuted, but to everyone who sits by and does or says nothing."

Syrians.

"Blind complacency can allow us to ignore or even forget history's lessons."

Rohingya, then Makka Kaifar followed by the photo of a seven-year-old Sudanese girl who walked for seven weeks to escape death.

"It took me a long time to learn all this."

Druze. Somali. An emaciated Congolese boy in the Kibati refugee camp wearing a mismatched pair of worn-out shoes.

The vacuum of silence in the room was palpable. I changed the projection to a photograph of Hitler standing with a group of his officers, all wearing full-length leather coats—coats that looked just like the one I inherited from my grandfather. I returned to the front of the room.

Standing in the dimness, I surveyed the class. The young man in the front row—the one whose legs had been stretched far out in front of him—now sat at attention. Many of the other students had assumed the same posture.

"I've been talking to you about shoes. Shoes are proof. Proof of victims. Proof of atrocities."

The students sat. Waiting. Listening.

I paused—a long pause—one Saba would have approved of and admired. My heart felt him smile.

"We need something tangible to force us to confront the reality of the evil that people are capable of. Something tangible to caution us to be vigilant. Something tangible to remind us of our responsibility in this world.

"My grandparents were Holocaust survivors. They became refugees. They understood the importance of historical legacy and wanted me to understand it as well. So, when I was thirteen years old—the age when Jewish boys go through a ritual called a Bar Mitzvah—my grandfather gave me a gift; a full-length leather coat exactly like the ones you see in this photograph."

GLOSSARY

Aba (Hebrew): Father.

Adonai (Hebrew): Literally "my Lords." This traditionally refers to the plural of majesty. Used to refer to God.

Alter cocker (Yiddish): Literally, "old defecator." Used to describe a crotchety old person.

Alteste der Juden (German): Eldest of the Jews.

Amcha (Yiddish/Hebrew): In Yiddish—common folk. In Hebrew—your people.

Arbeit Macht Frei (German): Work sets you free.

Asher bara (Hebrew): He who created.

Ata medaber Ivrit (Hebrew): Do you speak Hebrew?

Banh mi (Vietnamese): Literally, "bread." Also refers to a type of baguette which is often split lengthwise and filled with various savory ingredients as a sandwich and served as a meal.

Bar mitzvah (Hebrew): Literally, "son of commandment/law" One who is obligated to perform the commandments. Also, a coming-of-age ritual for boys usually taking place when they turn thirteen.

Baruch Hashem (Hebrew): Literally, "blessed be the name." Used to say "Thank God."

Bat (Hebrew): Daughter.

Bat mitzvah (Hebrew): Literally, "daughter of commandment/law" One who is obligated to perform the commandments. Also, a coming-of-age ritual for girls usually taking place when they turn twelve or thirteen.

Beseder (Hebrew): Fine, alright.

Bima (Hebrew): The platform in a synagogue.

Bricha (Hebrew): Escape.

Bruchim habayim (Hebrew): Welcome.

Bris (Yiddish/Hebrew): The Jewish ceremony of circumcision.

Ca phe da (Vietnamese): Vietnamese iced coffee.

Challah (Hebrew): A braided Sabbath and holiday bread made with eggs.

Chalutz (Hebrew): A person who immigrates to Israel to join a settlement to help build the nation.

Chanukah (Hebrew): A Jewish festival celebrating the rededication of the Second Temple in Jerusalem. The only religious observance is the lighting of candles, one added each night of the eight-night holiday.

Charoset (Hebrew): A mixture symbolizing the mortar the Jews used during their time as slaves in Egypt. The type of charoset Seth would eat would be from the Eastern European tradition of apples, walnuts, matzoh meal, cinnamon, honey or sugar, and kosher sweet wine. Sephardic Jews use dried fruits instead of the apples.

Chaver (Hebrew): Friend, comrade.

Chaverim (Hebrew): Friends, comrades.

Chesed (Hebrew): Kindness.

Chevra kadisha (Hebrew): Literally, "sacred society." The volunteer group who sees to it that the bodies of deceased Jews are prepared according to Jewish ritual.

Chutzpah (Yiddish): Nerve, audacity.

Cocker (Yiddish): Literally, "shitter." One who shits. Derogatory term for an old person.

Czy mówisz po polsku (Polish): Do you speak Polish?

Daven (Hebrew): Pray.

Dvar torah (Hebrew): A talk on topics related to a section of the Torah.

El Maleh Rachamim (Hebrew): Literally, "God full of compassion." A prayer for the soul of the departed.

Eppes essen (Yiddish): I will give you something to eat.

Eretz Israel (Hebrew): The land of Israel.

Falafel (Hebrew): A Middle-Eastern deep-fried ball made with ground chickpeas, fava beans, or both.

Fleisch (Yiddish): Meat, flesh.

Gehennah (Yiddish): A place of spiritual punishment and/or purification for a period of up to 12 months after death.

Gehsperre (German): Literally, "curfew." Refers to the week in Lodz when the Germans hunted down Jews they considered to be unproductive.

Gideoni (Hebrew): Wireless radio operator.

Greener (slang): A greenhorn. A newly arrived immigrant.

Greyten zikh far (Yiddish): Prepare yourself/yourselves.

Hachshara (Hebrew): Literally, "preparation." Training programs and agricultural centers to prepare Zionist youth for immigration to Israel.

Hachsharot (Hebrew): Plural of *hachshara.*

Haftorah (Hebrew): On Saturday (Sabbath) and holiday mornings, the Haftorah is a selection from on the the biblical books of the Prophets that is read after that week's Torah reading.

Haggadah (Hebrew): Literally, "telling." The written guide and text for the Passover *seder* which celebrates the Jews' exodus out of Egypt.

Haganah (Hebrew): Literally, "the defense." A Jewish paramilitary organization during the British Mandate of Palestine which became the seed for the Israel Defense Forces.

Hamantaschen (Hebrew): Triangular, filled pastries usually served during the holiday of Purim.

Hashem (Hebrew): Literally, "the name." A term used for God.

Hatikvah (Hebrew): Literally, "the hope." Israel's national anthem.

Havdalah (Hebrew): Jewish religious ceremony that marks the symbolic end of Shabbat and ushers in the new week.

Ima (Hebrew): Mother.

Jiddische Landsberger Cajtung (Yiddish): The newspaper published by the Jewish population of the Landsberg displaced persons camp in Landsberg, Germany.

Judenrein (German): Cleansed or free of Jews.

Judenscheisse (German): Literally, "Jewshit."

Kaddish (Hebrew): An ancient Jewish prayer regularly recited in the synagogue service. One form of it is a prayer traditionally recited in memory of the dead.

Kaf Gimel Yordei Hasira (Hebrew): Literally, "I get off the boat" referring to 23 *Haganah* commandos who died when their boat sank.

Kapo (German): Literally, "overseer." A prisoner in a Nazi concentration camp assigned by the SS guards to supervise forced labor or carry out administrative tasks.

Karpas (Hebrew): The vegetable, usually parsley, celery, or a piece of potato, dipped in salt water and eaten during the Passover meal.

Kashruth (Hebrew): The set of Jewish dietary laws.

Katzets (German): K.Z. short for *konzentrationslager*, referring to the Nazi concentration camps. After the war, used to refer to those who had been imprisoned in said camps.

Kein ayin hara (Yiddish): Literally, "no evil eye."

Kein briere iz oich a breire (Yiddish): Literally, "Not to have any choice available is also a choice."

Kibbutz (Hebrew): Literally, "gathering, clustering." A collective community traditionally based on agriculture.

Kibbutznik (Hebrew): A member of a *kibbutz*.

Kiddush (Hebrew): Literally, "sanctification." A blessing recited over wine or grape juice to sanctify the Sabbath and Jewish holidays. Also refers to refreshments offered after prayer services on Sabbath or festival mornings and before the meal.

Kippah (Hebrew): Literally, "dome." Skullcap. A brimless cap.

Kippot (Hebrew): Plural of *kippah*.

Kleiderschrank (German): A freestanding wardrobe closet.

Kosher (Hebrew): Satisfying the requirements of Jewish law.

Kotel (Hebrew): The Western Wall/Wailing Wall in Jerusalem.

Kriat Shema al Hamitah (Hebrew): An extended version of the traditional *Shema* prayer, recited before going to sleep.

Kurta (Urdu & Persian): A loose, collarless shirt traditional to many parts of South Asia.

L'Chaim (Hebrew): A Hebrew toast "to life."

L'hitraot (Hebrew): See you later.

La Wanz (Yiddish): From the German *wanze*. Bedbug. In this case, referring to lice.

Lager (German): Abbreviated term for "konzentrationslager" (concentration camp).

Laila tov (Hebrew): Good night.

Latkes (Yiddish and Hebrew): A pancake, often one made with grated potatoes.

Leolam va'ed (Hebrew): Literally, "to the distant horizon and again," usually translated as "forever and ever."

Ma Nishtana (Hebrew): The first two words in the phrase "Why is tonight different from all other nights?"

Ma'apilim (Hebrew): Jews who immigrated illegally to Palestine during British control in the 1930s and 1940s.

Machon (Hebrew): Institute.

Mameleh (Yiddish): Literally, "little mother." Used as an affectionate diminutive: "little girl."

Mamzer (Hebrew): A child born as the result of a forbidden sexual union.

Maoz Tzur (Hebrew): Literally, stronghold of rock. A popular Chanukah song.

Matzah (Hebrew): An unleavened flatbread in Jewish cuisine. An integral element of the Passover festival.

Maydeleh (Yiddish): Little girl.

Mazel (Hebrew): Luck.

Mazel tov (Hebrew): Literally, "good luck." Used as a form of congratulations.

Megillah (Hebrew): Literally, "scroll" or "volume."

Meises (Yiddish): Fables.

Mensch (Yiddish): Literally, "human being." A person of integrity and honor.

Meshugge (Yiddish): Crazy.

Meyn brieder (Yiddish): My brother.

Minyan (Hebrew): The quorum of ten Jewish adults (traditionally men) required for certain religious obligations.

Mi Sheberach (Hebrew): Literally, "may the one who blesses." A central Jewish prayer for the ill.

Mitzvah (Hebrew): Literally, "commandment." May also refer to performing a good deed.

Mordei Hagetaot (Hebrew): Ghetto fighters.

Moshiach (Hebrew): Messiah.

Naches (Yiddish): Pride, joy.

Nachon (Hebrew): Correct, right.

Neshama (Hebrew): Soul, spirit.

Parshat (Hebrew): The weekly Torah portion read during Jewish prayer services.

Pesach (Hebrew): Passover.

Pesadick (Hebrew): Kosher for Passover.

Po nikbar (Hebrew): Here lies.

Potrzebuje pomocy (Polish): I need help.

Rosh Chodesh (Hebrew): Literally, "head of the Month." The name for the first day of every month in the Hebrew calendar, marked by the birth of a new moon.

Rosh Hashanah (Hebrew): Literally, "head of the year." The Jewish New Year.

Saba (Hebrew): Grandfather.

Savta (Hebrew): Grandmother.

Seder (Hebrew): The Jewish ritual service and meal in celebration of Passover.

Sephardic: Initially, a Jewish ethnic division originally from Sepharad, Spain, or the Iberian peninsula. More recently used to refer to the Eastern Jewish communities of West Asia and beyond who, although not having genealogical roots in the Jewish communities of Iberia, adopted a Sephardic style of liturgy and Sephardic law and customs imparted to them by the Iberian Jewish exiles over the course of the last few centuries.

Sha (Yiddish): Hush, quiet down.

Shabbat (Hebrew): Sabbath. In Judaism observed from a few minutes before sunset on Friday evening until the appearance of three stars in the sky on Saturday night.

Shanda (Yiddish): A shame, a scandal.

Shawarma: Meat, or a mixture of meats, cut into thin slices, stacked in a cone-like shape on a slowly turning vertical rotisserie, and roasted.

Shekel (Hebrew): Israel's currency.

Shema Yisrael Adonai Eloheinu Adonai echad (Hebrew): Hear O Israel, the Lord is our God, the Lord is One.

Sh'erit ha-Pletah (Hebrew): Literally, "Surviving Remnant." A term used by Jewish refugees who survived the Holocaust to refer to themselves and the communities they formed in postwar Europe.

Shesh, arba, efes (Hebrew): Six, four, zero.

Shikse (Yiddish): A gentile woman.

Shiva (Hebrew): A seven-day period of mourning starting when the immediate family of the deceased (spouse, child, parent or sibling) return home from the funeral.

Shlep (Yiddish): To drag or lug something.

Shlichim (Hebrew): Literally, "ones sent." Post-war emissaries from Israel who provided Jewish refugees training in preparation for immigration to Israel.

Shofar (Hebrew): An musical horn typically made of a ram's horn, used for Jewish religious purposes.

Shtetl: A small town with a large Jewish population. These existed in Central and Eastern Europe before the Holocaust.

Shul (Yiddish): Synagogue.

Siddur (Hebrew): A Jewish prayer book.

Simcha (Hebrew): Literally, "joy." A Jewish party or celebration.

Simchas Torah (Hebrew): The Jewish holiday to celebrate and mark the conclusion of the annual cycle of public Torah readings and the beginning of a new cycle.

Sukkah (Hebrew): A temporary walled structure covered with organic material for the holiday of Sukkot reminding Jews of the temporary dwellings the Israelites inhabited on their way out of Egypt.

Tarbouka (Hebrew): A goblet-shaped drum.

Tehillim (Hebrew): Psalms.

Tfillin (Hebrew): Phylacteries. Small black leather boxes with leather straps that Jews (traditionally men) wear on their head and arm during weekday morning prayer.

Shema (Hebrew): Literally, "hear." The oldest fixed daily prayer in Judaism, recited morning and night.

Tikkun olam (Hebrew): Literally, "fix the world." Acts of kindness performed to perfect or repair the world and bring about social justice.

Tilchas tizig gesheften (Arabic and Yiddish): Literally, "you-lick-my-ass business." The name of a group of Jewish Brigade members formed immediately following World War II.

Tisha B'Av (Hebrew): Literally, "the ninth of the month of Av." A day of mourning and fasting to commemorate the many tragedies that have befallen the Jewish people.

To dobra dziewczyna (Polish): She's a good girl.

Torah (Hebrew): In the context of this book, refers to a scroll containing the first five books of the Pentateuch. In a wider sense, Torah refers to the Five Books of Moses, the entire Hebrew Bible, and the entire corpus of religious Jewish knowledge.

Treif (Yiddish): Any form of non-kosher food.

Tzaddik (Hebrew): *Righteous one.*

Tzedakah (Hebrew): Literally, "justice" or "righteousness." The moral obligation of charitable giving.

Vy govorite po-russki (Russian): Do you speak Russian?

Wehrmacht (German): Literally, "defense force. The unified armed forces of Nazi Germany.

Yad Vashem (Hebrew): Literally, "museum of martyrs." Israel's official memorial to victims of the Holocaust.

Yasher koach (Hebrew): Literally, "may your strength be enriched." Good job!

Yingele (Yiddish): Little boy.

Yishuv (Hebrew): Literally, "settlement." Refers to the Jewish population living in Palestine before the State of Israel was established in 1948.

Yitgadal v'yitgadash shmei rabah (Aramaic): May His great Name grow exalted and sanctified.

Yom Kippur (Hebrew): The Jewish Day of Atonement. The holiest day of the year in Judaism.

Zol zayn mit mazel (Yiddish): You should have good luck.

NOTE FROM THE AUTHOR

Word-of-mouth is crucial for any author to succeed. If you enjoyed the book, please leave a review online—anywhere you are able. Even if it's just a sentence or two. It would make all the difference and would be very much appreciated.

Thanks!
April

ABOUT THE AUTHOR

April Grunspan became enamored of writing while studying under author Carole Klein at Goddard College during the 1970s. She worked as a journalist and an editor until she took a long break to raise a family. She has now returned to her love of crafting fiction. Her inspiration for *The Coat* is a Nazi officer's coat her son did, indeed, inherit from his Holocaust-survivor grandfather. This is her first published novel.

Facebook –April-Grunspan-Author
Twitter – @agru
Instagram – agruarts
LinkedIn – april-grunspan

Thank you so much for reading one of our **Literary Fiction** novels.

If you enjoyed our book, please check out our recommended title for your next great read!

The Five Wishes by Mr. Murray McBride by Joe Siple

2018 Maxy Award "Book of the Year"

"A sweet...tale of human connection...will feel familiar to fans of Hallmark movies." *–KIRKUS REVIEWS*

"An emotional story that will leave readers meditating on the life-saving magic of kindness." *–Indie Reader*